I0725311

BORROWED TIME

TIME

BOOK 1 - BROKEN PROMISES

Infinity Books

DÄNNA WILBERG

Copyright © 2020 by Dänna Wilberg

All rights reserved.

No part of this book may be reproduced in any form or by any electronic or mechanical means, including information storage and retrieval systems, without written permission from the author, except for the use of brief quotations in a book review.

Cover Designer: Karen Phillips at www.phillipscovers.com

Editors: Kirk Colvin, Michele Drier

Formatting: Tarra Thomas Indie Publishing Services

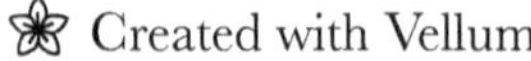 Created with Vellum

*To those who watch over us from the other side, your love
is forever etched on our hearts.*

ACKNOWLEDGMENTS

"Borrowed Time" began as a short story published in the Sisters in Crime Anthology in 2008. In 2011, I adapted my short story into a short film for "A Place Called Sacramento." Thank you to the Sacramento Chapter of Sisters in Crime, Capitol Crimes, for giving Suzanne Cash life and to Access Sacramento for providing the opportunity to show "Borrowed Time" on the big screen. I wasn't expecting my protagonist, Suzanne Cash, to stick around after the project was finished, but she did.

Psychic Linda Schooler was one of the first guests I interviewed on Paranormal Connection, a local TV program I produced and hosted for fifteen years. She not only impressed me with her psychic abilities, she impressed me with her integrity and her beautiful soul. I feel privileged that Linda allowed me to include her as a character in my book.

I've been blessed with continued support from mentor Kirk Colvin, The Eldorado Writers Guild, mentor Donna Benedict, critique partners, Michele Drier, Linda Townsdin, Tarra Thomas, June Gillam, Catherine McGreevy, and my sister Kathy, who doles out support when I need it most. I'd also like to thank one of my beta readers, Nancy St. Germain. Nancy and I have been friends since first grade and having her as a fan means the world to me.

Finishing a manuscript is a *big deal*. Thank you, Kirk and Michele, for editing, and Tarra for formatting my pages and taking on the task of all-around Project Manager. Choosing the right cover is a *big deal*. Karen Phillips, you've done it again! I am eternally grateful for everyone's incredible talent and expertise.

Thank you to my readers. It gives me great pleasure to write stories you enjoy.

Most of all, thank you to my family. Your love and support fuels my passion for writing.

Dänna Wilberg

2/20/2020

PROLOGUE

Amy Fitzpatrick sucked in her stomach, straightened her shoulders, and turned toward the Tabby cat sprawled across her bed. "What do you think, Rex?" Twelve weeks ago, she criticized her muffin top and super-sized chest. Today she relished the change. *Crossfit.* By summer's end, her abs never looked better, her arms and legs, defined. *Thank God for pull-ups and squats.*

She slipped into a pair of stone-washed jeans, a silky white tank top, and scooted her feet into strappy sandals. "Too plain?" But Rex didn't respond. He licked one paw and swiped it across his left ear. "I hope my date shows more interest than you, my friend," she said, brushing her long cinnamon colored hair.

Amy thought about her date, an older guy she'd met online thirty pounds ago. He said he was coming to town and wanted to meet her in person. His name was Jeff, and he suggested dinner. *Sushi, my favorite.*

She sometimes wished she could go back in time. Reset the clock. She didn't date much in high school, she preferred books to broken promises. When she graduated college and applied for a position at a local broadcasting company, she had no idea taking the job meant giving up the best years of her life. She ate her way through lonely nights and weekends. Starbucks became her new best friend, and she discovered Venti Frappuccino's with double whip. Coupons, received in the mail for pizza or buy one hamburger, get one free, upgrades for supersize fries with a large soft drink purchase, gave her something to look forward to. Until one day she looked in the mirror and no longer recognized herself.

Joining the dating site gave her a new lease on life. Whittling her weight down from a size 10 to a size 6 improved her confidence. She was ready for a relationship. "You know, Rex," she said, "if this guy works out, you may find your lazy ass sleeping on the floor."

Rex yawned and stretched.

At 7:48 p.m., Amy pulled into a parking structure on 11th and K Streets. She drove to the designated level and parked near the elevator as Jeff instructed. She thought the directive was odd and wondered why he didn't agree to meet at the restaurant. *Maybe he wants to check you out before he wastes his evening wining and dining you?* She took one last look in her visor mirror. *Don't be silly.*

A handsome, dark-haired man stood near the

elevator door. She recognized him immediately from his photo.

"Hello, Jeff."

He flashed a Hollywood smile. "Amy? Is that you?"

"Surprised?" Amy twirled around.

His lips puckered, and he whistled low. "Damn, you are even <u>more</u> beautiful in person!"

They rode the elevator to the ground floor and navigated their way through a courtyard with clusters of people enjoying Labor Day weekend. "This way," he said, ducking into the first doorway they came to. "I reserved a table for us in the corner—where it's quiet." His hand rested at the base of her spine. "We can get better acquainted."

The restaurant was nothing extravagant, but the food was spectacular. Jeff surpassed all expectations, and she wondered, *could he be the one?*

"This photo was taken last Thanksgiving," he said, sliding his phone across the table. "That's my grandma —she's 86, but boy can she dance up a storm. She's holding my fur baby, Penny."

Amy smiled at the photo, wondering if Penny and Rex would hit it off. She was getting ahead of herself, but he seemed to have all the qualities she dreamed of: funny, charming, attentive, talented and handsome. A career, family values—assets most girls put high on their wish list. *Almost too good to be true.* "Why are you still single?"

"Why are you?"

"I'm a workaholic?"

"I think we're in the same boat. I love my job."

"Does that mean we're destined to be alone?"

"Let's go to my place, we can talk about it there." His eyes traveled to her breasts and back.

"No. I don't think—"

His smile faded. His eyes turned cold. He slapped his hands on the table. "Hey, no worries," he said.

Amy needed a moment to assess his mood swing and excused herself to the restroom. She wasn't ready to have sex on their first date. Then again, maybe she was over-thinking the way he looked at her. A cartoon image of a wolf licking his chops came to mind. Maybe her mother had been right, maybe online dating wasn't such a good idea. When they connected on the dating site, she thought he'd be more mature than guys she dated in college, because of his age. *Less pushy*.

When she returned to the table, Jeff had ordered more Saki.

"I have to get up early, Jeff, I don't think I should—"

"Please, one more drink. I don't want the evening to end. I'm sorry if I rushed things, but I really like you."

He held her in his gaze until…

"Okay—I'm sure one more won't hurt."

my felt dizzy. Unsteady. Nauseous. "Where are we?" she asked. She didn't understand why her limbs were filled with cement, why bees swarmed in her head. *I only took a few sips.* "I don't feel right."

Jeff pushed a key into the lock.

"I have work tomorrow," she slurred, leaning against the heavy wooden door frame.

"I know. This won't take long," he whispered.

CHAPTER 1

"Let's put it over there," said events coordinator Suzanne Cash, pointing to the blank wall across the hotel ballroom. Julien, her assistant, dragged a gigantic cardboard cut-out of a bunny peeking out of a top hat across the room and lifted it as high as his five-foot-seven frame could stretch. Suzanne nodded and clapped her hands. "Perfect."

"Are you sure?" he asked, holding the cut-out in place.

"I'm sure."

"You were sure the last *two* times. Are you positive this is where you want it?"

"One hundred percent positive."

"You know these kids aren't going to care if the purple letters in ABRACADABRA clash with the wall sconces or the carpet, they're coming to see the *magic*."

She buried her hands in the pockets of her maxi skirt. "Geez, Julien—don't the kids deserve perfection in their imperfect world?"

"They're kids. Not experts in Feng Shui."

Suzanne brushed past Julien. "Did you get the black curtains I asked for?"

"Sure did. They will be hung tonight before I leave."

"We have to be finished with the stage decorations and the props by three o'clock tomorrow afternoon. Catering starts their set-up at four. Doors open six o'clock sharp. Can you check the weather again? Someone mentioned rain."

"Nothing until next week. We may be in for a wet Halloween."

"Damn, I still have my dress to collect from the cleaners."

"The kids are going to love you no matter what you wear. And I promise you, we <u>will</u> be done. Now scoot. You look bitchy with puffy eyes."

Suzanne smirked. "Do you need anything before I go?"

"No. Get some rest. Recharge your batteries."

She didn't argue. Her eyes *were* puffy, her long auburn hair needed washing, and her make-up had melted off hours ago. She was beat. Her feet throbbed; she couldn't remember the last time she had eaten. She was oblivious to everyone around her. Her bones yearned for bed. *I hate when he's right.*

The wind stirred leaves along the walkway. The sun, long gone, left the moon in charge. *Nothing looks familiar.* She turned to go back inside the hotel only to find the door locked. Frustrated, she walked towards a fenced area, noticing the hotel marquee in the distance. "Making Magic for Wish Kids."

After tomorrow night she'd get her life back. *No hurry there.* She loved her work. Whether the kids went into remission, or journeyed into the next astral plane, she rallied for every dime that went towards helping them forget their illness, pain, and struggle.

Suzanne walked toward the pool area and paused. *Presto!* The moon disappeared behind the clouds. *Now you see it, now you don't.* It was dark. *Too dark.* She must've gotten turned around. She stopped to listen. *Footsteps?* "Don't be paranoid," she mumbled, and inched her way towards the pool's eerie glow. She reached inside her purse for her phone, about to dial Julien, when an arm snaked around her neck and a large hand covered her mouth. Something hard pressed beneath her right shoulder blade. His hot breath seethed in her ear. "You shouldn't've meddled."

Then came a pop, and searing, hot, pain impaled her. A blow to the back of her head sent her reeling. She saw stars, heard a splash. Cold. Falling. Plumes of blood escaped her body as she descended to the bottom of the pool, her arms flailing like *snow angels.* Loving eyes acknowledged her despair. Tender arms enfolded her.

She closed her eyes and listened to the familiar voice. "Don't fight it," he whispered, "relax."

There was no mistaking the voice. *Jack.*

No longer falling. *Floating.*

Jack…my first love.

CHAPTER 2

Samson Metzger picked up the phone on the fifth ring. He hated being called in the middle of the night. Sleep was a commodity, not to be wasted. The desk sergeant's voice shattered the final fragments of his REM state. "He's at it again."

"Son-of-a—" Sam grumbled, pulling himself upright. "Where?"

"Diamond Springs, 515 Afton Street. I called the coroner. Johnson and Schuster are already on the scene. Dixon wants you there. Now."

"Fine." Sam plunked the phone back on its receiver. Twenty minutes later, he ducked under the yellow tape securing the scene. He flipped his badge at the officer standing vigil and donned the gear he had tucked under his arm. Once he was gowned from head to toe, he wiggled his fingers into a pair of nitrile gloves, dreading what lie ahead. He was well acquainted with the smell of death.

"What do we have?"

Rob Schuster lowered his mask. The camera around his neck dangled from a thick black strap. "If it isn't sleeping beauty."

"Not in the mood, Rob." Sam stood in the doorway to the living room of the rundown Victorian performing his usual overview of the crime scene. Starting at the far corner of the room, he began working in sections. "Same guy?"

"Looks like it," Rob said, holding up an evidence bag.

"Orange twine?"

"Yep. We'll know more once we get all the samples collected. Johnson's in the other room with the body." Before Rob reseated his mask, he added, "She's been here awhile."

Sam navigated his way down the hall. When he reached the bedroom, he pulled his mask over his nose and mouth. Inside, Dove Johnson, Goldorado County's finest crime scene investigator and forensic specialist, stood over the body of a young woman. Sam cleared his throat, and Dove jerked his head around.

"Hey partner—"

"Where's Dixon?"

"It's Friday night, probably bangin' some cheerleader." Dove shook his head. "Who knows? He said he'd be here. That was over an hour ago." Dove maneuvered his way around the body like a ninja. He lifted the dead girl's hand and carefully extracted an orange fiber embedded in her wrist. "This one fought like a hellion, just like the others."

Sam scanned the room. "No signs of struggle here in the house?"

"Nope—drop off, just like the Wheeler girl. I imagine when we find the scene of the crime it'll be horrific."

Sam squatted next to Dove. His eyes traveled the girl's body assessing decomposition and lividity. "How long?"

"Three to four weeks, give or take a few days."

"What kind of sick fuck does this?"

"The kind we'd better catch quickly." Dove nodded toward the girl's pelvic area. "I extracted the broom handle for prints."

Sam's stomach clenched. He moved away from Dove and tore at his mask. "When can I expect a report?"

"I'll be finished here in a couple hours. I should have something for you by midmorning."

Sam reached his hand in his pocket and pulled out the cell phone vibrating against his thigh. A grimace flashed across his face. "Detective Metzger."

"Just got a call from Mercy," Kelly, Goldorado County's bubbly dispatcher announced. "They pulled a body from the pool at the Marriott. She's still alive. Dixon wants you to check it out."

"It's freaking 2:00 a.m."

"I'm just the messenger—he said to get over there ASAP."

"O.D.? Suicide?"

"Not unless she shot herself in the back first."

"Jesus H. Christ," Sam hissed, flipping a page on his notepad. "Who called it in?" He scribbled the info on the page. "All right, I'll get over there as soon as I finish here." Sam clicked his phone off and slipped it in his pocket. "Like they say, no rest for the wicked," he said, slapping Dove's back. He took a last glance at the body. The girl was about his sister Audra's age. He shuddered.

On his way out, Sam approached Schuster, who was down on his knees photographing the Persian rug. He squatted beside him. "Anything?"

"One hundred-seventy-eight knots per square inch. Doesn't match the rest of the décor."

Sam noticed the furniture in the house was mismatched, shabby or broken. He lifted one corner of the rug. "The floor isn't faded," he said.

"No." Schuster snapped a series of photos. "Our guy carried the body here inside the rug, then staged the body in the bedroom."

Sam balled his mask inside his fist. "I got another call. I'll check in later."

Suzanne's brother, Steven, perched on the edge of her hospital bed and held her hand. "Hey Suz, you had us all worried."

Across the room, her husband Ben sat engrossed in a magazine. He'd barely lifted his eyes when she regained consciousness.

"Hurts," she whispered. She felt weak, her head pounded, pain radiated from her back in places she couldn't pin-point. Brightly colored scrubs swam across her vision, poking and prodding her body. Pliable tubing snaked from an IV pole to the PICC line delivering medication directly to her heart. Tiny lights flitted into black space and pulsated along her peripheral vision. She struggled to keep herself from falling back into the abyss.

"Do you know where you are Mrs. Cash?" a woman's voice came from the blur of colors above her head.

She tried to speak.

Steven lifted her hand to his cheek. "You're at Mercy Folsom," he said. "They brought you in last night." His voice quivered, "You were shot, found floating in the pool at the Marriott." He paused, choking back tears. "We thought we lost you."

Suzanne's fingers closed around his.

Ben circled to the other side of the bed and loomed over her fragile form. She tried to turn in his direction but couldn't. Her head spun. She felt nauseated.

Steven covered her hand with his. "The doctor said you're gonna be fine. You were in surgery for a good part of the night. The bullet nicked an artery. A centimeter to the left and—" Steven cleared his throat. "The Doc said you were lucky, the wound was clean, he said it would heal in no time. He also said you have a nasty concussion. I asked him how he could tell."

Suzanne couldn't laugh. Her brother always teased her about being the only "dizzy" brunette on the planet.

"What were you doing at that hotel?" Ben's tone turned Suzanne's blood to ice. Her eyes shifted to her brother, hoping he would intervene.

"How about if we go get some coffee Ben," he said. "Let Suzanne get her beauty sleep. We'll be back to check on you later, Sis."

Suzanne's lids closed, and she began to dream…

She was fifteen. A leaden sky, not unusual for December in Chicago, promised at least six more inches of snow. Suzanne trudged home from school. Three months into her sophomore year, and she wasn't doing well. A misfit with poor grades, not a good start. Her dad worked long hours, her mom worked part time, but between Rotary Club meetings and bake sales, mother-daughter time dwindled. When Suzanne's older brother, Steven, needed a favor he was her best friend, otherwise she didn't exist. Destined to be invisible.

She didn't notice the Chevy parked on the street in front of her bungalow until it was too late. Upon impact, Suzanne was jolted from one type of pain into another. A goose egg formed on her knee-cap, and she swore under her breath, "Dammit God! Why me?" Suddenly, large wet flakes tumbled from the sky. "Oh great. Just what I needed," she said and tromped inside the house.

"You're all wet," said the stranger sitting at the kitchen table.

"Is that YOUR stupid car out there?" Suzanne pulled at the torn fabric stretched across her knee. "My tights are ruined."

"I'd hate to see the other guy," he said, and bent down to touch her throbbing knee.

His touch took her breath away. It was gentle, soothing, contradictory to his tough guy appearance. His sagging jeans and worn leather jacket made her wonder if he was trouble. Trouble wasn't her type.

While Suzanne assessed his shaggy blond hair, the boy glanced up. She inspected his face; warm eyes, one brown, one green; dark lashes; faint freckles splashed across a nicely structured nose; a full mouth, centered on a square jaw. "I'm going to have a fat bruise," she said. The hand touching her knee had little nicks and cuts; the fingernails embedded with black grease. Casualties of maintaining the Chevy? Perhaps, but when their eyes connected, she felt kindness, generosity, and sensed a desire to know her better. The pain in her knee vanished.

"Who *are* you?"

"I'm Jack. And you—"

Suzanne examined her knee as if she were part of a hoax. "How did you do that?"

"Energy healing. You know, physician heal thyself?"

"Aren't you a little old to be playing doctor?"

Steven appeared from his room toting a classic car magazine. He flipped through pages, rattling off features of the new Mustang without acknowledging Suzanne's presence until his friend spoke up.

"You didn't tell me you had a sister," Jack said, nodding towards Suzanne.

"Oh, yeah. Jack, meet Suzanne."

She recognized the tone in Steven's voice as her cue to leave the kitchen. She gathered her things and started for her room when Jack blocked her path.

"Drop something?" he asked, dangling a glove from his pinky finger.

"Are you flirting with me?"

She grabbed the glove, and brushed past him, grazing his thigh with the back of her hand. A soft moan rumble in his throat.

Later that evening the storm let up, but high winds and drifting snow made it impossible to drive. Jack didn't seem to mind being stranded. Jack, Steven, and Suzanne bundled up and went outside to shovel the steps, walkways, and driveway.

The boys were piling the last hour's accumulation on the side of the drive when Suzanne threw the first snowball, hitting Jack on his right shoulder. It was war.

Suzanne hid behind the mound of snow closest to the back door, and bombarded the boys, clearly having an advantage. Jack shielded his face against the onslaught of loosely packed ammunition.

"Wait till I get a hold of you," he yelled.

She screamed, throwing snow quickly.

"Did you really think a little thing like *you* was going to stop *me?*" he asked, holding a handful of snow inches from her face.

"You underestimate me," she said, batting the snow out of his hand.

"And y̲o̲u̲, young lady, underestimate me."

"Steven, help," she cried, knowing her brother wouldn't come. *Don't fight.* She pretended to weaken, but when Jack relaxed his grip, she pushed hard, sending him reeling into a deep drift of snow.

"I give up," he said, brushing himself off.

"You want to call a truce?"

"Come," he said, reaching for her hand. She didn't resist. Something about him made her feel spontaneous, *daring*.

He led her to a patch of flat ground. "Turn around," he said.

Suzanne stood with her back to the virgin snow, arms stretched wide.

Jack turned to her; his eyes filled with a promise of something more—*a future.* "Ready?" he asked. "On my count—1-2-3."

"**M**rs. Cash?"

Suzanne didn't recognize the voice. Her eyes refused to open.

"Mrs. Cash, I'm sorry to bother you," the voice insisted. "I'm Detective Samson Metzger with the Goldorado County Sheriff's Department. I'd like to talk to you about what happened."

Suzanne's ears strained to hear.

"Mrs. Cash, we're losing time. We need to catch the person who did this to you. If you could answer some questions for me, I'll be as brief as possible." Sam pulled a chair next to her bed. "You were found in the pool at the Marriott, do you remember being there?"

She couldn't speak. Caught between worlds, she chose the past.

It was her sixteenth birthday. She was on the swing at the playground of her grammar school. Jack pushed her from behind. She pumped her legs to go higher.

"Go steady with me," he said.

"Steady?" She gasped.

He released the swing and planted himself in her path.

She gripped the chains. "What are you doing?" She dragged her feet until she skidded to a stop. Dust and gravel sprayed on Jack's shoes.

"I'm not moving until you give me your answer."

"Why should I go steady with you?"

"Because I love you," he replied. "I've loved you from the moment I saw you. I love everything about you." His thumb brushed a strand of hair from her cheek. "Don't you love me? Don't you want to be my girl?"

"Of course, I do."

Jack pulled his class ring from his finger and slipped it on hers. The ring was huge and wouldn't stay on her finger. Jack pulled orange twine from his pocket and wound it around the shank of the ring. He slipped it back onto Suzanne's finger and kissed her tenderly. "I will always, always, love you," he vowed.

"Mrs. Cash? Can you hear me?"

"Orange twine?" she mumbled weakly. *Funny. Why would Jack wrap orange twine around his class ring? He was a mechanic's apprentice. He always carried black tape.*

"Orange what?" The detective's voice sounded urgent. "Can you speak up? Were you meeting someone there?" Metzger pressed on. Suzanne's eyes fluttered. She fought to stay awake. "Tell me what happened, ma'am," he said. "Who did you go there to see?"

"Ki–" The word wouldn't form on her tongue. She wasn't making any sense.

"Were you there to meet a friend?"

She sensed his impatience. "Ki–" She repeated.

"Kids?" he said, remembering something about Wishes For Kids on the hotel marquee. "Is this about the fundraiser?"

She nodded.

"Did you *see* the person who attacked you?"

"Dark." As much as she wanted to cooperate, she couldn't describe the pictures in her head. She couldn't figure out if the drugs they were pumping into her system were the cause of her wooziness, or if her injured brain insisted on defaulting to sleep-mode. She wanted to explain to the detective that all the exits looked alike —somehow, she ended up in the rear of the building by the pool. *I needed to get home—on my feet all day. Lost.* She envisioned her attacker's arm wrapped around her neck; the muzzle of his gun pressed between her shoulder blades. She remembered his foul breath, his accusing words—

"British accent," she whispered, as a final "bang" rang out in her recall. Fear and exhaustion sucked her into an abyss.

Suzanne barely heard the detective rise from his chair. "I'll be back when you're feeling better," he said. "If there is *anything* you remember from last night, please have one of the nurses contact me immediately. I'll leave my card by the phone. You get some rest now." His hand touched hers. "Take care."

The sound of trays rattling on a metal cart in the hallway jarred Suzanne's senses. The smell of food wafted into the room. A woman's voice hummed a soulful tune. She heard rustling near her bed. The humming stopped.

"Mrs. Cash? My name is Veronica. I'm going check

your dressing. Is there anything I can get for you? How is your pain, sweetheart?"

Suzanne saw Jack standing in the corner of the room, dressed in his Army uniform. *He looks so young.* He had that smile on his face, the kind that made her melt, and she wanted him to come closer. *Why is he here?* She raised her hand to beckon him, but plastic tubing restricted her movement. A beeping sound pierced her brain.

The nurse began yelling. "Mrs. Cash? Suzanne, look at *me.*"

Another nurse rushed into the room. The blood pressure cuff squeezed Suzanne's arm. She felt a slight tug on her PICC-line. A warm sensation rushed over her, but she couldn't take her eyes from the corner of the room. *Falling.* She willed Jack to come with her and he did.

They were walking back to her house from the playground. Jack was kissing her hand, admiring his class ring on her finger. "One day," he said, "you'll be wearing a diamond."

"A diamond?" she said, although she couldn't imagine being any happier than she was at that moment.

"I'm going to take good care of you Suz. We'll live in a nice house, have a bunch of kids." When she gasped, he gave her a nudge. "Okay, how about two?"

Suzanne didn't answer. Something was wrong. "This isn't my house." She turned to Jack, expecting him to explain. She'd never seen him look so intense.

"You have to go in there with me, Suzanne. We need to find out what happened. Don't be afraid, I'll be with you." The three numbers below the porch light caught her attention. *515.* Panic rose before her hand touched the handle on the door. Her heart pounded in her chest, each beat–too hard, too fast. She knew what waited on the other side.

The girl's body wasn't cold yet.

"Suzanne, it's Steven." She opened her eyes. "How are you'?" he asked.

What's with the scruffy beard? The last time she saw him he was clean shaven.

"You've been knocked out for the past couple of days."

Days? She was here a few minutes ago with–
"Where's Ben?"

"Who knows, I'm sure he'll stop by later. You're pale again." Steven poured water into a glass from the pitcher on the nightstand.

"Nightmare—" She shuddered. "It seemed so real."

"Here, drink this," he said, handing her the cup.

"What day is it?"

"Tuesday. Detective Metzger is still hanging around

the hospital, says it's imperative he talk to you. Are you up to it? The last thing you need is stress. The doctor said your heart's been acting wacky. I can tell Metzger to go away if you want."

"He'll have to wait," she said, her voice cracking. "I need to tell you something." She took a sip of water.

Concern wrinkled Steven's brow. "What is it, Sis?"

"I saw Jack. He was here, in my room—I saw him as clear as day. He was in the pool too."

"That's impossible, Jack's been gone since—" he said, choking down his emotion. "He was my best friend. I would know if…he died in Iraq."

"But he was there." Suzanne pointed, "Standing in the corner."

"Jack? A ghost? No way. You're hallucinating—must be the morphine."

"Maybe," she said. Seeing Jack did seem preposterous. Still, *I know what I saw.* What she couldn't figure out was why Jack had been with her since the night at the Marriott, she hadn't thought of him in years. Head trauma and morphine could cause hallucinations. "He saved my life. How do you explain that?"

"I can't—I—I'm just glad you survived."

As if her physical pain wasn't enough, she reflected on Jack's last night on leave—the two of them together, his promise to write the moment he got to Iraq. Weeks went by without word. At first, she worried, and then she felt foolish. Weeks stretched into months and she wondered if he had jilted her. She convinced herself their love-making was something they needed to get out of their system, nothing more. She wrote to him every day, desperate for him to love her the way she loved him. When he didn't respond, she knew it was over. Three days after she mailed her farewell, the news came. Jack had been killed in an explosion. Three months later, she married Benjamin Cash at City Hall.

She remembered their marriage started on shaky ground, Ben, a wanna-be rock star, struggled with undiagnosed anger issues. She still silently grieved for Jack, the love of her life. Ben put up with her moodiness—she patched holes in the walls. Ben bounced from one band to another. She buried herself in charity work. Dysfunction took its toll on their relationship. They separated many times but reunited because *that's what dysfunctional people do.* Fifteen years of resentment and disappointment shaped their roles as husband and wife.

Steven interrupted her thoughts. "Ben off his medication again?" Her frown confirmed his suspicions. "Want me to have a talk with him?"

"Asenapine changes his pH, he doesn't like the way it makes him smell. I don't know, maybe he'll listen to you. I'm not up for one of his tantrums."

Steven nodded, "The detective asked him a few questions, now he's obsessing about what you were doing at the Marriott." Steven searched her face. "If you were —I mean, who could blame—you'd tell me, right?"

Her eyes grew large. "What?"

Steven knew better than to push. "Have you seen the doctor today?"

"Apology accepted, and no, I haven't talked to the doctor. But the nurse explained the results of my MRI, and the tear in my artery."

"Good news?"

"Yes, I'm healing nicely," she said. Suzanne's focus shifted to the corner of the room. "Scary. I don't remember having any tests. They said the pain will go away eventually, but what about my memory lapses?"

"Concussions take time to heal, Suz. In a few weeks, when the swelling is gone, you'll be back to eh, normal."

Suzanne touched the stitches on the back of her head. They were stiff and rubbed against the pillowcase when she moved. "I want to go home. Do you think you can arrange that for me?"

"I'll see what I can do. What about Metzger? He has a toothbrush tucked in his breast pocket. He's not going away."

Suddenly she remembered. "The event! I'm the committee chairman for the Wish Kid Foundation, I need to call Elaine."

"She called Ben, he explained what had happened."

"Did she say how it went? Did the kids have fun? Did we reach our goal?"

Steven crossed the room and peeked through the blinds. "Looks like we're in for a storm."

"It took months to put it together. The kids were excited about wearing masks. The mystery we chose was brilliant—the pledges—all those prizes? Steven, you're my brother, tell me—what happened?"

"Ben didn't say much, only that some lady named Elaine left a hundred messages on the answering machine and used up all the recording space. He was pissed, he erased 'em all. You know how he is."

"I need to call—"

"Knock-knock." Suzanne and Steven turned to face the man in the doorway. His voice was deeper than his stature called for. "Do you remember me? Detective Metzger. Samson Metzger. Sam. I've been waiting to speak with you, Mrs. Cash. I hope now is a good time."

Suzanne waved him forward. Salt and pepper hair framed a face etched with laugh lines, complexity, and at least forty years of sunshine. Bright blue eye, fringed with black lashes sparkled beneath nicely shaped brows. His tone dipped another register, "Sorry for the interruption, but the last time we spoke, well, we really didn't speak, I did most of the talking. You were heavily sedated." He re-introduced himself to Steven and shook his hand. When he turned back to Suzanne, images flashed in her mind; cathedrals, palaces, cliffs, a winding river… a feeling of contentment came over her. It was as if she had known him all her life. "Your father--he's German descent, he migrated to Austria after the war," she blurted. "Your mother was born in Sicily."

Sam took a step back. "Whoa. Thought I was the one running background checks around here."

"Sorry. That popped into my head. I don't know what came over me."

"I checked with the Wish Kid Foundation," he said. "I was thinking how ironic it was that the person responsible for organizing a 'Magical Mystery' event is now subject to a mystery of her own. Can you tell me more about the man with the accent?"

How did he know? "Did I *say* he had an accent?"

"You don't remember?" He moved closer. Spice, vanilla, and a hint of peppermint lingered in the air. "I want to find the person who tried to kill you *before* the town goes vigilante. People tend to freak out when the body count goes up."

"515." The number came out of her mouth like a hiccup. The detective moved closer still.

Steven stood up, ready to intervene, but Sam held up his hand.

"Say again?"

When Suzanne repeated the number, the detective pulled a notepad from his pocket and began to write. "What about 515, Mrs. Cash?"

"I don't know." She felt confused. "In the nightmare, it wasn't my house–" Her stomach began to pitch. The color red flooded her vision. "515" flashed neon in her mind. She was caught in a series of violent images and gore.

"Tell me what you're seeing."

"A wooden floor. She's face-down," she heard herself

say, "Her hands and feet are bound with orange twine. Her clothes, crumpled in a ball."

"Go on," the detective insisted, but it wasn't him talking any more–it was Jack. He was there, like he had promised.

"What else do you see?"

"Blood," she cried. "I see bloodstains on a white blouse, on faded jeans."

The hospital door burst open, spitting Sam to the curb. Twenty years on the force, and *never* had he experienced anything like that. *Who the hell is she? What does she know about Amy Fitzpatrick?* More women had been found brutally murdered over a course of eight months: Twila Averose, Melinda Carlisle, Dillyn Wheeler, and Amy Fitzpatrick. The only people privy to the details found at the crime scenes were guys he had worked with for years. Nobody leaked a case. *Nobody.* How did she know about his father? His mother? *Austria?*

To make matters worse, she had an effect on him. Even in her injured state, she was beautiful. He dipped his hand in pocket and grasped the sobriety coin. *Ten years. Don't blow it now.*

Alcohol had kept the demons at bay. Numbed his heart. Served as a catalyst between reality and the underworld. And then one day he was called to a scene, a child had been severely beaten, set on fire, and thrown into a dumpster. After dowsing his anger with a fifth of whiskey, he had an epiphany. You can't medicate a conscience.

～

"Nooo," Suzanne cried out. The kink in her IV sounded an alarm. Jack hovered near the edge of the bed. His eyes sad.

"Mrs. Cash, calm down. *Shhhhh*," the nurse said, patting Suzanne's hand. "I'm Belinda. You had a bad dream, that's all."

"I saw her—she's—" Suzanne said, catching her breath. "Is Detective Metzger still here?"

"No, I haven't seen him all morning."

"Morning?"

"Yes, Mrs. Cash it's morning."

"Can you call Detective Metzger for me? It's urgent."

Belinda called the number on the card Detective Metzger had placed on Suzanne's nightstand and handed her the phone. "Her name is Amy. I see her with a man, a dark-haired man. She's in trouble."

"I'll be right there."

"I don't understand, why come here? Find her before it's too—"

"She's already dead."

"But she can't be I just saw her—"

"Her body was found at 515 Afton Street."

Suzanne dropped the phone. A small voice echoed in the distance, "Mrs. Cash? Mrs. Cash, are you there?"

~

S am pulled up a chair and drew his pad from his shirt pocket. "Tell me what you saw."

Suzanne ached more for the dead girl, than she did from her gunshot wound. "I saw her getting ready for her date. She lost thirty pounds and was excited about fitting into her new jeans. After dinner, he took her to a place—the hallway had green carpet with sort of a diamond pattern in the center. Small sconces lined the walls—she was wobbly."

Metzger stopped scribbling on his pad, his gaze, hard around the edges.

Suzanne hiked her cover up an inch or two. "You think I'm making it up?"

"I'm trying to wrap my head around what you're telling me. Go on."

Suzanne felt sick inside. "What good is this information if she's dead?"

"Amy Fitzpatrick died weeks ago. She was found in an abandoned house on Afton Street."

"But I saw —"

"We did a thorough exam of the crime scene. She was murdered somewhere else. Green fibers were found beneath her fingernails. The house on Afton had hardwood floors."

Suzanne's scalp tingled from the top of her head to the nape of her neck. Her stomach knotted. Jack appeared in the corner of the room; his arms tight across his chest.

"Have you talked to anyone else about your dreams, Mrs. Cash?"

"Suzanne, please."

"Deal, if you call me Sam."

"No, I didn't tell anyone about the girl," she said, diverting her gaze.

"There's more?"

"You'll think I'm insane."

"Try me."

"I have been seeing my dead boyfriend from long ago in these dreams."

"I see. And?"

"And—I see him here, in my room."

Sam raised one eyebrow. "And?"

"And—he's standing behind you."

While Sam took an incoming phone call into the hallway, Suzanne dozed. She dreamt of the summer she turned sixteen, she and Jack were cleaning the pool. Suzanne was a poor swimmer. Jack insisted she learn to float.

"Suzanne, *floating* is part of *swimming*."

"I'm afraid," she cried.

"Of what?"

"Sinking."

Jack's face softened. "C'mere, let me show you." He pulled her close and turned her around. "Lean back against me," he said, placing one hand at the base of her head, and one on her lower back. "Relax."

She obeyed, closing her eyes to the blazing sun. His touch made her shiver.

"No monkey business, this is serious." His hand moved lower, resting too close to one of her "off limit" zones.

"No tricks—promise?" she said, moving his hand higher up.

"I promise," he said, lowering his mouth to hers. His kiss, gentle at first, grew more urgent. It felt as though he was sucking air from her lungs. She tried to scream. The had sun vanished from the sky. *Darkness.* Suzanne struggled to free herself from the orange twine around her wrists, and feet. Something impeded her movement. Her eyes felt gritty. A damp earthy smell, a scraping noise. Realization hit her. *Buried alive.*

Suzanne woke with a start, tearing at her face, gulping in as much air as her lungs could hold. Sam took her hand. "What's wrong?"

"I can't—I can't breathe."

It didn't take Sam long to understand. "Jennifer Richmond's body was found a half mile from the Kingsvale exit. The Goldorado County coroner determined her death as strangulation by suffocation. The

Sheriff's Department withheld news about her being buried. They didn't share little details—like orange twine imbedded in her hands and feet." Sam paced once around the room and returned to Suzanne's bedside. "An autopsy will reveal whether she was still alive when she was put in the ground."

Suzanne winced. "She struggled."

"How can you be sure?"

"I felt—" She gripped the side rails of her bed to steady her hands, she could still recall shovels of dirt filling the hole. "She was still alive."

CHAPTER 3

Ben parked in Calvin's driveway. "Fucker better be home," he grumbled. Calvin Cook headed the band, booked their performances, controlled the money. He dreamed of quitting his job at the hospital—*We'll take the show on the road.* Ben knew better. Calvin talked more crap than a porta-potty, which was okay most of the time. What wasn't okay was cancelling the last few practices.

Calvin still owed the guys money from a gig they'd played Fourth of July weekend. With Suzanne in the hospital, Ben needed money to live on until she could make a deposit into their account. He knew not to force the issue. She'd question money spent on things most people didn't understand.

Ben had met Calvin through Suzanne. They'd worked together on a few projects through the hospital. When Calvin told her he was a musician, Suzanne invited him over for a beer. He brought his guitar and he and Ben jammed. Ben had to admit, at first, he envied Calvin. Calvin was tall, handsome and a smooth talker. When he sang, women couldn't get enough. Especially during their British oldies set, when Calvin sang lead on Herman's Hermits, "Mrs. Brown You've Got A Lovely Daughter," and the Beatles, "Love Me Do." Ben shined more on their hard rock set—AC/DC, Billy Idol. The band was good. *Goin' places.*

Ben knocked on the door and peeked through the window. No answer.

"Calvin? Open the fucking door, man." Ben looked through the window again. It was dark inside. His temper sent a potted geranium smashing on the side-walk. He needed his *medicine.*

He slammed his car door and peeled out of the driveway. A quarter mile down the road he pulled over to make a call. Calvin wasn't the only game in town.

Two weeks passed before Suzanne was discharged from the hospital. Ben drove her home, then said he was going to work. *Work.* Hanging out in his buddy's basement all day, smoking pot. *Being creative.*

Suzanne fixed herself a cup of tea and turned on the news.

"Are criminal investigators calling the latest murder part of a crime spree? Is there a serial killer on the loose? Stay tuned for more—"

The cup slipped from her hand and crashed to the floor. Jack stood in front of the 55-inch TV screen, hovering inches from the floor.

"You can't keep scaring me like this, Jack. I don't want you here. You're dead!"

"You know why I'm here. You need to trust me."

"Trust you? I trusted you once—you broke my heart. Now you're filling my head with horror. Why?"

"Come with me."

Suzanne was blindsided by an image of an ax hitting bone. "Stop," she cried, but Jack grabbed her hand, and pulled her into another place, another time.

The house was dim.

Shards of light squeezed between faded draperies. Italian Provincial furniture beneath fine art hanging above a dingy mantle. Papered walls, wooden floors. Blood stained the center of a green, diamond-patterned, ornate rug. The man's back was turned. Legs dangled across his forearms.

She followed unseen, down a flight of stairs. A large wooden table stretched across the width of the room. He laid the body down, careful of her long hair. He fanned her chestnut tresses around her head, turned her palms up, and crossed her bare feet, right over left. A sharp metal object gleamed under florescent light, its wooden handle, stained with blood.

"Stop," Suzanne pleaded.

"You've seen enough, Suz. Come."

Stepping back in time, Jack and Suzanne were in a swimming pool.

"Try it again," he said.

"You're trying to drown me, I know it."

"Why would I hurt you? I love you."

There, he said it. Said the words she had longed to hear. "I love you too, Jack. But if you don't stop trying to drown me, I may change my mind."

"If you're going to learn to swim, you have to learn to float."

Why did he keep saying that?

Before she could object, she was back in her living room. The TV blasted the news.

"—body parts found along the American River."

The feeding frenzy had begun.

She Googled most recent 'brutal murders in Sacramento'. She scrolled down. Twila Averose, Melinda Carlisle, Dillyn Wheeler, Amy Fitzpatrick, most recent, Jennifer Richmond. She grabbed her phone.

"Detective Metzger," she demanded, her hand shaking. The receiver had a hum she didn't remember hearing before her near-death experience. Her senses seemed to be on overload. She smelled flowers that weren't there, perfume, smoke. Doctors chalked it up to her brain injury. She knew different.

When Metzger identified himself on the other end of the phone, she blurted out, "He's setting me up."

"Suzanne? Who's setting you up?"

"Jack."

"You said he's dead, how could he—"

"From the beyond. He's showing me the murders after they happen, but he's teaching me to float, and once I learn to float, he'll teach me to swim, and once I can swim, he'll show me the murders before they happen—can't you see? He's preparing me, setting me up!"

"Take it easy." His voice calmed her. "Want me to stop by? I can be there in fifteen minutes."

"Yes. And Sam? Please tell me I'm not going insane—because it feels like I'm losing my mind."

After they hung up, Suzanne hurried to the kitchen to make a pot of coffee. Sam was a coffee kind of guy. How she knew didn't register.

Fifteen minutes later, the doorbell rang. Suzanne opened the door.

"Is that coffee I smell?"

"Yes, come in." She led him to the kitchen. "Sit," she said. "Sorry. Ben hates when I order him around."

"Nothing wrong with being direct."

He could've taken offense, but he hadn't, and she

was beginning to like the way he made her feel comfortable. It had been a long time since she'd been able to be herself. When working with people in charity, she kept her opinions to herself. Charity work was about the cause. The cause always took priority over any feelings she may have had about how the goals were met. She chose her profession to keep sunshine in her life. *Purpose.* If it were up to Ben, he would've sucked the joy out of her life long ago. *Contrast.* As a couple, they were not only opposites, Ben's bi-polar disorder kept her on her toes. She watched what she said and learned to walk on eggs without cracking the shells. And then there was Sam…

"Tell me again," he said. "I'm not clear on how Jack is setting you up."

She poured coffee, filling two mugs. "When we were young, Jack promised to teach me how to swim, but he said I had to learn to float first. He believed in taking things one step at a time. I think that's what he's doing—taking it one step at a time. Seeing how much I can take—how long I can float before I sink."

"What did he show you this time? What did you see?"

"An old house, ornate furniture. A tall, husky, man. I couldn't see his face. The woman was maybe early twenties. Long hair, brown." Suzanne shuddered. "I saw an ax."

"Dear God."

She wanted to reach over and touch him. He moved first, taking her hand, holding it in his. *Strong hands.*

"Are you okay?" he asked.

His concern melted her heart. "Yes. No. I threw-up."

"That's not cool." He smiled. "I don't know what to think about all of this 'spooky' stuff—about *you*."

Ben walked in the back door. When he saw them, his face twisted in rage. "What the hell is going on here?"

"Ben, you remember Sa—Detective Metzger?"

Sam rose and extended his hand.

Ben's eyes were wild. "I don't give a fuck who you are — What are you doing sitting in MY kitchen with MY wife?"

Suzanne intervened. "Calm down. Nothing is going on. He came because I asked him to. I don't expect you to understand. I was upset. Detective Metzger was merely consoling me, that's all."

Ben slammed his hand on the table spilling coffee. "Look what you made me do. Clean it up."

"Hey—" Sam stepped between Ben and Suzanne, "Chill. Your wife is instrumental in a murder case I'm working, nothing more. A young woman was found butchered along the American River. Did you hear about it?"

Ben stepped back. "No shit," he said. His eyes, cold, and fathomless, gave Suzanne chills.

B en retired early. Suzanne sat up, alone in the dark, mulling over conversations with Sam. As foreign as her visions seemed to him, he tried to understand. He couldn't deny that she knew things. Sam didn't judge. Ben did.

And Jack? The visions brought back bittersweet memories she had spent years trying to forget. *Pain.* She let her mind drift back to a time when she questioned his love. She was sixteen, working at a restaurant. Jack and Steven had come in for a bite to eat. Another waitress, whom Suzanne considered a rival, and whom Jack said he detested, made a point to tell him it was her birthday. Suzanne watched as Jack rose from his chair, grabbed the girl's face and kissed her passionately. *I was crushed.* He had laughed at her jealousy, said it was all in fun, but she didn't see it that way. She never fully trusted him after that.

"Why did you agree to marry me then?"

Jack's voice made her flinch. He sat beside her, took her hand and held it to his cheek. "I loved you the moment I saw you. I love you still. The other side doesn't erase the love we feel for those we love when we're alive." He turned her face toward his. "Look at me."

"This is insane—the visions—they're terrifying—"

"I'm sorry, but you're the one. I have to make you see."

In an instant, she saw herself in a hallway. The green diamond-pattern on the carpet was familiar. A man, his back towards her, turned his head, allowing her a partial view of his profile. His ball cap shaded his features. *He's dragging something.*

"No—Please don't!" Suzanne covered her eyes. When she looked up, the figure standing in the doorway was *Ben*. She was back in her living room.

"What the hell is wrong with you?"

"I'm sorry, I didn't mean to wake—"

"Hell if you didn't."

"You're free to go elsewhere if my yelling bothers you so much."

"Why don't you? Maybe that little pissant you were coffee-klatching with today will put up with your shit."

"Go back to bed, Ben." Suzanne sighed. "I'm in no condition to fight with you."

"Serves you right for being at some hotel instead of home, where you belong."

"Leave me alone. We'll talk in the morning."

"The hell we will. I'm DONE, done with your weirdo woo-woo shit. Done with you thinking you can save the world when you can't even save yourself. Look at you—you used to be pretty, you took care of yourself. Now you're like all the other plain Janes fighting for the *cause.* How 'bout the cause at home? When's the last time we had sex?"

"I'm not going anywhere until I'm healed. Stay with your friend, you know—the other rock star, the one you *work* with. I'm sure he has room in his basement for his good buddy."

"Screw you, Suzanne." Ben stormed out of the room. Their fights had progressed over the years. She knew he had mental issues, but she was tired of putting *his* health first. She warned him that going on and off his meds would mess-up his brain chemistry but nagging only escalated his anger.

She got up and went into the kitchen. Tea wouldn't fix things, but it would busy her hands until she calmed down. Reaching for a cup aggravated the stitches in her chest. She plopped down on a kitchen chair and began to cry. A hand reached for hers, startling her.

"Dammit Jack."

"He's a jerk, I hope you plan to leave him."

"Go away."

She was about to sip her tea when she heard a crash upstairs. Something hit the bottom of the stairs with a thud. She peeked around the corner. *My pillow?* Next came her blanket, a shoe, her hair-brush. She prayed he would stop.

Ben barreled down the stairs, his arms filled with clothes from her closet, his eyes wild, his face red. She reached for the phone, ready to dial 911. *He's out of control.*

"Ben, this isn't going to solve anything."

"You think you can leave me? Have at it—here you go." He threw clothes at her, whipping a handful at a time. The zipper on one of her skirts nicked her cheek.

She held the phone tight, her thumb hovering over the 9. The pain in her chest burned. Tiny lights danced in the corner of her eye. It felt as though she were moving, picking up speed. Ben's voice echoed in her brain. His mouth moved in slow motion, he raised his fist, but before he struck her, her world went black and she was gone.

∽

"Can't leave you alone for a minute," Steven teased. "Someone should be down in a bit to take you for your MRI."

"MRI?"

"Doctor thinks you may have another concussion. You hit your head hard when you passed out. He said it's a wonder you didn't crack your skull open. I told him you've always—"

"Been a hard head, I know. Do you ever say anything nice about me? Where's Ben?"

"He's staying with his buddy."

"I'm leaving him. I can't take the abuse anymore. He's going to be the death of me if I stay."

"Where will you go?"

"Your house."

"I thought you'd never ask."

"You're my brother. Brothers look out for their sisters, right?"

"You know you don't have to ask. I'll have Karen prepare the guest room for you."

"I promise, it won't be for long, as soon as I get on my feet, I'll—"

"Quit worrying. With all the traveling I do, Karen will be thrilled to have the company."

"I hope *I* still have a job when I get out of here."

"Elaine can't run that place by herself, and it would take a millennium to train someone to fill your shoes."

A young orderly pushed a wheelchair into the room.

"Ready for a little ride?" The orderly double-checked the name on Suzanne's wristband, and helped her out of bed. After he put terry socks on her feet and placed a blanket over her lap, he wheeled her toward the door.

Suzanne lay on a cold, stainless steel table, her hands pressed to her side. A woman hovered near by.

"You're not claustrophobic, are you?" A young technician donned in turquoise scrubs smiled as she spoke.

"Not that I know of."

"Good. I'm going to strap your head in place. It will prevent you from moving during the MRI. The less you move, the sooner we finish."

Suzanne felt her body being maneuvered into place. "Once you're in the tube, you're going to hear a rat-a-tat-tat noise. Please keep your head as immobile as possible. Feel free to close your eyes, relax. It will be over soon."

She closed her eyes. The table moved. The noise began.

Jack was with her; it was late summer.

"When are we going to the lake?"

"When you can swim."

"I thought I was doing really well."

"You still can't float."

"I can do the breaststroke pretty good."

"I know, you're making progress, but if you get in trouble, you'll need to float."

"What kind of trouble?"

She heard another voice. A man's voice. *Him.* "You're doing just fine Mrs. Cash," she heard him say with a *British accent*, and without warning, she was at the Marriott. It was dark. She stood by the edge of the pool, confused. She didn't know where she was. *All turned around.* Go back? Julian would help. While digging in her purse for her phone she felt his breath on her neck. His words hissed in her ear. *"You shouldn't have meddled."* Meddle? And then hard, cold, steel pressed against her back, and hot pain seared through her. He hit her in the back of the head with the gun, and she plunged into the water. She heard beautiful music, angels singing. *Jack's voice.* "I'm here." *Cold air on my face.* "Breathe, Suzanne, breathe."

"Mrs. Cash?"

Suzanne's eyes squinted into the light.

"Are you all right?"

"What?" All Suzanne could see was the mid-section

of the young woman dressed in turquoise. The table moved forward.

"You stopped breathing. Are you okay?" The technician's eyes expressed her concern.

"I must've—who else is here?"

"Dr. Reynolds was here a bit ago. He got called to the ER. I checked the images," she said, loosening the strap across Suzanne's waist. "Everything looks good. We're finished." She helped Suzanne into a sitting position. "Are you all right?"

"I'm—fine."

An orderly wheeled Suzanne into her room. Steven was on his phone. He placed his hand over the speaker. "It's Metzger."

"Let me speak to him."

Steven handed her the phone.

"Detective Metzger, I know who shot me."

Sam walked in the door ten minutes later and asked, "What do you have to tell me?"

"There's a Dr. Reynolds that works here. He has a British accent. He shot me."

"How can you be sure?"

"I recognized his voice."

"Why would a doctor shoot you?"

"I don't know. But I know it's him."

"I'll check into it." He brushed her hand with his

fingertips. A warm sensation reached a part of her she had long forgotten.

"Why are you so nice?" Her M.O., *trust no man*. Too many let-downs. Too many broken promises.

"I like you." His hand reached for hers. She pulled away. "I intend to find the creep who put you here," he said.

"Sounds like you're going to be *very* busy."

"You're worth it."

After the detective left the room, Steven sat beside Suzanne. "What's going on? Are you falling for this guy?"

"Who's falling for who?" Suzanne and Steven turned toward the voice coming from the doorway.

Steven stood up. "Ben, what are you doing here? Don't you think you've put my sister through enough?"

"I'm her husband, asshole, I have a right to be here."

Suzanne grabbed Steven's arm. "Steven asked me if I was falling for the excuses the doctor made—regarding my condition."

"Oh, so now you have a <u>condition</u>?"

Steven stepped between her husband and the bed. "Suzanne is staying with me and Karen until she's back on her feet. Doctors' orders. She needs full time care, and Karen is happy to play nursemaid. Beats having to pay someone to come to the house."

"You're up to something."

"Dammit, Ben—can't you think of someone besides yourself? I need to be with someone who can care for me, not a ticking time bomb." Suzanne could tell by Ben's expression that he would store this moment and use it against her later. "Karen is home, you're not. I need to rest, not battle with you."

"Fine. Have it your way. You'll regret talking to me like one of your little volunteer twits."

"Please go. Just let me get better."

Ben left.

Steven stood in the doorway. "Tell me you're done taking his abuse."

"When it's right—"

"You've been saying that for the last five years— what's it gonna take? Him beating the crap out you? Slicing your throat?"

"Don't be so dramatic. He's not going to make it easy. Please, let me take care of things my way, in my own time."

"If he gets any crazier, we'll have to put him away."

"You think committing a person is that easy?"

"Fine."

After Steven left, Suzanne closed her eyes. She knew Ben would make her life hell. She remembered how persistent he had been at winning her back when they separated the last time. He'd sent flowers, showed up at the house, then at her office. He was charming, apolo- getic—*sincere*. When she agreed to give it another whirl it didn't take long for his horns to emerge. The flowers stopped. His phone calls became more frequent. His questions accusing. "Where are you? What are you doing? Who are you with?" By then, she was exhausted. *Dating wasn't my thing; I didn't trust other men.* She knew what to expect with Ben, so she settled, once again.

She thought about Detective Metzger. Wondered what it would be like to live in *his* world. How she longed for normalcy.

Being shot, thrown in a pool, and left to die changed a person. *Not to mention being visited by your dead boyfriend.* Maybe her head injury had knocked some sense into her. She couldn't go back. She couldn't spend another day with Ben. *I'm done.*

Jack stood at the foot of her bed.

"Go away. I'm done with you, too. I'm making changes, and I'm starting with you, Jack. Stay out of my head, my dreams, my—"

Without warning, she saw a house with dingy windows. She smelled urine, mixed with Lysol and bleach. The stench was enough to make her retch— but how could she? *This isn't real. Wake up!*

Jack let go of her hand and she froze. A man busied himself collecting tools from a rack on the wall. A saw. A drill. A large file. She could see a bottle of bleach beneath the bench next to a shoe? *Dear God.* The foot was still attached.

"Mrs. Cash?" Suzanne's lids fluttered. Bile rose in her throat. "Mrs. Cash, wake up."

Jack leaned against the wall; his arms crossed. How many times had she seen that pose? Him waiting patiently for her to *get it*? "Leave me ALONE!"

"Mrs. Cash, calm down. It was just a dream. You're okay. You're safe, now. Do you know where you are?"

"Do you see him? There—in the corner?"

"No ma'am, I don't see anyone. You were having a dream."

"There was a—foot—it was—"

"Shhhh, now. You're at Mercy General, and you are safe. I'm Justine, your nurse this evening, and I am going to make sure nothing bad happens to you. Understand me?"

"Yes," Suzanne whispered, but she knew it was a lie.

CHAPTER 4

Weeks turned into months. Christmas had come and gone. Budding trees, blossoms, promising spring. And then came summer, almost without notice.

Sam parked on the street and made his way up the winding drive. He checked the address against the paper in his hand. The conversation he had with Dove about Suzanne being spooky played in his head. "If you want to know more about that kind of stuff, ask a psychic. I know a good one." Dove wrote her name and number down and handed it to Sam. "She's the real deal."

He tucked the paper in his pocket and rang the bell.

A face peeked through the crack in the door. "May I help you?"

"I hope so. I'm Detective Samson Metzger, Goldorado County Sheriff's Department. I'd like to talk to you about a case I'm investigating."

"How I can help," the woman asked, inching the door open.

"You're Linda Schooler, the psychic?"

"Yes. Do you want a reading? I only take clients by appointment—"

"I really need your help." Sam presented his badge. "Please?"

"I'm expecting a client shortly. Can we make this quick?"

"I hope so. May I come in?"

The psychic scanned him from head to toe. "Okay, but for just a few minutes—as I said, I am expecting a—"

"Thank you," he said, brushing past her.

The woman closed the door. "Come." Sam followed her into a quaint parlor furnished with a loveseat and two sapphire-blue velvet wingback chairs. She offered him the chair across from her. "What is it you'd like to know?"

"Can people see the dead?"

"Are you seeing dead people, detective?"

"Not me, it's—"

"A friend."

"Yes."

"Does your friend have a name?"

"Suzanne."

The psychic closed her eyes. He watched her eyes move back and forth beneath her lids. Her head moved from side to side.

Her eyes opened and she spoke. "Suzanne is a vessel. What she brings from the beyond is a gift. She lost someone very dear to her, that's the connection. Love. The love they shared was severed. He is gifting her *sight*, showing her things that will propel her journey here on the earth plane. You see, what we undergo on this level is an experience. Once our journey at this level is complete, we move to the next realm. Like a video game. Each level presents a challenge before reaping a reward."

"The 'gift' as you put it, is information. It's not pleasant."

"I see that. Your friend not only wants to shut it out, she fears the unknown. She'll adjust. She needs to believe in her higher self, and let the information flow to its destination, which is—*you*."

"Me?"

"You're in a quandary—there's more to come."

Sam didn't have patience for riddles. "Thank you for your time. How much do I owe you?"

"Nothing. Catch your killer. The world is full of checks and balances. Good cannot exist without evil."

"Tell that to the parents of the murder victims."

"Right. And tell her what's in your heart."

"Pardon me?"

"You're falling in love with her."

Sam drove home dissecting the information he had received from the psychic. How had she pick up on his feelings for Suzanne? *Am I that transparent?* He had spent a lifetime guarding his heart, putting up walls. The last thing he wanted was a complex relationship. He liked women, liked the pleasure they gave him when he was in need, but that was the extent. He'd never been in love, or even cared about a woman long enough to establish more than a casual friendship. Suzanne was different. He loved her eyes, and the way her lips formed words when she spoke. Her beauty, masked behind the stress of her situation, presented itself when she looked his way. *I can't wait to see her again.*

Who was he kidding? His time was eaten up trying to solve a puzzle with too many obscure pieces. Another young woman missing, and he and his men were no closer to catching the killer. The man who shot Suzanne was still at large. No wonder Dixon gave him shit.

Angela Foxworthy stood on her tip-toes, suspended from a beam overhead. Shackles bit into her flesh, pain radiated from her head to her feet, but that was nothing compared to the burning sensation she felt having her skin stapled to the wood pressing against her spine.

She had given up smoking two months ago, now she wondered why. Like the diet her mom went on before she found out she had cancer. All that struggle for nothing. Angela knew she fucked up. She knew she shouldn't have been walking home late at night, but she wanted to go to the party. She thought she had a better chance of getting home safely walking three miles, than riding with one of her drunk friends. When the car slowed, she was apprehensive, but when she saw who it was, she hopped in without a second thought. He offered her a soda. The can was open, but he said he hadn't drunk any yet. She had no reason to doubt him. She was thirsty.

She danced around the sticky blood, screaming each time her skin tore, and fresh blood added to the mix. It seemed as though she had been in and out of consciousness for days. Her captor hadn't returned. No food. No water. *No cigarettes for you.*

She wished she hadn't been so trusting. She wished she could go back, do things differently. She wished he would kill her and get it over with.

CHAPTER 5

"I'm not hungry." Suzanne pushed her plate away. "The chicken is delicious, Karen. It's my stomach. Must be the meds."

Steven looked up from his meal.

Karen said, "Try and eat another bite or two. You need your strength."

"Okay, Mom."

Steven scowled. "What the hell has gotten into you?"

"I don't know." Suzanne dropped her fork on the table. "I'm going to go lie down."

She closed her bedroom door and laid across the bed, burying her face in her pillow. Words and images, cyclones spinning in her head.

The knock on the door made Suzanne bristle. "What?"

"Can I come in?"

Sam. Shit. Suzanne hadn't thought about brushing her hair. *What's the use?* She opened the door. "Hi."

"Bad time?"

"What makes you say that?"

"The brush you're holding like a led pipe."

Suzanne tossed the brush on the bed. "Let's go outside. Boys aren't allowed in my room."

"Boys?"

"The whole male species, brothers included. Why are you here?"

"I checked out your Dr. Reynolds."

"And?"

"He doesn't exist."

"I heard him—he was there!"

"Someone was there. The nurse collaborated your story, but there is no Dr. Reynolds on staff."

"The nurse called him by name."

"She didn't know him, she identified him by his badge."

"So, who is he?"

"Million-dollar question."

Sam's hand gravitated toward Suzanne's.

"Why do you keep touching me?" she asked.

His smile was sheepish, his voice dropped a notch. "A psychic told me I liked you."

"You talked to a psychic? About me?"

"I needed more info on near death experiences, thought I'd consult an expert."

"And she just happened to mention that you like me?"

"Well, yes, sort of. Have you ever been?" he asked.

"Ever been what?"

"To a psychic?"

"Once. A séance. I thought maybe I could summon Jack— the table shook a little—that's all. It was a long time ago. What else did she say?"

"She said you were given a gift."

Suzanne studied the sky, lost in thought. Steven took a lounge chair next to her. "You're acting like a shit, Suz."

"I know, I owe you and Karen a huge apology. I don't know what's come over me." She shrugged. "I don't sleep—may be why I'm so cranky." She heard Steven sigh.

"You were born cranky."

"Thanks."

"Truth hurts, what can I say?"

"You can say you've been through a lot—you deserve a break."

"Mom and dad taught us to suck it up."

"Yeah, well someone didn't shoot them in the back and throw them in the pool to die."

"I'll let you slide this time but take it easy on Karen.

She doesn't deserve to be treated like your personal whipping post."

"You're right, I *am* a shit."

"Bygones. What were you and Dick Tracy talking about?"

"Psychics. He talked to a psychic about me."

"I thought he'd consult a psychiatrist, not a psychic. You did hit your head. Who knows what kind of damage you did?"

"The MRI didn't show any tumors, the bleeding has stopped. But the radiologist kept shaking his head while he was reading it."

"Meaning?"

"Meaning whatever he was looking at wasn't the norm."

"I could've told you that."

"Why does everything have to be a joke? These visions scare me."

"How often are you having them?"

"It's been a few days. The last one was while I was in the hospital." Suzanne massaged her temples. "Whenever I see Jack, it happens. It's like watching a horror movie and I—"

"Are you still on that kick?"

"You don't believe me?"

"I thought when you felt better—"

"So, as long as you thought I had brain damage, seeing Jack was acceptable?"

"I just can't wrap my head around it."

"That's what Sam said. Only *he* went to a psychic to try to understand."

"Sam?"

"Stop." Suzanne folded her arms across her chest.

"You want me to go to a psychic?"

"Let's both go."

"No thanks. I don't need to know the extent of your—"

"My what?" Tears welled in Suzanne's eyes.

"Fine," he said. "I'll go with you to see a psychic."

That night Suzanne couldn't sleep. Karen's Pinterest ideas had transformed the guest room into a magazine-worthy retreat. Pale yellow walls trimmed in white, garage sale cast-offs refinished into shabby chic treasures with crystal knobs. Sheer, pale grey panels framing tall transom windows, billowed in the summer breeze. All she had to do was close her eyes and drift away on a moonbeam, but when she closed her eyes, she saw Jack.

"It's okay. Take your time." They were in the pool, Jack's hand supporting her back. "Relax." His hand moved away. *I'm floating.*

Floating. Drifting. Suzanne could feel the sun's heat warming her body. Water droplets sparkled like diamonds on her skin. But before she reached nirvana, clouds bruised the sky and she was tumbling down a flight of stairs.

"Get up you stupid bitch." Leather slapped against denim. "I said, get up!" The whimpering she heard was not hers. She scrambled for a place to hide. From the corner where she crouched, as small, and inconspicuous as possible, she saw a girl, sprawled on the floor, her chin split, and bleeding. Her teeth had gone through her lip when she hit the concrete floor. Blood oozed from her mouth, and she spit out something small and white. The girl crawled on her belly as the leather strap broke the skin on her back.

"Please," she cried. "Help me, dear God, please."

God was not in the room.

Suzanne woke, gasping for air, her hair and nightgown drenched in sweat. The wind whipped the curtains into a frenzy. The air smelled like rain. *It doesn't rain in Sacramento. Not in June.* The wind came to a halt, the grey panels settled in place, and crickets chirped a summer's concerto. The damp smell was gone.

The next morning Suzanne dialed Detective Metzger. "You wouldn't believe the dream I had."

"Good morning to you too."

Suzanne glanced at the clock. *7:08.* "Did I wake you?"

"No, no. I'm up."

Suzanne could tell by the smoky tone of his voice that she woke him up. "Late night?"

"Very. A few bad guys and vampires. What can I do for you?"

"I had another dream."

"Interesting. I don't have any new victims."

"Perhaps I should save it for when you do."

"I didn't mean—tell me about your dream."

"He kicked her down a flight of stairs, I'm assuming she is in a basement. She was bleeding. He whipped her with a belt."

She heard Sam suck in a breath. "California homes typically don't have basements."

"One flight of stairs, the floor was concrete."

"I suppose I could check with my realtor friend to see what's around here."

"I don't think she's in the vicinity."

"Why?"

"I smelled rain." Suzanne closed her eyes remembering the scent.

"It doesn't rain here in June."

"Exactly."

"Do you think the vision is from another time? I can check the almanac, see when we had rain in June and cross reference to our crime data base."

"Sounds like a plan."

Awkward silence fell between them, until he asked, "Did you get any sleep?"

"Not really. I'm becoming quite the bitch. It won't be

long before Steven and Karen get out the holy water or start smudging the house."

"What-ing the house?"

"People smudge their house with sagebrush to get rid of evil spirits. Steven said he'd go see a psychic with me. Is it okay if I call yours?"

"Sure. Let me get her number."

She heard him rummaging through stuff while she waited. Ben would've complained, crabbed about the inconvenience.

"916-555-3255, her name is Linda. Linda Schooler."

"Great, I'll let you know what she has to say."

Suzanne checked the address as Steven pulled against the curb. "Do I have to go in?"

"She's a psychic, not a witch. C'mon, Steven, Sam said she's nice. Don't you want to hear what she has to say?"

"Not really. You know how I feel about this stuff. I'm a pragmatic person. I work with numbers. Numbers add up. If they don't, I haven't done my job. Simple explanation, end of story."

"Jack believed."

"Jack believed in a lot of things, flying saucers, little green men."

"I see him."

"I don't. Let's just get this over with."

~

L inda opened the door wide. "Welcome."

"Thank you. I'm Suzanne, this is Steven."

"Yes, the vessel and the non-believer. C'mon in." She led the two into her parlor and pulled the chain on a Tiffany lamp, filling the room with a soft glow. She placed a deck of Tarot cards on the table. "Just in case."

"Just in case, what?"

"Just in case you run out of questions before our time is up. I read both ways. Your choice."

Suzanne twisted a lock of her hair. "This is my first time. What do I do?"

"What would you like to know?"

"I have a spirit, Jack—he saved my life. Now he appears to me—shows me horrific things. Why?"

Steven snickered.

"A young man is telling me you collected cars." She cocked her head and listened. "He says you can't throw a snowball for shit."

Steven sat back, his eyes big.

"What has Jack got to say about me?"

"He says he loved you when he went to the other side. He loves you still, that's why he is coming to you. You see, on the earth plane we experience emotion. That's our biggest challenge. We all have a job to do before we ascend. Jack is helping you overcome something. You two share a bond— you don't need me to tell you that. You've been together in many lifetimes. Reincarnated. You'll be together in many more." Linda placed her hands flat on the table. "You're special," she said. "You have cheated death because it's not your time. The experience has changed you," she tapped her head, "up here." She placed her hand on her heart, "And here." Linda closed her eyes and listened. "Uh, huh. Yes."

Steven and Suzanne exchanged puzzled glances.

"Yes, I'll tell her." She opened her eyes. "The young man says when you can float, you'll swim."

Steven squeezed Suzanne's hand. "What does he mean?"

"Jack was trying to teach me in my dreams, Steven. You thought I was crazy." Suzanne turned to Linda. "Why is he scaring me?"

"He is not trying to scare you. He is emotionally detached from what is going on in this dimension. His task is to give you the tools you need to do the job you came here to do."

"But I don't want the job—I don't want to see young girls being tortured. I don't want Jack sitting on my bed watching me sleep. I don't care if I ever learn to swim!" Suzanne rose to her feet. Steven grabbed her arm.

"Sit. Let Linda finish."

"What can I do?"

"Set your boundaries—tell Jack what is acceptable, what is not."

"Jack was never one to listen." She thought of Jack insisting she learn to float. And Ben, another controlling male in her life. What was she thinking back then? At this moment love was a four-letter word: DUMB.

"We all have choices," Linda said. "These choices determine how our life plays out, but the destination is often the same no matter which way we go. Lessons are learned on a divine level. Sometimes the choices we make are those that bring the lesson to us in a more friendly or timely fashion." Linda leaned back in her chair.

"You're saying that being shot and almost drowning was part of the plan?"

"Ever read a movie script?"

"No."

"When we watch a movie, we are oblivious to the script, and all it took to bring the story to the screen. To be a part of the process, from start to finish, you come to realize that making a movie is a lot like life. Sometimes it takes several takes to get a scene just right." Linda leaned forward. "Imagine yourself in an episode of CSI. Your character has been chosen to solve the mystery, catch the bad guy. It's that simple. Once he's caught, you can move on to the next episode."

"But why me?"

"On a soul level, you auditioned for the role and got it."

"That's bullshit. What about Metzger? How does he factor into my *episode*?"

"He may be your happy ending."

"Never."

"Love is eternal. We bring it with us each time."
Linda paused. "Your friend agrees with me."

"Jack? Tell him to quit scaring me. I'll float when I'm ready."

Linda closed her eyes and listened. "He says *relax*."

Steven held Suzanne's arm and helped her into the car. "That was mind blowing. I don't know what to think."

"Try being on this end."

"I have to say, what she said made sense. I never thought of life in terms of a movie, but I guess that's kinda true."

"Well, you picked 'When Harry Met Sally,' I got stuck with 'Silence of the Lambs.'"

"Let's get some dinner. Karen has yoga tonight."

"How about you pick the place?"

Steven did a quick turn into a diner. Neither one spoke.

Suzanne sat quietly, contemplating Linda's advice. She wondered if Linda had actually seen Jack, or only heard his voice. Perhaps it was less unnerving to be clairaudient than clairvoyant.

Steven interrupted her thoughts. "She saw him, didn't she?"

"How did you—"

"I think that's what she said, you know when we first got there. And she knew I didn't believe in hocus pocus."

"You just read my mind. I was thinking the very same thing."

"Perhaps you read my mind. Don't clairvoyants know stuff *before* it happens?"

"I don't think I want to know."

"Face it—something happened to you. As a result, you have this extraordinary talent. Imagine what this could mean."

"My sanity?"

"Naw, you were a little crazy before the accident."

"It was no accident. Just the kind of support I need from my brother."

"Shouldn't you be able to tune into the guy who shot you?"

"It doesn't work like that."

"How do you know?"

"I just know."

Steven ordered Sushi. Suzanne picked at tempura fried shrimp. The sauce, salty and slightly tangy, reminded her of blood. She gagged.

"You're not becoming anorexic, are you?"

"It's the sauce, it tastes like—never mind."

"Eat the rice. A little iron might help."

"I can't eat. I don't know why, but food—maybe it's the antibiotics. I don't have an appetite."

To add to her misery, Jack was sitting next to Steven. His face, devoid of emotion, gave her the creeps. She glanced at the tempura sauce she had dipped her shrimp in moments ago and saw it was no longer brown. *Red.* She bit her tongue, suppressing the urge to scream.

~

When they got home, Karen was in the kitchen, toasting bread. "How did things go?"

"Toast smells good, may I?" Suzanne grabbed a plate from the cupboard.

"Help yourself—after you tell me what the psychic said."

Steven said, "She told Suzanne she's been chosen to be a messenger."

Karen looked to Suzanne. "Is that true?"

Her situation felt more like a curse than a gift, yet Karen seemed impressed. "Yes. Basically, that's what she said."

"Now what?"

"I guess I take it as it comes." Suzanne pushed the lever down on the toaster. The heat, and the glowing metal strips reminded her of hell. Music filled her ears. Heavy metal. Raw, unbridled shrieking lost in maniacal chords. *Blood dripped from her eyes.* The lyrics pounded in her brain, *Truth oozed from her lips. Kill me now, I beg of you, kill me quick.* And then she saw her.

"Suzanne?"

She didn't respond. She watched the girl twist and turn, trying to free herself from the chains holding her captive. Chunks of flesh clung to the wall. The man taunted her with a chicken leg.

"Want some, bitch?" He waved the leg under her nose. "Too bad. All mine."

She whimpered, and pulled on the chains, writhing in time to the beat. When he finished tearing the meat from the bone, he flung the chicken bone at her chest and laughed. "Dead girls don't eat."

Suzanne felt strong fingers dig into her armpits, hoisting her from the floor. She felt herself being dragged across the room. "No," she cried, echoing the girl's cries. When she opened her eyes, she was lying on the couch. Steven held a cold cloth on her forehead.

"A warning might be nice."

"Sorry. I saw her and—"

"And what?" Karen sat beside her. "What did you see?"

"Another girl. He's going to kill her."

"I'll call Sam." Steven rushed for the phone. Karen patted Suzanne's hand. The smell of burning toast came from the kitchen.

Sam leaned against the kitchen counter. Suzanne paced the room.

"This time it was different."

"How so?"

"Jack wasn't there."

"What do you think it means?"

"I haven't a clue. One minute I'm mesmerized by the toaster, next I'm witnessing this—this monster." She hesitated and faced him. "God, how I wish this would stop."

"I haven't heard anything—I mean, no one's been reported missing."

"I guess that's a good thing. Still—I feel something tragic is about to happen."

CHAPTER 6

A month went by since Suzanne moved in with Steven and Karen. Ben still hassled her every chance he got. He refused to move out of the house, and she refused to move back home. Her welcome was wearing thin at her brother's. Karen remained kind, yet distant. She knew it was just a matter of time before she'd get her eviction notice. She needed a plan.

"Your scar looks great. How are you feeling?" The doctor folded his arms and waited for her answer.

"Still getting strange visions. Are you sure I don't have a blood clot? Or a tumor?"

"I assure you, you're fine."

"Does that mean I'm free to go back to work?"

"Sure does. But are you ready?"

"No. But I need to work. I'm not only going stir crazy, the bills are piling up. My husband and I are—well, it's time to take my life back."

"Sounds like you could use some counseling." He jotted the name and address of a psychotherapist he thought would be a good fit. "Grace Simms understands your kind of trauma. Give her a whirl. Let me know how you're doing."

When she got home, she called Elaine. She didn't expect her tone to be so short. "What did you expect? I tried to reach you—you haven't returned my calls. We had work to do, the accounts payables had to be turned in. I know what happened to you was tragic, and I'm really sorry, but you really didn't think we would just limp along until you came back, did you?"

Suzanne's heart reached her throat. Tears welled in her eyes. "No, Elaine. I get it, thanks. I'll stop by to pick up my things."

"I already dropped off the contents of your desk, didn't Ben tell you?"

"No. No, he didn't."

"Son-of-a-bitch!" She wanted to strangle her husband, throw his sorry ass out in the street. She knew her only recourse was to file for divorce and try to get the house. *But without a job...*

"You okay in there Suzanne?" It was Karen.

Suzanne opened the door. "Sorry. Having some anxiety. Lost my job."

"Oh. Now what?"

"I got my all-clear from the doctor today, guess I'll look for another job."

"How long do you think—"

"Listen, I know you're tired of my crap. I'll be out of here as soon as possible."

"Why are you being so—"

"What? A bitch?"

"I didn't—"

"Of course not. You're too kind." The tears Suzanne had been holding back spilled down her cheeks.

Karen embraced her. "I'm so sorry this is happening to you. Your brother and I care about you. We both want to help. But it's hard sometimes, you're like a wounded animal. We're struggling to communicate with you, but you lash out so easily."

"I know. I'm angry. Some guy is walking around free after devastating my life, my husband is an asshole, my dead ex-boyfriend is scaring the living shit out of me. I 'm being crushed from the inside out and I'm not being fair to you or Steven."

"Come, let's have a glass of wine, sit on the patio, and enjoy the sunset. Steven won't be home 'til late. I have chicken Vesuvio in the crock-pot."

"Okay, I'll meet you outside."

Suzanne ran cold water and submerged a washcloth. The water turned red. She shook off the vision, hoping it was just a misfire in her brain, but the color of the water deepened until it was almost black. She looked around the room for Jack. He wasn't there.

She dipped her hands into the water, grabbed the washcloth and squeezed. The water was clear. *Odd.*

She brushed her hair. The medication she had been prescribed to prevent infection made her hair lackluster. But in the last couple of weeks, the shine had returned. Her eyes seemed brighter, and the redness of the scars on her chest were beginning to fade. She had lost ten or more pounds, which she couldn't afford, but with Karen's cooking she was filling out again. *I may be able to land a decent job if I keep it up.*

She needed to make things right. She vowed to be more civil, and grateful. She heard a familiar voice coming from the patio. *What's he doing here?*

"What brings you out this way, Sam?"

"Thought I'd stop by with an update."

Karen poured three glasses of wine. Suzanne expected Sam to refuse, saying he was on duty, but he claimed to be on his own time.

"I spoke with the X-ray tech who told you the doctor's name. I reviewed the surveillance footage from the camera outside the lab. The man posing as a doctor covered the lower part of his face when he entered and exited the room, but we were able to zoom in on his eyes. I cross-checked his eye pattern with immigration and didn't get a match." He leaned forward. "My hunch? Our guy faked the accent."

"Why bother?"

"I think you know this guy."

"I don't know anyone who would try to harm me except—"

"Except, who?"

"Ben wouldn't be that crazy—or have the balls."

"You said yourself he's unpredictable."

"Volatile, yes—but premeditate something like that? I'd bet a million bucks he's not capable of—" The word *murder* lodged in her throat.

"The nurse's description matches Ben's."

"Ben is a lot of things, but a cold-blooded killer isn't one of them. Besides, what about motive? We can't even separate without him unraveling. Why would he want to kill me?"

"That's the million-dollar question."

"He's sick. He may get violent, but he—" Ben's band played a lot of British oldies. They were good, *authentic*. "I'm sure I would've recognized Ben's voice, accent or not."

"I'm not here to badger you. I'm trying my damnedest to figure out who tried to kill you. I need to eliminate any possibilities." His angst morphed into concern. "Any more visions?"

"Strange you should ask. I'm getting flickers, snippets, nothing that adds up. And Jack is still missing from the equation."

"Maybe he felt you were ready to 'swim'."

"And maybe I should visit your friend, Linda."

"Despite your extraordinary talents, we're no closer

to catching your assailant *or* our serial killer. I'm for good ol' fashion detective work."

"Have it your way."

"Let's get back to Ben."

"Trust me, he's not your man."

"Is he yours?"

Sam's eyes smoldered in the glow of the setting sun and she wanted to reach for him. Lose herself in his arms. It was as if their souls mingled in the last remains of the day, and she wanted him. "No. Ben and I are through. It's a matter of formalities, that's all."

"I should be going." He rose. "Early court call. Laundry to do, shirts to press."

"You do your own ironing?"

"I find it therapeutic. I watch a few of my recorded programs, nuke a microwave dinner, or make a sandwich. It's a good life."

"Karen made chicken Vesuvio, perhaps you'd care to join us?"

"Thank you, but I need to get home. Raincheck?"

"Sure."

Stars appeared in the sky. She wished on every one of them.

S am dialed up the volume on his car radio and sang along to a Beatles tune. "Listen, do you want to know a secret? Do you promise not to tell, whoa, whoa—

oh, closer. Let me whisper in your ear, say the words you want to hear— I'm in love with you-ou..." How he loved the oldies. He loved the simplicity, the poetry. Boy meets girl. They fall in love. *Happy ending.*

Sam knew getting involved with Suzanne on a personal level was unwise. He'd seen too many times when a cop fell for a "vic" and got his heart stomped. *Not me.* He concentrated on the British invasion playing on the radio. Why would someone want to kill Suzanne? What was "elaborate" about it? Why the British accent? Because she knows him. Did disguising his voice alleviated some of the guilt? But was it Ben? Suzanne was convinced no. He wasn't so sure.

He began to station surf; "Tears of a Clown," he flipped again, "Will you still love me tomorrow..." He joined in. He didn't have the heart to tell Suzanne about Angela Foxworthy. An elderly couple found her body while on their morning walk. Her body appeared to have been bitten by something, a chicken bone lodged in her throat.

Ben chugged another beer. He set the empty between two cans, completing the second row of his pyramid. When he reached the top, he planned to take a photo and send it to Suzanne. "See what you made me do?"

His life was in the shitter. Suzanne was gone. The band had kicked him to the curb, and he was flat broke. Out of drugs, out of luck, just plain out of it. The best he could do was a beer buzz. He had pawned his gold wedding band for $160. Not a whole hell of a lot, considering.

Rage ebbed and flowed in his head. He hated the world. He hated Suzanne more. But he'd give his left testicle to have her back. *Why?* He didn't know. That notion came from the sick part of his brain. Why would anyone want a woman who betrayed him? He popped opened another beer. The sound gave him a thrill. The extent of his love song.

～

Sam clicked his mouse to refresh his screen. Ben Cash. *Run-of-the-mill loser.* High school education. No job in the last eight months. Before that, truck driver, delivery man, 7-11 clerk. One arrest for drunk and disorderly. Six calls for domestic violence, charges dropped each time by spouse. Seven parking tickets, all paid. *Nothing.* The "why" still niggled at his brain. Perhaps a call to Suzanne would help. *Who you trying to kid?* He simply wanted to hear her voice.

Suzanne answered her phone on the second ring. "Hello?" Her tongue felt tacky, like wet paint.

"Did I wake you?"

"Sorta."

"Shall I call back?"

"No, that's okay. The ceiling won't look any different twenty minutes from now."

"Are you okay?"

"I'm fine. Trouble sleeping. What else is new?"

"I'm drawing blanks. I thought maybe you could help."

"I'll try."

"I'm back to motive. You stated the man said you shouldn't have meddled. Do you have any idea why he would've used those words?"

"You asked me before. My answer is still I don't know."

"Tell me about the fund raiser…"

"What's there to tell?" Suzanne cast her mind back to before the fund raiser.

"What kind of people do you come in contact with? Surely there's a little drama now and then."

"Drama? These kids are sick. Drama is not allowed."

"Even behind the curtain?"

"Our donors are solid. Staff is minimal—we love what we do. Or I should rephrase. I loved what I did."

"You quit?"

"Not exactly. I got replaced."

"That must've stung."

"Yeah, big time. Let's move on. Don't want to drown in my sorrows this early in the day."

"Their loss."

"Yep. What's next?"

"Motive. You know something, saw something, or heard something," Sam said.

"What if the guy thought I was someone else?"

"I checked the hotel. There were eight women staying there. One was on business. Blond. 5'7", 210 pounds. Seven were traveling with spouses. None matched your description. What about the people attending the fund raiser? Anyone seem out of place?"

"No. I'm stumped."

Metzger tapped a pen on the blank sheet of paper on his desk. "Me too. If you think of anything…"

"I want the guy caught too Sam, but right now I think you have bigger problems."

"Why's that?"

"I just had another dream."

Suzanne gripped her cup with both hands while Sam busied himself with cream and sugar. "I didn't recognize the area. Or the train. People were speaking in foreign languages. I remember Belvedere Palace. The girl was alive. In fact, she was excited. She was with a man."

Sam sipped his coffee. "What do you make of it?"

She tried to avoid his eyes. "The dream was definitely different from the others. Where is the Belvedere Palace anyway? Is it a new casino or something?"

"There's the Belvedere Palace in Vienna, Austria." He set his cup down slowly. She watched his shoulders sag. "What's wrong?"

"It's creepy enough that you dream about murdered women. Austria is—well it's sacred to me. I vacationed there as a child." He looked away. "I have fond memories of the Belvedere."

"Care to share?"

"My parents had their hands full keeping me from playing in the fountains. My sister and I chased birds and smelled the flowers." His face softened. "I had to know how each bloom was assembled—my mother fussed over grass stains on my trousers."

"How many siblings do you have?"

"My parents were older when they married. Audra came along the day before my eighth birthday, change-of-life baby."

She imagined him having to share his parent's attention with a new baby, a girl no less. Steven had gone through the same thing. But they were only three years apart. They had become closer in later years. "Where is your sister now?"

"Budapest." Sam shifted in his seat, added more sugar to his coffee and stirred. "Tell me more about your dream. Did this man resemble the man in your previous visions?"

"I didn't see his face. He didn't speak."

"Maybe we should pay a visit to Linda Schooler."

"We?"

"It wouldn't serve any purpose me going alone." His fingertips brushed her arm.

"Oh," she said, ignoring the tiny bumps on her skin.

With Sam gone, Suzanne was free to breathe. Why he affected her the way he did was still up for speculation. She didn't want to feel anything for anyone right now. The hole in her chest would heal more quickly than the ache in her heart. Jack hadn't appeared for some time. What if he was a figment of her imagination? The more time that passed, the more time she had to re-evaluate her state of mind. And? *Can't debate the fact that you knew things about the murdered girls.*

"Hey?"

Suzanne jumped. "Steven—you startled me."

"Did I see Sam?"

"He just left. He wants to see Linda Schooler with me."

"I think he has the hots for you."

"Don't be ridiculous. He wants to know more about my crazy dreams."

"Another murder?"

"No. But it was really weird. I was in a foreign country."

"Speaking of foreign, any thoughts about work?"

"Is this the eviction speech?"

"No speech. But when do plan to move out?"

"If Ben would leave—"

"Forget Ben. You've been here eight weeks. Do you have a plan? That's all I'm asking."

"I've been looking at the want ads."

"What about some kind of healing work? I'm sure working with terminally ill children all these years qualifies you for—"

"The jobs I'm qualified to do won't support me."

"Fat chance you'll get alimony."

"Puts me in a pickle, huh?"

"Keep looking. Karen is a saint, but I think she misses our 'us' time."

"I don't blame her." Suzanne's words trailed as she watched her brother leave. "Damn." She collapsed into a chair and dialed Ben.

Ben lazed with one leg propped on the arm of the sofa. Black Sabbath competed with the announcer pitching an anti-psychotic drug on TV. Smoke hovered over his head each time he took a drag off the joint, held his breath. His self-entertainment was interrupted when the light on his phone caught his eye. Suzanne's picture made him cringe. He picked up the offending object and examined the pretty face ruining his high. He slid the bar to accept the call.

"What the fuck do YOU want?"

"Ben, we need to talk."

"About what? I thought I made myself perfectly clear. I am not giving you a divorce, and I am not moving out of this house. What more is there to say?"

"How are you?"

"Fucking amazing with you gone."

"I can't stay with Steven forever."

"That's your problem."

"California is a fifty-fifty state. I can force you out."

"Is that right?" He drew on the burning stub between his thumb and forefinger and blew smoke into the phone. "You go ahead and try." He ended the call. Laughter rumbled in his chest. He felt victorious until he closed his eyes and images of Calvin's house filled the blank screen behind his eyelids. "Fucker," he seethed.

He launched himself off the sofa, grabbed his car keys and slammed the back door. "Calvin, you better be home, man."

Ben had no sooner pulled onto the ramp to highway 50 when flashing lights filled his rearview mirror. Tempted to give the law a run for his money, he tapped the accelerator upping his speed.

"Pull over," reverberated into the night.

Ben pulled onto the shoulder, but the black and white flew past. "Holy fuck." He broke into fits of laughter. "Shit, that was close." He pulled back onto the road and headed toward Calvin's.

When he turned onto Calvin's street, he slowed down. Calvin's house was lit up like Christmas. Black and white cars filled the cul-de-sac. Lights swirled everywhere. Neighbors came out of their houses like moths drawn to a flame. "Holy shit. This cannot be good."

Suzanne's phone rang at 11:04 P.M. She stretched one arm across her pillow, resenting the intrusion. She didn't remember falling asleep. Her voice, groggy and weak, managed "Hello." Sam's voice sounded excited.

"Sorry to wake you, Sleeping Beauty, but we need

you down at the station. We arrested a guy we're interested in for your case."

"Can it wait until morning?"

"Of course, I just thought—"

"I'm happy you caught him, but I'm in bed and I—"

"No worries. I'll swing by to pick you up at 9:00."

"I can drive myself—"

"I thought maybe we could get a cup of coffee before I take you to the County jail."

"Okay." Silence filled the distance between them.

"Sleeping Beauty? You sounded like you were asleep and—"

"And?"

"Well, the beauty part goes without saying."

"Sam, don't you think you're being—"

"Unprofessional? Forgive me. Go back to sleep, Suzanne. See you in the morning." Suzanne heard the click on the other end of the line. *Mission accomplished. It's all over. He's going to slip out of my life.*

S am shoved his phone into his pocket. He grabbed the cup of stale coffee he had reheated twice and headed for the interrogation room. It was going to be a long night. Another young woman was reported missing.

S uzanne fluffed her pillows, straightened her covers and took three deep breaths. The fourth exhale caught in her lungs. "Jack. Dammit."

"It's not over."

"Sam said they caught the guy who shot me."

Jack extended his hand. Suzanne pulled the covers to her chin. "No more. I have to move on."

"He's still out there."

"Who? Why can't you just tell me?"

"It doesn't work that way."

"I didn't sign up for this, Jack, never."

"We don't have time to argue the details, look—"

Suzanne couldn't move. Her ears heard a scraping noise. Her legs were frozen beneath something heavy. Pain radiated up her spine and reached her temples. The smell of blood assaulted her nostrils. Her eyes gravitated toward her knees. She screamed. Her legs were gone.

A t 7:45 A.M., she awoke to the sound of her alarm. Her hair was damp. Her nightgown clung to her skin. A veil of perspiration covered her face and chest. Panic set in as she reached beneath the covers for her legs. "Thank God," she whispered. She flopped back against the pillows. One hand balled into a fist and pounded the mattress. Jack loomed behind her eyelids. His face held no malice, only the love she saw during the years they spent together. "What do you want from me?" she cried. His face disappeared behind a bright orange glow. She opened her eyes to golden light pouring through her bedroom window. Outside, birds chirped. A breeze stirred the leaves, scattering them across the patio. Although the moment was picture perfect, deep inside She was sad. *The slow death we embrace as part of life feels too close to home.*

Karen was already up, dressed and starting breakfast in the kitchen when Suzanne shuffled toward the coffee pot. Karen's greeting hit her nerves like nails on a chalkboard.

"Good-*morning* Suzanne. Sleep *well?*"

Too early for a pissing contest. "I've slept better. How 'bout you? You're up early."

"Work to do."

"Can I help?" Suzanne mustered her best game face.

"Thanks, you wouldn't—"

"Wouldn't what? Now I'm incompetent?"

"God, why do you have to make things so hard?"

"I'll be out of here as soon as I can."

"I didn't—"

"No, Karen, you didn't. I said it for you." Suzanne stomped out of the kitchen and barricaded herself in her bedroom. She flopped down on the bed, intending to get a grip on her anger. Until Jack showed up.

"This is all your fault," she cried, pulling a pillow over her head. "Why can't you leave me alone?"

"You know why."

"Who is this monster? Why can't you show me his face so I can describe him to police and be done with this? How many more have to die?"

"I wish it were that simple."

"Do you see what you're doing to me, Jack?"

"We can't disrupt the circle of life, Suzanne."

"That's bullshit."

"I know. Come."

"No."

"You must see this."

Jack didn't wait for her permission. He snatched her and plopped her in a dank room. She didn't have to see a thing. She knew. Death enveloped her, seeped into her soul.

She sank to her knees. Growling and laughter assaulted her ears. The girl screamed each time he bit into her flesh or carved little semi-circles into her skin and stapled them to the wall. She couldn't move. Her hands dangled from the orange twine securing her to an overhead beam. He twisted chunks of her long, fawn-colored hair, and stapled them to the beam. She begged him to stop.

Suzanne felt his mood shift from euphoria to anger when blood oozed from between her legs. He dug through his bag. She heard a cracking sound when he shoved a steel pipe down the girl's throat. Next came the saw.

~

S am tilted his head. "How long?"

"A day." Dove Johnson handed him a baggie containing orange twine.

"He's getting ballsier."

"He's expediting his kill. The ligature marks were made hours, not days earlier."

"What's the C.O.D.?"

"Suffocation. He shoved something down her throat. Her trach is shattered." Dove squatted beside the body and moved the girl's jaw back and forth.

Sam could see the jaw was unhinged. "Son of a bitch." He wiped his brow. "What else?"

Dove sighed. He scooted on his knees until he was next to the girl's hips. He lifted her T-shirt, exposing bite marks and flesh wounds the shape of a fish on the girl's lower abdomen. "God only knows what this means," he said.

Sam bent down to get a closer look. "None of the others indicate ritual. What are you thinking?"

"Can't say for sure. We'll know more when the M.E. takes a look at her."

"Anything else?"

"Besides her legs missing? She was menstruating.

Evidently, our boy found this offensive. She wasn't raped like the others."

"And you're sure we're looking at the same killer?"

"Unless someone else knows about the orange twine—"

"It's hard to imagine one sicko, let alone two."

Both men turned when the door opened and Rob Schuster came in. "Sorry I'm late. Traffic."

"Where's Dixon?"

"Let's see, what day is it?"

"I want that guy's life." Dove peeled off his gloves and sniffed his fingers. "Anyone notice how toxic these smell?"

Sam and Rob exchanged a glance.

Dove pulled another pair of gloves from his pocket, gave them a sniff, grimaced and put them on. "Let's get her ready for transport. I have a movie date with my better half. Dixon will have to catch up on his own time."

"We all can't be a lady's man," Rob said, performing his cat-walk around the victim.

Sam's phone hummed in his pocket. He pulled it half-way out, checked the caller ID and let it drop back into his pocket. "You guys good to go here?"

"Call me Later. Lambert's on call tonight. He's sharp. We should have a C.O.D. report by quitting time."

Sam rushed his goodbyes and hurried to his car, phone in hand. "Suzanne? What's up?"

Her sobs made him shiver. "Shhh. Calm down." He gave her a moment to compose herself. "Suzanne?"

"I'm here," she said. "I need you."

Her soft, breathy words filled holes in Sam's heart he didn't know existed. But the moment shattered into hardcore reality. *She needs your help. Not you.* "What's wrong?"

"There's a girl. Another victim."

Suzanne showered, dressed in navy leggings, an oversize, dusty blue sweater and tan boots. She twisted her long auburn hair into a knot and secured it with an iridescent-blue clam shell clip that complimented her lapis-colored eyes. She had long given up make-up. A swipe of tinted lip balm would have to do. Her reflection confirmed her suspicions. *You need more sleep.*

She didn't wait for Sam to come to the door. When he pulled up, she jumped into the passenger seat of his car. "Drive," she said, looking straight ahead.

Sam stole a side glance as he pulled into traffic.

"He cut off her *legs*."

"I know. I just came from the scene."

Suzanne buried her face in her hands "I can't take this anymore."

Sam pulled into a Starbuck's drive-thru, ordered two Grande black coffees. "I can't imagine how horrific this must be for you," he said. His hand reached for hers, then stopped mid-way. "We haven't identified the victim yet. My team got the call at 4:00 this morning. She was killed some time yesterday."

"I'm sorry," she said. Her fingertips brushed his as she accepted the cup of coffee.

Sam parked the car at the far end of the parking lot, facing the street. He sipped his coffee in silence, but his eyes darted in all directions, like he expected the killer to pop into view.

"There's a place in Raleigh, North Carolina—a research center. They test paranormal stuff. Interested?"

"In what?"

"Perhaps they could help you understand what's going on. Help you control the visions or something. I don't know, just heard about it—thought I'd pass the info along."

"What about Linda Schooler?"

"I just thought maybe…"

"Maybe what? I could get my head shrunk along with an exorcism? I want it to stop. That's all. Just *stop*." She set her coffee in the cup holder and dug through her purse for a tissue.

"Let's take care of business first. Put away the bastard who shot you and worry about the rest later." His compassion proved overwhelming, and she looked away. "I'm not free, Sam."

"Doesn't mean I can't help."

"As long as you keep that in mind."

CHAPTER 8

When they arrived at the County jail, they entered a sparsely furnished area adjoining the interrogation room. A heavy glass window separated her from a man dressed in an orange jumpsuit.

"I know him!" Her face lost color. "Calvin Cook shot me? Why?"

"How well do you know this guy?"

"I considered him a friend. He and my husband—" She turned to Sam, "Is Ben involved too?"

"Not at this point. What can you tell me about him?"

"As the event coordinator for Wish Kids, I often had business at the hospital. I met Calvin in the cafeteria, about three years ago. We got to talking. He said he played guitar. After getting to know him better, I introduced him to my husband. They started playing in a band—a British tribute band." Suzanne's mind whirled. What motive would Calvin have to shoot her? *We were friends*. And how had she "meddled"? Why did he accuse her of meddling before he shot her?"

"We are bringing your husband in for questioning. He may be able to fill in the blanks."

"Is that necessary?"

Sam needed a shave. His eyes were tired. "We need to find out the extent of his involvement."

"He should be at home." She touched Sam's arm. "Be careful. He's been off his meds. Calvin was the closest he came to self-medicating."

"How's that?"

"They smoked a lot of marijuana."

"Anything else?"

She remembered a run-in she had had with Calvin at the hospital days before the fundraiser. She had caught him pocketing a patients' meds. When she confronted him, he turned hostile, swore he wasn't stealing, said it wasn't what it looked like. At the time she had so much on her mind. The kids, the banquet, rehearsing magic acts. It all made sense now. "Calvin may have been stealing drugs from the hospital."

"Do you have proof?"

"A couple of days before the event, I was meeting with one of the nurses on the pediatric ward. She had volunteered to dress as a clown and do face painting. I wanted to make sure she was still available. Sometimes shifts change and people have to drop out. I saw Evelyn, that's her name, talking with Calvin. She was the charge nurse that evening, and she was prepping the med cart for rounds. While she and I were talking, I thought I saw Calvin slip a few of the capsules into his pocket. He did it so quickly, I wasn't sure I saw what I saw. When I asked him about it, he not only denied it, he got angry. Later that evening, I asked Evelyn if she had come up short."

"What did she say?"

"She shrugged it off."

"And you took that for a yes?"

"I didn't take it anyway. Like I said, I had a million other things on my mind." She rubbed her temples. "What happens now?"

"We're holding Cook on suspicion of attempted murder and drug charges. His residence proved to be quite the dispensary."

"What about Ben?"

"I sent a couple of my men to the house to pick him up for questioning."

Suzanne covered her face with her hands. Sam pried them away.

"You know I'm going to make sure nothing happens to you, don't you?"

"How are you going to do that?"

"If your husband knew about Calvin's drug activity, that makes him—" Sam reached for her hand.

"Don't."

Sam scooted his chair until his nose was inches from Suzanne's face. She could feel his breath brush her lips. "I won't let him harm you."

"Ben is my problem, not yours."

"If he broke the law, he's mine." Sam pushed himself backwards and rose. Suzanne flinched when the door slammed behind him. She laid her head on her arms. What else could go wrong? She hated the "poor me" voice taunting her. She wanted to trust Sam, trust that the nightmare would be over, but she didn't know him. Her one leap of faith had ended badly when she had married on the rebound. Ben would seek revenge whether he was Calvin's accomplice or not.

Sam wanted to nestle Suzanne close, make her realize how deeply he had come to care for her. *Stubborn.* Would he want her any other way? *No.* She wanted his help, she didn't want him smothering her, he got that. So why did he feel like a buffoon? *Love, buddy. Love does that to a person.* But first he had a job to do. With a serial killer at large, and Calvin to put away, he had no time to ponder his feelings. Besides, Suzanne was married. He suspected leaning on Ben would make him leave town. *One can only hope.*

CHAPTER 9

Ben peeked out the window. The car pulling into the drive wasn't company. He heard car doors slam, footsteps coming up the walkway. When the officers pounded on his door, he broke into a sweat. Not that he had reason to be nervous, *he* had done nothing wrong. Were they here about Calvin?

"Benjamin Cash? Open the door, sir. We need to speak with you."

"What about?"

"Open the door, sir. We don't want any trouble." The officer at the window took a step back and unsnapped his holster. "We just want to ask you some questions."

Ben sorted possibilities in his head. Paranoia flickered between rational thoughts. He hadn't broken any laws. Proving he smoked a little reefer at Calvin's would be difficult. Even if Calvin had ratted on him, it was

Calvin's word against his. He reached for the deadbolt, gave it a twist, and opened the door.

When they grabbed his arms, he felt trapped, his adrenaline surged. He kicked at everything within range, but then he was face down on the porch, cold steel circling his wrists.

"We've got Ben in a holding cell." Sam pushed a chair next to Suzanne. "He got feisty, my men had to secure him."

"He's sick, Sam. He's not a monster."

"We'll take that into consideration. Is there anything you need from the house? I can take you."

"When can I leave?"

"You're free to go anytime. I'll give you a lift."

"How long are you going to hold him?"

"Until I'm convinced he had nothing to do with your attempted murder."

"What makes you think he did?"

"Just making sure the facts add up. I'm like that. Especially when it comes to someone I care about."

"Don't let concern cloud your judgement." Suzanne rose. "Can we go now?"

Sam escorted her to his car without words. When he dropped her off, his goodbye was professional. Suddenly she felt *alone*.

Calvin cringed when he saw Ben walk past the interrogation room. *Why is he here?* Ben had issues. Big ones. Calvin knew Ben didn't play with a full deck. Once Ben had lit up a bowl or two, he was as pliable as Silly Putty. Their only disagreements were over money. Okay, so what if Ben was right about him skimming off the top. He did most the work. He picked the songs. He booked the gigs. He called the practices, got everyone "fired" up before a performance. They owed him.

Suzanne. *Bitch.* Why did she have to stick her nose in his business? Copping a few pills now and then didn't raise any red flags with the hospital staff. He suspected he wasn't the only one with his fingers in the pie. Besides, most of those kids were gonna die anyway. Right? Bleeding hearts, like Suzanne, didn't keep them from the pearly gates. Pain? *Part of life.* Get sick? *You die.* His mother, father, two sisters and Aunt Judy had died of cancer. *Nasty shit.* He didn't care one way or another. Here today? Make the most of it. Get high, *stay high.* Cannabis fed his muse—pain meds were a bonus. All work, *no play*— Suzanne had no right to meddle in his affairs. *She deserved to die.* Miss goody-two-shoes. She didn't notice he was following her. A few OxyContin and a six-pack of Abeita "Purple Haze" had helped with his decision to shoot her. *Seemed like a good idea at the time.* "Just wanted to be a rock star," he whispered to the wall.

Ben's 6'2" frame slammed into a chair across from Detective Sam Metzger. "You needn't go to such extremes to sleep with my wife, Detective. Suzanne is her own person. In case you haven't noticed, she's independent to a fault."

"I'll keep that in mind," Sam said. He leaned back in his chair. "Speaking of Suzanne, how do you know Calvin Cook?"

"What's Calvin got to do with my wife?"

"Whose idea was it to kill her? Yours? Or did you two rock stars cook up the scheme together?"

"I don't know what the hell you're talking about. I didn't conspire with anyone to kill my wife."

"So you didn't know Calvin planned to shoot the missus?"

"No!"

"That's not what your buddy Calvin says. He says you blackmailed him into killing your wife. Except, as we both know, Suzanne being independent to a fault, *survived*."

"I want a lawyer."

❧

CHAPTER 11

Sam followed the stairs to the basement where Goldorado County's finest were busy gathering data, testing theories and charting "current events." The basement was known as the "war department."

Dove Johnson stood with hands on hips assessing photos of the latest victim. "Mackenzie McElroy. Twenty-three. Reno posted the MP on her this morning. According to her folks, she was in Sacramento visiting a friend. They gave up asking for details when she turned eighteen. Parents said she was a Virgo. Private. The only thing she shared was instructions; water the orchid on Tuesday. Four ice cubes, no more no less."

Sam said, "Maybe it's a Virgo thing."

"Maybe." Dove moved closer to the photo. He pulled a magnifying glass from his lab coat pocket and zeroed in on the mark near the girl's left breast. First impression was the mark was a bite. The possibility of DNA got Dove excited.

"What is it?" Sam asked.

"I know what it's not. Our boy doesn't bite. Could be a hair clip, tongs, or a clamp of some sort. The punctures are cone shaped and symmetrical, not rectangular and irregular like teeth would make."

"We have the guy that shot Suzanne Cash, if that's any consolation."

"Every douche bag we get off the street is a plus. Hey, we on for dinner Friday night? Nancy would love to see you. She asked me to invite Dixon. Should I be worried?"

"Don't tell me you're jealous of Dixon."

"Cautious, that's all. Guy's a babe-magnet."

"Nancy only has eyes for you."

"How do you know?"

Sam shrugged. "I need to get back upstairs. I've got Suzanne's husband on the hot seat."

"He was in on the plan to shoot her?"

"Probably not." Sam shrugged. "His lawyer should be here *sometime* today. Until then, I want to imagine he's guilty."

"Masochist. You'll never get the girl that way."

On his way upstairs, Sam mulled over Dove's reaction to Dixon. The guy was good looking, smart, made good financial decisions and was single. However, he lacked something. A heart. Sam wondered if that's what it took to survive. Not that he didn't consider himself a good catch. He'd never make the cover of GQ, but he cleaned up well. He wasn't a mush, but he was kind. Sobriety helped with the kind part. Once he became sober, he had thought about settling down, raising a family. Somehow, the job always sucked the hours out of his day. Dixon seemed to have plenty of time on his hands. "He does his job, doesn't rock the boat," is what his men had to say. When Dixon didn't show up at a crime scene, they all figured it was because he was getting laid by a woman most men fantasized about. Dixon's social life was filled with women worthy of the red carpet or the cover of Sports Illustrated. *Big deal.* Sam concluded Dixon would never know the true meaning of love.

T he warm evening encouraged Suzanne to join Karen on the patio. "The police have the man who shot me in custody."

Karen set her drink down. She rose and closed in for a hug. Suzanne stiffened, but then relented and let the hug ease her pain.

"Doesn't mean it's over. Ben might be involved. Can you believe it?"

"Ben? How?"

"The police brought Calvin Cook in for questioning. Evidently, Calvin and Ben were doing more than making music. Calvin's house was raided for drugs. We both know Ben's a lot of things, but drug dealer? Murderer? I know he smokes pot, but chemicals? I can't get him to take his medication—"

"What about the money? Ben seemed to be doing okay while you were in the hospital."

"That's because he was stealing from me. I stashed money in the bookcase. He found it. Ben is sick. He's not a killer."

"How do you know? It's not like you kept tabs on the guy. You've always done your thing. He did his. How many times did he say he was going out of town for a gig and come home broke? Then, suddenly he has money to blow."

"I've been giving him an allowance from what's left of my inheritance."

Suzanne reached for Karen's drink, chugged the remnants, and handed her the empty.

Karen examined the glass in the fading light. "Nothing tequila can't fix. Ready for another?"

She disappeared into the house and returned with two tumblers filled with ice, liquor, and extra lime wedges. "Over here." Karen moved their party to a double glider and began to swing. The soothing motion triggered Suzanne's memory of another time. *Jack. Love.* Her dreams ended by war. Now, she was past her prime, jobless, broken, a vessel for nightmares. She swallowed some tequila along with her bitterness. Life was meant to be sweet. Jack had promised her a future. Instead she had ended up with the first person who'd wanted her, sabotaging any chance for happiness.

"Penny for your thoughts." Karen nudged Suzanne's shoulder.

Tequila warmed her words. "What do you think about Sam?"

CHAPTER 12

Ben had been sitting in the same room for six hours waiting for a court-appointed lawyer to show. The burger and fries brought to him an hour ago rumbled in his stomach. He wanted to go and smoke a joint. "This is crap," he mumbled. He crumpled the burger wrapper and squeezed it into a tiny ball.

Sam Metzger watched Ben from the other side of the one-way mirror. He wondered what Suzanne saw in the man. He was average looking, barely a high school graduate and didn't have a pot to piss in. Not to mention his bi-polar personality and volatile disposition. But who was he to judge? He wasn't the lady's man Dixon was, rich, powerful—but he was intelligent, kind, good-natured. *I clean up well.*

When Sam entered the room, Ben growled, "How long are you going to keep here?"

"As long as it takes. Seems Calvin is pointing the finger at you."

"I didn't do anything. You can't arrest me for smokin' a little weed. I have a medical condition. Cannabis calms me down. Ask any shrink."

"I'm more concerned with the plot to kill your wife."

"That's bullshit and you know it."

"Not according to Mr. Cook."

"He's lying. I would never hurt my wife."

"You have quite a temper, Ben." Sam slapped a manila down on the table. "These domestic violence reports don't lie. And from what I hear— you still refuse to take the medication prescribed by your doctor."

"That crap makes me sweat, smell funny, and it doesn't do shit. Besides, smokin' weed or getting a little pissed off doesn't make me a murderer."

"Where were you the night your wife was shot?"

"You asked me that at the hospital. You know damn well I had nothing to do with Suzanne being shot. And until my lawyer arrives, I have nothing further to say—" Ben turned toward the mirrored wall. He wanted to be sure he was heard by whoever stood on the other side of the glass. "Except stay away from my wife."

CHAPTER 13

S ac State student, Sheena Bradford, hurried along the walkway leading to the parking lot. She had a two-hour window between classes and had been craving a latte since morning. Cravings were becoming more frequent. *Dammit Dixon.* He had the upper hand when it came to condoms. If she wanted him in her bed, she had to stick to his terms.

"Get one of those apps to track your cycle," he insisted. Why she obeyed him wasn't entirely clear. She thought she'd grown past stupid when it came to men. Dixon was different. His eyes, his touch. His lovemaking. *Best I've had with anyone.* His mouth, capable of pleasure no woman should live without. *Too late for regrets.* She was addicted. She'd do anything to feel his lips on her skin.

Sheena sent Dixon a text. Latte in ten. Join me? She got into her car, started the engine. Her heart sank when he replied.

Busy. Later.

It's just sex, she reminded herself. He never pretended otherwise. Why did she feel dejected? Being a week late contributed to her bleak mood. She wondered how he was going to react. She suspected he had a dark side. *Won't be pretty.*

Any chance of having a relationship with Dixon was merely a figment of her imagination. "You're barely eighteen," he had said, "I have to protect my image, being in the public eye and all—" but in her heart, she knew, *he's a player.* At that moment, the latte she'd been craving didn't sound so good. Sheena opened her car door and forfeited her dignity along with her breakfast.

Ben Cash was released by 8:00 p.m.. First stop, his beloved brother-in-law's place to have a chat with Suzanne.

When he arrived, he smelled smoke and heard music coming from the backyard. He used the back gate, rather than ring the bell.

Suzanne and Karen were huddled near the fire pit roasting marshmallows when he interrupted their girl talk. "Shouldn't you two be singing Kumbaya or some shit like that?"

Suzanne jumped to her feet. "What are you doing here?"

"Just wanted to stop by to thank you for siccing your

boyfriend on me. Always wanted to spend a day at a police station. Got a free lunch out of it though."

"Perhaps you should think twice about the company you keep."

Ben moved closer. Suzanne smelled his stale breath. "Who introduced us, huh? Calvin was your friend first."

"I tried to help you. Music was the only connection Calvin and I had."

"I had nothing to do with you being shot. If I wanted you dead, dear wife, I would've killed you myself. Seems Calvin fucks everything up."

Karen stepped between them. "Time to leave, Ben. I don't think you want to spend any more time downtown."

Ben's hateful glare frightened her. "Enjoy your evening ladies."

Once the gate closed behind her husband, Suzanne exhaled. "Life keeps getting better."

"Divorce him. Take your power back. Find a job, start over."

Suzanne hugged herself and shivered. "Let's go inside. I'm cold."

Karen rescued the sticks from the fire. "I have a couple of Hershey bars stashed in the pantry. Let's make s'mores and put on a movie."

"Thank you for understanding Karen. I know you and I clash sometimes, but I can never repay you for your kindness."

"We're family. You drive me crazy, but I love you all the same."

Suzanne lounged on the sofa with a fluffy blanket, s'mores and the 1983 movie, "Svengali" starring Jodie Foster and Peter O'Toole.

"I never saw this one," Karen said, settling next to her on the sofa.

Ten minutes into the movie, a voice invaded Suzanne's brain. *Jack.* Jodie Foster morphed into a young brunette, Peter O'Toole no longer her handsome captor. The man was faced away from the young woman on the screen. His words made her flinch. "Get rid of it." The brunette backed away from him. *Beautiful.* She held her breast as if she could no longer bear the pain. Suzanne wondered what he had meant by "Get rid of it" until she heard a baby cry. The woman screamed.

"Suzanne?" Karen shook her.

"He's going to kill her," she cried.

"Who?"

"Him!" She pointed at the TV, but a Ford commercial segued into a Farmers Insurance promo.

"It was just a movie. I can change the channel." Karen pointed the remote at the TV and scrolled down until she found a comedy. "There. All gone. Only funny stuff from now on."

"She's pregnant. I heard a baby cry. He wants her to get rid of it."

"Maybe you should take Detective Metzger's advice

and go to Raleigh. They can help you decipher your visions."

"I'd have to dip into my savings. I can't support Ben *and* go to Raleigh."

"Let Ben take care of himself. If he's that sick, let him get professional help. Quit making excuses for him."

"You're right—I'll talk to Sam."

CHAPTER 14

Calvin Cook signed his confession at 9:15 p.m. Sam helped escort him back to his cell before leaving the station. His stomach grumbled from lack of food. He considered calling Suzanne to reassure her that her assailant was behind bars, ask her to have a bite to eat with him. Dove was right, *masochist*. The more he wanted her, the more it hurt. He dialed her number.

"Sam? It's late."

"I'm calling to give you an update. Cook confessed. He's at County, you're safe."

"Thanks for the good news." Dead air lingered between them. "Are you still at the station?"

"Yeah. Thought I'd grab a bite to eat. Care to join me?"

Suzanne looked at Karen, who had been eavesdropping.

"Give me ten minutes. I was ready for bed."

"See you then." He disconnected the call. His fatigue had faded.

When Sam arrived at Steve and Karen's house, he parked on the street. He walked to the door, his step light. Karen opened the door before he had the chance to ring the bell.

"Suzanne's almost ready." She stepped outside and closed the door behind her. "I wanted to speak with you. She had another episode. I think sending her to Raleigh would be a good idea. Before she loses her mind."

"That bad?"

"We were watching a movie, she blanked out, started screaming. She needs help, Sam."

"It's her call—"

"I have a feeling you can be pretty persuasive. You're good for her."

He wondered if Suzanne would agree. "I'll see what I can do."

Suzanne appeared in the doorway. Sam admired her quick transition from "ready for bed" to ravishing. Her auburn hair tied back in a low pony-tail, showcasing high cheekbones and silver hoop earrings. Her sapphire scoop-neck top revealed a hint of cleavage, tight jeans hugged her petite frame. She flung a charcoal leather jacket over her shoulder.

"Hope you like burgers," he said. "Not much open at this time of night."

"If we're talking Burgers and Brew, you'll make me a happy girl."

"You didn't tell me you read minds."

He followed her to the car, admiring the scenery on the way. The butterflies were back. When he opened the door for her the moon lit her face in an ethereal glow. He wanted to kiss her. But before the thought turned to action, she shut him down.

"This isn't a date."

"No. Dates are off limits. You're married."

"I'm glad we're on the same page."

She's here with you now, be happy with that. "I respect your decision to keep our relationship professional," he said, sliding behind the wheel, "but don't expect me to be a machine. I like you. I like being with you. You're pretty, funny, and intriguing. This isn't about you being a damsel in distress. If I had met you under different circumstances, I would've felt the same. This is new for me. I don't date co-workers, clients, or cousins of co-workers or clients."

"Do you date at all?"

"No. You're the first. Ever." They both laughed, easing the tension. By the time they reached the restaurant, they were talking as if they were old friends.

Over burgers, Suzanne described her vision. Sam listened. "Do you feel the woman is local?"

"Yes. I also think she's pregnant. Which means, they've been together before."

"And it's always the same guy?"

"Yes. I still can't see his face, but I get the impression he's handsome."

"Handsome?"

"Svengali."

"He's the guy who hypnotized his victims, right?"

"Yes, one woman in particular. In the Jody Foster, Peter O'Toole version, he wanted to make her a star."

"You think Peter O'Toole is handsome?"

"He had the power to make Jody Foster believe he was."

"Quite the age difference, don't you think?"

"I get the feeling the monster you're looking for *is* older than the women he targets."

"Interesting. What else?"

"I want to go to Raleigh."

Sam sat back assessing Suzanne's sudden mood change. "Have you looked into the Durham Center?"

"Karen told me about the place. She said it's a great experimental facility. It's more scientific than hoo-doo."

"Let me see what I can arrange. It would be beneficial to the department, but with all the budget cuts lately, I'm not sure if my boss will go for it. If not, I can pick up the tab."

"That's asking too much. I have a little money saved. I'll make it work—best there's no strings."

"Please, let me help. No strings. You have my word."

"Let me check whether I can get in. They may be booked solid."

"I have a sneaking suspicion this is going to work out for you."

"Predicting the future, Detective?"

The urge to kiss her returned. "Hope so."

CHAPTER 15

The next day, Sam dropped by Steven and Karen's to confirm Suzanne's decision to contact the Durham Research Center. She described her visions in the online form provided by the center. When she hit "send," she felt as if she had sent piece of her soul across the country. "I feel silly," she said.

Sam patted her shoulder. "Let's see what happens. In the meantime, I booked us an appointment with Linda Schooler."

"Us?"

"It's easier for me to witness what's going on, than to hear it second-hand."

"What about work?"

"What we're doing *is* work. And I intend to compensate you for your time."

"I don't remember getting on anyone's payroll."

"Whoever this killer is, he's eluded us for over a year.

You're the closest we've come to any leads. I consider you a valuable resource, one the department is fortunate to have."

Suzanne slammed her laptop closed. "We had dinner last night. Please don't think that makes me one of the boys. Ben is furious with me as it is. He thinks–"

"I know what Ben thinks–and maybe he's right. Maybe I do have a thing for you–but my feelings will never interfere with this investigation. I intend to conduct myself as a professional. Do we have a deal?"

"Depends."

"On what?"

"How much are you paying me?" The stunned expression on Sam's face made her smile.

When Sam and Suzanne arrived at Linda Schoolers', Linda greeted the couple with a warm welcome. "Gotta new dog, this is Katie," she said, holding the black Lab's leash tight. "Make yourselves comfortable in the parlor, I'll be right there." Linda disappeared with the dog and reappeared with a tray of tea and cookies.

"Sam told me you were interested in the Durham Center—"

"Yes. I filled out the form this morning."

"Would you like to test your gift?" Linda poured tea in three cups and handed one to Suzanne. "We can start with playing cards. It's a fun way to see how intuitive you are."

Suzanne sipped her tea, her eyes taking in the crystal balls and Edgar Cayce books on the shelf across the room. Linda withdrew a deck of cards from her pocket and shuffled them. She laid ten cards in front of Suzanne, face down. "Can you tell me the suit and number of the first card without turning it face up?"

"Jack of hearts."

Linda turned the card over. "Correct. How about the next one?"

Suzanne glanced at Sam.

"Eight of clubs?"

Linda flipped the card. "Eight of diamonds. Try the next."

Suzanne focused on the third card. "Ten of spades."

Linda lifted one corner of the card for a peek before flipping the card. Sam clapped his hands, encouraging Suzanne to go on to the next. When she correctly identified the remaining seven cards, Linda reshuffled the deck and laid out ten more cards. Once again, Suzanne got them all right. "Lucky guess."

Linda rifled through her desk drawer for pens and paper. "I'm going into the other room and I am going to do something, like nod my head, turn around three times, whatever … I want you to write down on the piece of paper what you see. Sam? Come with me, you're going to witness my actions and write them down as well. When I finish, we can compare notes."

Sam followed the psychic into the other room. Suzanne expected Jack to show up to help her. When he didn't appear, she became unnerved. After all, it was Jack who showed her things. How could she know what was going on in the other room without his help? When Linda shouted "Ready," Suzanne picked up the pen and closed her eyes. She could see Linda's arms extended from her body. *Arm circles.* Suzanne jotted down her answer. When she closed her eyes again, Linda stood motionless. A moment later, she raised her right foot, put it down, and repeated the motion three times. Suzanne saw what she was doing very clearly, however, she couldn't see her face. Once the exercises were over, Linda and Sam returned to join Suzanne.

"Show me your answers," Sam said.

She handed him her paper. His scent was pleasant, clean. "I did this without Jack's help, so I'm not sure…"

Sam glanced at Linda. "You nailed it."

Linda said, "You have a powerful gift, young lady."

"So how do I explain Jack?"

"A mother holds a child's hand when crossing the street until the child is capable of crossing on their own. Those who help us from the other side have an agenda. They come in love, hold our hand until we're no longer in need of their services. You've proved something to yourself today."

"What's that?"

"You've lifted the veil. You're the one in charge. You still have work to do, but I think you understand that these visions are accurate. You are able to tap into certain frequencies and acquire information."

"I couldn't see your face."

"Practice. In time you will." Linda reached for Sam's arm. "Do you need further proof, Mr. Smarty-pants?"

"I guess, I…"

Suzanne said, "At least you know now that I'm not crazy. Not *yet* anyway."

"You're getting closer to the truth, but be careful," Linda advised. "We don't need you ending up in the river next time."

"What do YOU see?"

"I see a young woman who has a real chance at love, if she allows those around her to protect and care for her. Keep in mind, stubbornness delays manifestation."

Suzanne blushed. "Now look who has super powers?"

S am handed Suzanne the keys to his car. "I'll be a moment." Suzanne headed out the door while he paid Linda her fee. "Thank you," he said.

"Take it slow, Sam. Love shouldn't be rushed."

He shook his head "I've never felt like this before."

"Keep a close watch on her. I have a feeling she hasn't seen the worst of it yet.

When he got into the car, he hurried to close the door so her sweet scent didn't escape. "Hungry?"

"I need to get home."

Once again, he stuffed his feelings inside. When he was with her, he begged time to stand still. *Someday*, he vowed. *Some day*.

Suzanne checked her email when she got home. To her delight, she found a response from the Durham Institute.

"Dear Ms. Cash,

Thank you for contacting us. We have an opening. Please phone us for the date and time.

Sincerely,

Beverly Klein

Durham Psychic Institute Administrator

1-888-555-1212

Suzanne picked up the phone and dialed.

CHAPTER 16

Sheena Bradford struggled to get through her morning art classes. She'd managed a few soda crackers and ginger tea without vomiting, but the urge remained, and all she wanted to do was go home and sleep. She intended to stop by the pharmacy and pick up a pregnancy test. She wouldn't dare alert Dixon to the possibility of a baby without proof. She hurried through the parking lot to her car.

"Hey."

She flinched. Dixon leaned against her car his posture self-assured. He was the last person she had expected to see at this time of day, and his presence was unwelcome. Her nausea was getting the best of her. Seeing him sent her over the edge.

"Got the flu, Dix." She popped the trunk, grabbed a grocery bag, opened it, and puked.

"That's disgusting."

"Yeah, well—" The ginger tea left a sweet aftertaste in her mouth.

A gentleman would've turned away or offered assistance. Not Dixon. He made everything about him. Her predicament was not his problem.

"Your tits look bigger," He said, brushing past her.

She watched him walk away. She had never imagined herself as a mother, but an abortion was out of the question. Even if she had to give the baby up for adoption, she would carry the pregnancy to term. Goodbye dreams. So long aspirations of becoming the world's finest female architect. *Hello nine months of big mistake.*

Sam hung around the station going through old files. He still felt stuck. Same guy, different methods. Victims came from different counties, social groups, hair and eye color varied—he finger-drummed his frustration on the scarred surface of his desk. One commonality. Their age. He needed Suzanne's help. But first, she had to help herself.

He dialed the number of his bank. He would transfer money into his checking account, then prepay Suzanne's stay at the Durham Institute. She needn't know the money hadn't come from the department. One way or another, she would identify the killer. He prayed it would be before he killed again.

Sheena arrived home to find a bouquet of flowers leaning against her doorjamb. She rushed inside to open the card. Maybe Dixon wasn't a dick after-all. She expected an apology, instead his message chilled her to the bone. Watching You. *Why would he say that?*

She dumped the flowers in the kitchen sink, rushed to the bathroom and collapsed on the floor. The room began to spin and she spent the next hour dry-heaving into the porcelain bowl.

She heard a familiar sound in the next room. Her cell phone lay in the bottom of her purse collecting text messages. She peeked inside. Dixon's private number. *He knows.*

Dixon strolled through the station around 4:00 p.m., his vibe less approachable. Sam knew attempting to converse with his boss at this time would be pointless. Dixon's behavior seemed rigid at times. A drill sergeant who didn't refrain from kicking your ass when you didn't comply with the rules. *His rules.* One of which was knowing when he required privacy. Unless the building was on fire, or Air Force One landed on the front lawn, Dixon's office was off limits.

Dixon didn't tolerate whining, chit-chat, or bullshit. On the flip-side he could charm the bark off a tree when he wanted. He could make a person feel ten feet tall, or like dog shit on the bottom of his shoe. There wasn't an in-between.

Dixon had a way with the ladies. Sam figured women were no different than men when it came to admiring good looks. Pretty people were desirable, and Dixon rated twenty on the pretty people scale. Perfect build, perfect hair, perfect teeth. His educated, intuitive, savvy demeanor won him lots of votes during election time. Dixon was competent, he got the job done, but as a team player, he remained apart from the rest. He was the Sheriff. He gave the orders. His rules.

Sam was searching for the file on Amy Fitzpatrick when Dixon appeared at his desk.

"Still at it?"

"I'm working with Suzanne Cash, the woman who was found floating in the pool at the Marriott awhile back."

"As I recall, her case has been resolved. What are you doing, Metzger?"

"She's a proven psychic. We need her help."

"Proven by whom?"

"I had her tested. She's going for training. She's an asset." Sam plopped a photo of Amy Fitzpatrick's mutilated body on the stack of papers on his desk. "A person we can count on to help us catch a psycho."

"I don't recall you asking my permission."

"Don't you want to stop the killing?"

"Don't twist my words."

"I realize I haven't brought you up to speed on our last victim, my apologies."

"You going rogue on me, Sam?

"Just doing my job."

"What makes the information this woman provides so useful?" Dixon's argumentative tone riled Sam.

"She actually sees the murders. In time—she'll be able to identify the killer.

"Are you seriously expecting me to believe your woman is tapping into the guy's head?"

"So far she's been accurate with details. The timeline is still off, but she's closing the gap. At first, she saw the murders after they happened. Lately, her visions have gotten closer to the actual time of the crime. The vision she had recently hasn't happened yet."

"What did she see?"

"A young woman in her early twenties, most likely a student. She saw her carrying books. She also believes the girl is pregnant."

Dixon paled. "Is that so?"

Sheena decided she'd wallowed enough, vomited enough, cried enough. Time for action. She thought of her cousin who had moved to upstate New York after high school. Renee was two years older and ten years wiser. She would know what to do.

"Renee? It's Sheena. Yes, I'm still alive," Sheena chuckled, "but I need your help."

The conversation had gone better than she expected. Renee had changed jobs recently and moved into a two-bedroom apartment. Renee admitted that although single life was the way to go, hanging out in clubs and bringing home "strays" was getting old. "You'd love it here."

Sheena agreed. A change of scenery and lifestyle would do her good. She pulled a blank sheet of paper from her binder and began a list: sublet apartment, arrange for transcripts to be forwarded. Perhaps she could finish school in New York. Maybe life wouldn't be so bad after all. Renee seemed cool with the idea of her pregnancy but advised her to be sure before she went all wiggy. She grabbed the pregnancy test off the kitchen counter and headed for the bathroom. She was about to pee on the stick when her doorbell rang.

She remained silent, willing her visitor to go away. The bell rang again. And again. She finished her business and stuffed the pregnancy test under the sink behind a stack of Architectural Digest magazines and a box of tampons. She knew who was at the door even before the pounding began.

"Open up," Dixon yelled. A man down the hall opened his door and peered into the hallway. "She's upset with me," Dixon said, rolling his eyes. The man nodded. He understood. "I'm not going away, Sheena. If I have to stay here all night, I will." Dixon put his ear to the door. *Nothing.* His fist came down on the door once more.

The last thing she wanted was let him in. "Dix?" she called her voice weak. "I'm really sick. Can we talk tomorrow?"

He lowered his voice. "What the fuck, Sheena—why haven't you answered me? I've been texting and calling all afternoon."

"I must've crashed, Dix. I have a fever. 103. I ache all over. My head feels like it's breaking in two." She stood by the door waiting for his reply.

"Fine. Call me tomorrow. We have to talk."

"Ok, baby." Sheena pressed her ear against the door. When she thought she could breathe again, she heard him ask. "Did you like the flowers?"

CHAPTER 17

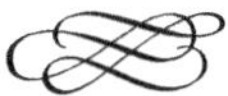

For Suzanne, time was her nemesis. She had promised Steven she would find a job and move out soon, however, enrolling in the program at the Durham Institute would delay all plans.

"I'll be gone a month," she said.

"I'm happy you decided to go, Steven said. "I'm hoping you come back prepared to move forward."

Karen set aside a pot of pasta and joined the conversation. "Have you told Ben?"

"Not yet." Suzanne opened the fridge and gathered ingredients for a salad.

Steven popped a black olive in his mouth. "California's a 50/50 state. He can't keep what doesn't belong to him. Mom and Dad didn't leave you an inheritance to blow on a deadbeat husband. That money was to provide for your future. Ben will find another woman to squeeze."

"You make it sound oh-so-simple."

"He's a loser, and the sooner you realize that cutting him off doesn't make you a bad person, the better you'll be."

Suzanne placed the vegetables on the counter and walked away. Her appetite was gone. Her self-respect, iffy. She called Sam. Despite her promise not to involve him in her personal life, she needed his positive energy to boost her spirits.

"Hello?" Sam answered Suzanne's call.

"Ever been to Raleigh?"

"No, can't say I have." Sam opened a jar of pickles.

"I don't know what to pack."

"I hear layering is always good."

"I like that suggestion. I imagine the classes are casual dress. Jeans, T-shirts."

"For sure," he said, conjuring her in tight fitting-denim, thin fabric stretched across perfect breasts. "Wear one of those T-shirts with a profound saying on it like, Got Ghosts? or I Know What You're Thinking and I'm Telling Your Mother."

Laughter bubbled through the phone. "When do you leave?"

"Next week. I plan to book my flight tonight."

"Need a ride to the airport?"

"Not sure yet."

"You should be getting a call about the check in the next couple of days."

"Check?"

"The department will be picking up the tab for your enrollment, lodging, and food."

"But I thought—"

"I spoke with Dixon this afternoon. He's all for it."

"Dixon?"

"My boss. You haven't met him yet."

"When did I become one of the boys?"

"You could never be one of the boys. Is that the reason you called?"

"Would you like to join me for a beer?"

"How would you feel about ice cream instead?" Silence stood between him and destiny. "Beer's good too."

"I love ice cream, but it has to be just ice cream."

"Fine. No toppings for you."

Dixon powered on his computer and waited for the monitor to blink into life. One site he dearly loved and had planned to visit again produced a pop-up reminding him what a lonely man he was and invited him to play. He clicked on the link and typed in a credit card he maintained in a fictitious name. Soon, his screen blossomed with naughty teens. Firm breasts and tight assets jiggled and wiggled in hi def. He increased the volume so as not to miss the moaning and dirty talk. He watched two co-eds get it on, while a third critiqued and graded their efforts. The "A" she gave them came with two "Ss". Dixon sighed. The *ménage a trois* bored him before they reached a climax. He'd seen it all. Time to hunt.

He entered the link to one of his favorite dating sites. With a three-day weekend approaching, he could afford to take a little trip. A place where surveillance was minimal, someplace remote.

He scrolled down the list of singles, reading each bio as if he were shopping for a new car. Too shiny, too many miles, bumpers too big, headlights too small. He scrolled through fifteen pages until he spotted the one. *Patti.* Cute, perky tits, slim in the hips. Porterville, California. *Hello, Patti.* Her fresh face didn't fool him one bit. He knew her type. "Oh, Patti. I have a big surprise for you."

His fingers flew across the keyboard. His file held information fabricated from a death certificate he confiscated while working in Fresno. According to his profile, "Jerod Warner" was born in 1991. Dixon attached a photo, sun-bleached hair, muscle shirt showcasing nicely developed biceps with press-on tattoos he picked up at a Dollar Store in Reno. Sunglasses hid his eyes. His square jaw with three days of growth gave him a rugged look. It was an attractive photo, woman loved it. He received twenty-five to thirty e-mails a day from women all over the world wanting to date him. For now, Patti was his one and only.

"Hi, Patti. Love your name. Patti is fun to say. Like *sugar*. Spunky, sweet. Your profile says you're twenty-two, and although you don't *appear* older, your age defies your years. What I mean is that your eyes are soulful, like someone who has accumulated an extra decade in their head. Someone with depth. Quiet intelligence. Beauty and brains. My kind of woman.

"I'll bet you like country music one minute and classical the next. Am I right? If I'm wrong, forgive me. I love it all, so whatever genre you're into, I'm there. I listen to country when I'm grilling a steak, Andrea Bocelli when I'm my creating my special pasta sauce, but I have to admit I go totally old school and put on Luther Vandross when I'm hot tubbing under the stars. I like it all, even Bieber and Taylor Swift.

"I was quite shocked to discover you live in Porterville. My grandmother lives in Bakersfield. I'll be visiting her this weekend. Do you think we can get together for coffee, or dinner? I would love to meet you. Always, Jerod."

He attached his file number and hit send.

Dixon reread his lies, confident his identity could never be traced, he waited. Ten minutes later, Patti responded.

"Hi Jerod. I'm new at this. Am I supposed to make you wait before responding? You're very attractive and no doubt can get any girl you want, so imagine my surprise that you like country music, know who Andrea Bocelli is and like to cook. I would be happy to meet for coffee. P-Ville Coffee Shop is off 99, first freeway exit when you hit town, on your right. Can't miss it. I'm available after 2pm."

Dixon liked the eager beavers.

Patti, Patti, Patti, you made my day. P-Ville Coffee shop it is. I'll look for you at 3pm.

Dixon leaned back in his chair. He imagined little Patti on her knees, pleading in her sweet Patti voice. *Life is good.*

Patti phoned her best friend Christine. "I have a date with a hottie."

"Please don't tell me you met on the internet."

"Don't be a kill joy—I'm not running off to a motel with him."

"I'm serious, Patti. How do you know he won't slip you a roofie, take you over the border, and sell you to some brothel in Tijuana?"

"I'm not some moony sixteen-year-old. I told him to meet me at a coffee shop."

"Let me be a fly on the wall. I can sit in a booth nearby. Just in case."

"Just in case what?"

"I just don't have a good feeling about this."

"So I was safer going home with Ricky what's-his-name last week? I was drunk, I knew him for twelve-and-a-half minutes, and you tossed him my keys."

"I knew people who knew him. That's different."

"I'm a big girl. If I wanted this kind of treatment, I would still be living with my parents."

"Fine. I'll text you every ten minutes. If you don't respond? I'm calling the police."

"You watch too much CSI."

Patti hung up the phone. She and Christine had been best friends since pre-school. She texted,

OK but I don't want to see you!!!

What she really wanted to say was, "I don't want <u>him</u> to see you, because then he'll be more interested in you than *me*."

She gathered her chestnut brown hair in her hand and twisted it into a French knot. She sucked in her cheeks and did fishy kisses at the mirror. She pulled down the front of her T-shirt until she could see the swell of her breasts. She squeezed her arms together making the flesh pop into view. "Hi Jerod," she said in her best Marilyn Monroe voice. "It's so nice to meet you." Her eyes grew large. "Really? You think I'm pretty?" She batted her lashes. "You say the sweetest things."

Patti turned to examine her backside. Not bad. Cherry-cheeks. Not apple cheeks, like most men liked, but her two little bubbles looked great in Daisy-Duke shorts, and the bra she purchased the other day would give her that Victoria Secret look that men drooled over. She let go of her hair, letting it fall around her shoulders. "Who are you trying to kid?" Her cat, Friskme, gave her the answer. "Meow."

"That's right my little friend. MeOW." She threw herself on the bed and stared at the ceiling. "On the other hand, he may be the man of my dreams."

CHAPTER 18

Sheena's insides churned as she ushered her friend Robert into her apartment. She prayed Dixon wasn't keeping an eye on her. She needed to move quickly. Robert was a big guy, capable of throwing a punch, clearing a path at a heavy metal concert, or getting an ignorant skater boy to move his car at 5a.m. when he had blocked Sheena's car, but she wasn't sure how he would measure up to someone like Dixon.

Robert minded his own business, never hit on Sheena, or made her feel uncomfortable in any way. He confessed one night after numerous margaritas that he preferred men, which made him accessible, but unattainable. When Sheena called to inform him of her dilemma, he was at her door in a heartbeat to hatch a plan.

"I know someone who will take the furniture off

your hands, put some extra cash in your pocket." Robert ran a beefy palm along the arm of the sofa.

"Do you want my TV? It's two years old. Media friendly."

"I could put it in my spare room, but—"

"I can't take a thing, Rob. You'd be doing me a favor."

"Okay, but if you change your mind—"

"What about my bar stools? Can you use those?"

"Yeah, mine suck."

"Lastly, my bed. Mr. Asshole bought it for me. It's practically new."

"I don't know—I'd feel weird."

"It's all weird. But I'd rather see the bed go to a friend. Mr. Asshole paid a fortune for it."

"Ok. I can turn my den into a second bedroom, put it in there. Maybe even invite my sister to come down from Wisconsin. She's been dying to visit Sacramento."

"It's settled then." Sheena exhaled. "If you take the stuff to your place after I'm gone, that would be great."

"I'm gonna miss you like crazy. You're the only decent person in this shithole."

"I always considered this shithole affordable housing."

"I'd rather just beat the snot out of Mr. Asshole and keep you here."

"Promise me you won't tangle with him."

Robert puffed out his chest. "As long as he doesn't mess with me."

"Chances are he won't. And please, not a word to anyone that I'm gone. My rent is paid until the end of the month. If you move stuff discretely, no one will know I'm gone."

"Are going to let me know how you're doing?"

"In time. For now, you have to trust me. *No one* can know where I am."

"Why don't you just go to the cops?" he asked, throwing up his hands.

"It's complicated. I need to stay off the radar as long as possible."

"Okay. Give me your bags. I'll put them in my trunk and meet you like we planned."

Sheena reached up for a hug. "Thanks for being my friend."

He wrapped his arms around her and squeezed. "I'll see you in a couple of hours."

She watched Robert take the suitcases to the door. In two hours, it would be midnight. He would drive her to Orangevale where an Uber driver would take her to the airport in San Francisco. Her flight to New York was scheduled for 5:04 a.m.

At 11:42 p.m. Dixon did a little housecleaning on his laptop to make sure his history was clean. He picked up his phone and texted Sheena.

You still sick? Maybe I should come over and take your temperature. From the rear.

Sheena panicked.

Very funny. Temps down to 101. And my rear? Sprung a leak. Called the advice nurse at Kaiser. It's the flu all right. Want to come over and watch a movie?

Yeah, right. Dixon worked his thumbs.

"And expose myself to the flu? No thanks. I know plenty of HEALTHY women."

Sheena's eyes welled with tears. How could she have been attracted to such a monster? Yet, she was about to give up everything to carry his child.

Dixon popped open a beer, and flipped through channels on his TV. He subscribed to all the premium channels, but never went beyond the package. He couldn't afford a footprint of lusty purchases on his cable bill. He went over to the closet where he kept an assortment of goodies under the floorboard. He moved his hiking boots and pulled up a wooden floor plank and grabbed a handful of DVDs. He chose the disc labeled "Sheena", slid it into his DVD player and settled into his favorite recliner. He wondered if she ever posed in front of the mirror like she posed for him. When she bent over in the video to give him a better look at her ass, he imagined a sharp object piercing her bowel. "You'd better not be lying to ol' Dix now, darlin'. That would make me very, very, *angry*."

Although Suzanne usually dressed to please herself, in the back of her mind she remembered Sam mentioning his favorite color. Yellow. She rummaged through the box of clothing she had grabbed last time she had gone to her house and found the perfect top.

The mustard colored swing top worked nicely with her faded denim jeans and camel suede booties. After slipping five silver bangles over her wrist and jangling them, she removed them. Since her "incident," she felt uncomfortable wearing jewelry. Metal made her wrists ache. Rings felt too warm against her skin. Ben had noticed right away that she had stopped wearing her wedding ring.

Suzanne peeked out the window as Sam pulled up in front of the house. *It's just ice cream*, she thought, hoping he hadn't seen her in the window. She ran to the closest mirror to check herself. She brought her hands to her face, as if their coolness could lessen the heat she felt whenever he was near. When the doorbell rang, she took a deep breath. *Just ice cream.*

Sam took in the sight of her. "Wow, you look…"

"I'll grab my purse." She wanted to run, change her clothes, and undo the feeling of wanting to please. She hurried down the hallway and ducked into her room. When her heart slowed, and the lump in her throat disappeared, she picked up her purse and returned to Sam.

"All set?" She tucked her purse under her arm, avoiding his stare. "Sure you don't want to go for a drink?"

"Go to a bar? A noisy one, where intimacy is out of the question? Lose ourselves in the buzz, and not be responsible for fragmented conversation or misguided signals? You're not going to discourage me. And for the record, I don't bite."

"Perhaps you're the one who should be going to Raleigh."

"Being able to read people comes from being a cop. I'm especially good with lying."

"Who's lying? I thought maybe—" *How dare he be right?* "Okay, I'll give you the noisy part."

Sam yearned to tell her how delicious she looked in yellow, but although he sensed her interest in him, he'd play it cool. Suzanne's behavior reminded him of a horse he contended with when he was eleven years old. His Aunt Deb had given him a handful of carrots to make friends with the horse, which he did, at first. Once the carrots were gone, the horse played hard to get. Sam tried daily to win the horse over, but Aunt Deb assured him that the horse had a mind of her own, and that Sam need not take the horse's behavior personally. "She's fickle," his Aunt had said, "We got her that way. Someone must've mistreated her."

From then on, Sam took a different approach. He let the horse come to him. He always greeted her with a carrot but didn't expect her to do more than take the carrot and bolt. One day the horse surprised him. Instead of bolting, she nudged his hand. By the end of the summer, Sam rode her around the dirt track.

When they arrived at the "Ice Palace," Sam opened her door, but didn't offer his hand.

"What are these things?"

"They're little doughy balls, called Bobas. Try some."

Suzanne scrunched her nose. "I don't know—"

"Live dangerously!"

"What are those?" she asked, pointing to a container of colorful candies.

"Peanut butter drops." Sam spooned a few on his ice cream and moved to the next row of treats. He loaded his cup with sprinkles, fresh raspberries, marshmallow bits and chocolate shavings. He drizzled hot fudge and squirted a generous amount of whipped cream on top. Suzanne lagged, investigating each container's contents. She filled her cup with gummi worms and Oreo cookie bits. When she finished, she presented her masterpiece.

"What do you think?"

"You're sure you've never done this before?"

"I swear on my Mother's—" Suzanne paled. Her spoon bounced on the floor.

"What's wrong?" He grabbed her elbow to steady her. He led her to a table and sat her down.

The cashier rushed over. "You have to pay."

Sam handed the cashier a twenty. "Keep the change." He knelt by Suzanne's side.

"It's not her," she said.

"Who?"

"It's not the pregnant girl."

CHAPTER 20

By noon Saturday, Patti had modeled six outfits for Christine. "Here's the plan," she said, pulling a lime green chiffon top over her head. "I'll drop you off in back of the café, then park in front. Give me five minutes before you come in, and for God's sake, don't look at me."

Christine threw a top at Patti. "Oh, that's right, I'm a fuckin' idiot."

"I didn't say–"

"Green doesn't go with your skin tone. Try the orange."

"I didn't mean—"

"I know. Trust me, I won't blow it. Just don't leave me sitting there forever."

"I promise. But just in case, you have an Uber app, right?"

"How many times have I Ubered your drunk ass home?"

Patti slumped on the bed. "What if he doesn't like me?"

"Don't be silly. What's not to like?"

"I'm not *hot* like you."

Christine handed Patti a pair of denim shorts the size of a toaster cover. Tiny rhinestones lined each pocket. "Put these on. You'll be fine."

D ixon circled the parking lot. If he parked near the dumpster in back, his car would be unnoticeable to anyone entering from the highway. The sun cast a shadow across his black sedan, making it almost invisible. He checked the clock. 2:55. Five minutes until show time.

A chartreuse-colored Beetle rounded the corner.

"Drop me off over there." Christine pointed to the far corner of the building. "I can stand in the shade."

"Wish me luck."

"Patti, he's gonna love you, stop worrying."

Dixon watched Christine slam the car door. *What do we have here?* He briefly thought about picking up the blond. Take her for a ride. Instead, he got out of the car and headed toward the café to meet Patti. He spotted her immediately, like a peach, ripened in the sun. *Easy-picking.*

"You must be Patti," he said, sliding into the booth.

"And you must be Jerod. Nice to meet you."

They both turned when Christine walked in and sat across the room. Dixon said, "You're much prettier than your photo."

"And you're much taller than yours."

"Really? Never heard that before."

"I have to say, I'm a bit nervous. You're my second online date, and the first one doesn't count because I had met the guy before. We went to the same high school."

"Lucky for me it didn't work out." Dixon said, "I think it will be different with us."

Patti smiled. "I hope so."

Dixon ordered coffee from the waitress, extra cream, and two glasses of water. "Cute place, never been here, as many times as I've driven past." He scanned the café. His eyes stopped at Christine. She smiled and reached for the sugar, her long hair spilling across her chest. She held his gaze until he looked away.

"You said you were visiting family—" Patti seemed to sense his interest had been pulled in another direction. "Your Grandmother?"

"Yes. She's eighty-three. I try to visit whenever I can."

"How sweet."

"She practically raised me when we lived in the Midwest. My mom worked."

"And your dad?"

"Which one?" He knew women were as attracted to

a man with a dysfunctional past as they were to puppies. *How can I fix this?* clearly written on her brow. "It wasn't so bad." His mournful expression buried a hook between her heart and her better senses. All he had to do was reel her in.

"That must've been difficult for you."

"We moved around a lot. That was the only bad part. I liked to play sports. It was hard getting on a team."

"My father was a naval officer. We moved every two years, like it or not."

The waitress set two coffees and a dish with assorted creamers on the table and went back to fetch two waters. When she returned, Dixon took the glasses from her and placed them on the table. He waited until Patti had finished preparing her coffee to put on his clumsy act. As he reached for the creamers, he bumped one of the waters, caught the glass, but not before it had hit Patti's cup, spilling coffee all over the table.

"Oh my God, what a klutz—are you okay?"

Patti gasped when the hot coffee splashed on her lap and dribbled down her leg. She grabbed her napkin.

"I am so sorry." Dixon rose from the table, napkin ready, but Patti held up her hand.

"It was an accident. No worries." She hurried for the bathroom.

Dixon scribbled a number on a sugar packet and walked over to Christine. "You must think I'm a jerk, but

I'm not. You are by far the most beautiful woman I have ever seen. Call me."

Dixon slapped a twenty on the abandoned table and walked out the door.

When Patti emerged from the restroom, Christine intervened. "He left. What an asshole. He spills coffee on you and leaves? So much for Prince Charming."

Patti saw the twenty on their empty table. What she didn't see was the sugar packet her friend slipped into her purse.

Christine listened to her friend cry all the way home. Patti was clueless when it came to men. And other things. Like friendship. Christine befriended Patti for one reason only. Patti provided her with a network of people to use. *Like Jerod?*

She thought of his eyes, his stare seductive, naughty. The way he responded to her smile. She imagined him stripping her naked, tracing every inch of her body with his tongue. Patti was right, she didn't stand a chance with a guy like Jerod. He wanted a real woman, one who could teach *him* a few things.

Once Patti was settled in with a deep-dish pizza, a box of chocolates, and a fifth of Captain Morgan, Christine complained of a headache. "My period must be early I never get headaches."

Two shots in, Patti began to unravel. "I don't know

what I would've done if you weren't there. I'm such an idiot," she sniffled. "When am I gonna learn? When am I gonna get it through my head that men are cretins, and I'm better off alone?"

Christine nodded, "I know, you deserve better." She hugged Patti. "Don't drink the whole bottle. I'll call you tomorrow."

Christine walked two blocks to her apartment. Before she went inside, she plucked the sugar packet from the zipped compartment in her purse and studied the phone number. After a few seconds of deliberation, she dialed.

"I hope this is the beautiful blonde from the café." The man's voice was low and sexy.

"I'm a bad girl," she said.

"My favorite kind. What's your name bad girl?"

"Christine. My friends call me Chrissy. I know yours. Jerod."

"How did you—"

"Patti couldn't cut it alone. I was her support system —in case you were a creep."

"You ARE a bad girl." Dixon loved stupid women. "Where are you?"

"Twenty minutes from the café. I can Uber there."

Dixon didn't want anyone to be able to track her whereabouts, he appealed to her vanity. "Save your money for a new lip-gloss, or something. I'll pick you up."

"How sweet. Let's meet at the gas station on Meyers

and the highway. If you're heading north from the café, it's the third exit. I'll wait for you by the—"

"If you don't want anyone to see you, meet me in the back."

"Yeah, it wouldn't be cool if Patti decided to—"

"*Exactly*. I get it, *bad girl*, see you soon."

Dixon patted the plastic pouch in his pocket. Enough Rohypnol to knock out a horse. *How I love the feisty ones.*

Christine ran up to her apartment for a quick change. She shimmied into a pair of hot pink thong panties, a matching push-up bra, a black mini skirt, and a tight black tank with cut-outs on either side of her mid-section. She lifted her breasts until they peeked over her neckline. She checked her image, sprayed herself with Victoria's Secret body scent and grabbed her purse and jacket. She had three minutes to reach her destination. No time for the phone buzzing in her purse. She was about to get laid and didn't want to spoil the mood with someone else's drama.

When she approached the gas station, she headed to the back, thinking about Jerod's hand up her skirt. She checked her watch. *He's late.* She checked her phone in case he had been trying to call. Sure enough, *1 Missed Call.* The number made her cringe. *Patti.*

Dixon watched Chrissy. People always did interesting shit when they thought no one was looking. For instance, Chrissy snuck a hand under her skirt to make an adjustment, exposing her bare cheeks. Then, she bent forward and scooped up one breast, then the other, until flesh swelled over her top. He wondered if Chrissy's mother ever warned her about guys like him. Did she warn her to be careful, choose wisely, and always have a back-up plan?

His own mom was too busy screwing everyone in the neighborhood to offer advice. And his dad? He didn't know the man, and he never bothered to pursue the issue. He grew up lying about everything, where he lived, who his parents were. Until he went to live with his grandfather, his mother pawned him off on one charitable person or another. She always found someone to take pity on their situation. Her fictitious family helped out when they could. "Uncle" Joe registered him for school, "Aunt" Bev intercepted phone calls when he got in trouble. Nobody showed him the ropes.

He was on his own. Like now. But he had a plan. First, he intended to ravage her body. Then, he would offer her a drink. The drugs would make her easier to manage until they arrived at his secret hideaway. Then he would get down to business.

S uzanne mulled over her disaster date with Sam. One moment she was eating ice cream, the next moment she was watching a girl being flung down a flight of stairs. Blonde hair caught on a protruding nail, ripping a clump from the girl's scalp. "How old is she? How do you know she's young?" Sam asked her again and again. *I could tell by her scream.* "I couldn't see her face." She couldn't see the man's face either, which frustrated her even more.

"Dammit, Jack." She closed her eyes, willing him to appear. "If you're going to torment me like this, show me their damn faces." She opened her eyes and looked around her bedroom. Silence. "I hate you," she screamed.

Her packed suitcase mocked her from the corner of the room. Who are you trying to kid? You'll never be a *real* psychic. You're getting space junk. Static. Magnetic waves meant for someone more receptive. Someone more committed. *Someone who wants to catch a killer.*

She examined her image in the mirror. *Is that true?* What she saw was too many sleepless nights, deep creases in the middle of her forehead. "I thought you loved me, Jack," she whispered.

Her phone rang just then, ending the pity party. "Hello?" Even her voice sounded beat. If Sam noticed, he didn't say.

"I guess we can try again."

"Try what again?"

"Ice cream."

"My flight is at 2:00."

"I'm driving you, remember?"

"Sure. We can talk on the way."

"What's wrong?"

"I'm not sure I'm cut out for this paranormal stuff."

She hung up the phone feeling low. The last vision had been a doozy. She could almost feel *her* hair being yanked from her scalp. I want to catch this bastard so much I can taste it. So fine—keep your distance, Jack. I'll find him on my own.

Sam felt drained. He couldn't insist Suzanne go to Raleigh. What if the institute wasn't the answer? He dialed Linda Schooler.

"Let her go, Sam. It will be good for her to be around like-minded people. She'll get a better understanding of her potential, how to manage it. It's not a gift until you accept it. Right now, seeing young women being tortured and killed is acid to her soul. Once she learns to detach herself from the experience and sees her 'sight' as a tool, she'll be able to get back to herself."

"I'm going to miss her."

"Let her go. She'll come back ready to work, and, perhaps, ready to love."

"Am I doing the wrong thing by asking her to help catch this monster?"

"She was given the gift for a reason. We never get more than we can handle. The universe supplies us with challenges so we may learn and grow. She's a cactus right now. Once she realizes what she's capable of, and follows her path, she'll become a rose."

"Great, one has needles, the other has thorns."

"Both are equally beautiful and need tender loving care."

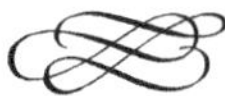

CHAPTER 21

Christine didn't know what hit her. The last time she felt this wasted was in eighth grade when she polished off a bottle of vodka, popped a hit of speed, and smoked two fat bowls of weed. She remembered being in self-destruct mode over Josh Bellner. Josh had asked Kimberly Asay to the graduation dance. *I was the one who gave him a blow job.* Kimberly wouldn't even kiss him, let alone gobble his schlong.

Jerod had brought wine. *I didn't drink that much. Did I have sex?* The ache between her legs answered her question. *That's right.* Jerod sure knew his way around *precious.* And boy, did *precious* love a big strong man taking her home. "Six orgasms," she slurred.

"Don't even think about getting sick."

Her head bounced off the passenger window. Jerod's voice wasn't gentle like it had been when they were making love beneath azure skies.

"Where am I?" Her head swam a couple of laps.

"It's a surprise," he said, his tone flat.

Her brain had turned to pudding. She couldn't feel her feet. She must've dozed. The moon was high against a black backdrop. *No cars*, either direction. She willed her hand to reach for her phone, but her hand lay dead in her lap. Words squeezed through the fissures in her mind. *This should be Patti, not me.*

When Suzanne touched down in Raleigh, a sense of foreboding flooded her senses. *No, not here, not now*, she begged the unknown. The feeling lasted the duration of her ride to the hotel, and through the check-in process. The concierge asked her twice if she was okay, and a bellman insisted upon getting her bags. Safely in her room, she began to shiver.

Her knees weak, the room spinning, she collapsed on the bed. The room was dark, with the exception of a small light in the entry. She wanted to tear open the drapes, open a window, get some air, but she felt paralyzed by the night. She was afraid the stars would converge into a monster and swallow her whole.

Her jaw clenched as snippets of horror danced behind her closed eyes. Images taunted her, daring her to make sense of the scene. Blond hair coiled around a pulley, painted toes desperately reaching for the floor, screams melding with painful cries. The sound of a whip. Metal hitting metal.

Suzanne's body jolted upright. She tore at the drapes, unlocked the window, and gasped for air. Below, the street was empty. The night still. The world around her oblivious to the torture unfolding in some Godforsaken place.

Suzanne reached for her phone. "Sam? Call me." Her chin trembled. "Another girl has been taken."

Dixon slipped into the driver's seat and started the engine. The car belonged to a rich man who wanted to stay out of trouble. *No questions asked.* California was a great state to keep secrets. So many dark roads. So many abandoned shacks. His Grandpa had surveyed land back in the seventies. Dixon had been a snot-nosed little varmint who got under everyone's feet. His mom had pawned him off on whomever she could. Dixon tagged along on Grandpa's jobs. When Grandpa wasn't trying to fondle Dixon's genitals, he was teaching him the lay of the land. When Dixon turned twelve, the poor man had an unfortunate accident. *Writhed in the dirt while crows gathered, eager to peck at his eyes.*

Dixon marveled at the stars. Clear nights launched him into a fantasy world where he piloted his rocket ship into the next galaxy. Driving the desolate highway made him feel as though he were in outer space, navigating the Milky Way. Chrissy's screaming and crying left behind...he was *free*. As he drove past the 'P'Ville Café,' the "Closed" sign glared at him. *Damn, I hate that place.*

S am sat behind his desk, a half-eaten burger churned acid in his stomach. His fries resembled boney fingers, his diet soda, now warm and flat. The room was quiet when the call came in, and he resented the interruption.

"Metzger," he growled.

"Sam?"

"Suzanne? Sorry, I didn't realize it was you."

"He's kidnapped another girl."

"Shit," he grumbled. "When?"

"I got the hit on the way to the hotel. I'm not really sure."

"Tell me what you saw." He ripped a sheet of paper from a pad he kept in his desk drawer and penciled in the date and time.

"She's blonde. About 5'5". Her hair is long, thick. I saw shackles. Chains. I can't see her face, or his." She paused. "He has a whip."

"What does the location look like? Is it the same?"

"Stairs. I saw stairs in the other visions."

"We haven't received any missing person reports fitting the description you gave me." He clicked on his browser and scrolled through the missing person alerts from other counties. "Are you okay?" he asked.

"It was all I could do to get to the hotel without passing out."

"I'm glad you made it there safely. What else can you tell me?"

"Stars."

"What about stars?"

"So many stars you feel like you're falling. I don't know what it means."

"I'm going over previous reports. There has to be something we're missing."

"I have a feeling these girls are going with him willingly. He's handsome, charming…"

"Ted Bundy? *Casanova?*"

"Svengali."

Svengali. She had used that reference once before. "You should get some sleep. I'll make sure I check my phone."

"You do the same."

"Goodnight, Suzanne." He ended the call, feeling unfulfilled. He wanted to chat about Raleigh, about her expectations, the food, anything to keep her on the line. He wanted to be there, tucking her in, kissing her goodnight. *What a fool.* He had promised himself he would never fall in love again, and here he was, feeling like a teenager with his first real crush. Cynthia Brightman had broken his heart in college. He had vowed never to endure that kind of pain again. And yet, the mere thought of having Suzanne in his life brought him joy. Once they caught Svengali, he would pursue her the right way.

Dove Johnson poked his head around the corner of Sam's cubicle. "Seen Dixon anywhere?"

"When's the last time you've seen Dixon in the office at this time of night?"

"I called him about an hour ago, his message referred me to the number here at the station, I just thought…"

"Thought what?" Dixon appeared behind Johnson.

"Surprise, surprise." Sam said. "Your date have a curfew?"

"Now Sam, don't gloat—my dates are all consenting adults. You know how I feel about breaking the law."

Dixon's grin said different.

Suzanne lay back on her pillow, her arm shielding her eyes from the bright lights. "Oh, Jack. How I relied on you." *How you broke my heart.* "And now this."

She slid her hand to the empty side of the bed, yearning to feel the warmth of another. *Sam.* She wondered what his touch would feel like against her skin. Would he be gentle? Aggressive? His lips appeared kissable, yet firm. His blue eyes softened at the sight of her. She had filed for divorce, despite Ben's objections. Once the fight was over, and she was free? *Free.* The word niggled in her mind, as if it came out of someone else's mouth.

Christine blinked. *Dark.* Pain radiated throughout her body. Heavy chains weighted her down. Her limbs were too weak to fight against her restraints. Metal circled her neck and ankles. Orange twine bit into her wrists. Her urine-soaked shorts felt cold against her skin. The air was dank. *Suffocating.* Her head pounded. Her ears rang. The welts on her legs pulsated in waves of pain. A stench assaulted her nostrils. Methane? *Cows.*

Her body shook, her teeth chattered. She opened her mouth to call out for help, but the tight metal collar turned her voice into a feeble whisper. She wished she'd never traded places with Patti. Too late. *I'm going to die.*

CHAPTER 22

Morning in Raleigh sparkled. Suzanne stretched in her bed. Time to get up and face the world. Her first workshop began in an hour, just enough time to take a shower and grab breakfast.

Hot water pummeled tender muscles. The discomfort grew until her arms ached and burned. She caught herself running her tongue along her teeth to make sure they were intact. When she looked down, she saw welts on her legs. *How?* She rinsed and stepped out of the shower. The welts disappeared. The smell of methane made her search the room for the source. Nothing. *Am I losing my mind?*

She hurried up the steps of the Durham Parapsychology Institute. As she rounded the corner, juggling a cup of coffee and a bagel wrapped in a napkin, she collided with another student.

"Let me help you," the woman said, holding

Suzanne's cup while Suzanne collected herself. "Name's Bunny Amendola. You here for the *woo-woo* classes?"

"I'm Suzanne. Suzanne Cash," she replied, shaking Bunny's free hand. "Woo-woo?"

"The family's been teasing me all my life about seeing stuff. 'There she goes with that *woo-woo* stuff again'" Bunny steered Suzanne down the hallway. "You don't get that from people?"

"I guess, a little. My brother thinks I'm a freak."

"So, what do you do? See ghosts? Bend spoons? What's your specialty?"

Suzanne wasn't sure how to answer.

"That's okay. I get it. It took me awhile to figure it out."

"If you have it all figured out, why are you here?"

"I died in a car accident, according to paramedics. I went from seeing dead people to being one of them, now I have an entourage."

"You have ghosts following you?"

"Spirits, actually."

"What's the difference?"

"Ghosts are more of an imprint in time. They're like stuck. They stay in one place. A spirit, however, can move about the cabin, so to speak. They show up wherever and whenever they please."

"I have—or had—a spirit. My late fiancé. He died in Iraq. He didn't appear until I almost died. Then he began showing me things."

"What kind of things?"

Suzanne broke free from the woman's company. She wasn't ready to divulge her reason for being at the institute.

~

Patti's thumbs worked the keypad on her phone, texting.

where are you? u mad at me?

Patti reread the dozen texts she had sent the day before.

wtf chrissy?? call me!!! thought we were friends. -:(

Patti tossed her phone on the bed. She sat at her desk. She tapped in her passcode and leaned back as her profile appeared on the screen. She scrolled through her messages, searching for a message from Jerod. "Asshole," she muttered. His profile no longer existed. No great loss, but what would she do without Chrissy? *Why can't I be more like her?* She decided to walk over to Chrissy's apartment. *Better to talk face to face.*

When Patti arrived, she noticed her friend's car looked like it hadn't been moved in days. Parking spots were unassigned, as a result, Chrissy took what was available. She never parked in the same place twice.

Patti walked up three flights of stairs and knocked on her friend's door.

"Chrissy? It's Patti." She put her ear to the door. "Chrissy?" She knocked again. "Come on Chrissy. Don't be mad, let me in."

Patti gave up and headed home. She didn't notice the black car parked close by. She didn't see the man watching her.

Dixon sank down into his seat. He watched Patti climb the stairs to Christine's apartment. He wished he could lure her into his car, take her far away where she would no longer pose a threat. He had never let one of them live before. He had taken a big chance with Patti. *Patti. Patti. Patti. Are you becoming a little sleuth?"*

Once she had given up on Chrissy, she walked toward him. He pulled his cap down, bent away from her line of sight, and began rummaging through his glove compartment.

After Patti had climbed into her VW Bug and driven away, Dixon relaxed. *Time is on my side.* He started the ignition and shifted into drive. He had an important meeting to attend. A serial killer was on the loose. *Can't have that can we?*

Christine's bladder burned. Perspiration beaded along her hairline. Occasionally a bead broke loose and trickled down her face. The smell of her own urine mingled with the smell of cows. She struggled against the orange twine digging into her flesh. "Patti!" she screamed. "This is all your fucking fault."

She had no idea how long she had been tied up. The muscles in her ankles and calves spasmed, her head felt like she'd been clobbered with a block of cement. *Stand up. Stretch.* She shifted onto her knees. Leaning forward, she rested her weight on her hands, intending to push herself upright.

"Ouch," she cried, plucking a sharp object from her knee. It was small, white, flat on one end, jagged on the other. "Nooo—" She kicked and screamed, but her memory froze at age eight, when she had placed an object like this one under her pillow. *For the tooth fairy.*

"What do we know?" Dixon settled against a scarred wooden desk, arms crossed, long muscular legs crossed at the ankle. "Who's first? Sam?"

Sam and his team had been working round the clock gathering evidence since the first murder had occurred earlier that year. Since then they had been scouring the internet and calling other precincts, collecting information on missing and murdered girls. One thing the girls had in common was their age. *Young and pretty*.

Sam said, "I've been working with a psychic. She's been providing me with details from the crime scenes. I feel we're getting closer to a description of the killer."

Dixon rolled his eyes. "Christ. That's all you've got?"

"She gets visions, sees the crimes being committed, pin-points details of the scene. I believe we're getting closer to finding the bastard."

"What happened to good ol' police work?"

Dove stepped forward. "Forensics concluded the girls have been brutally raped, beaten, and dumped in locations that are far from the crime scene. The lab verified the orange fibers found embedded in Amy Fitzpatrick's wrists and ankles matched the orange twine used on Jennifer Richmond and Twila Averose, the girl from Georgetown. Although the victims have been tortured using various methods, we believe there is just one perpetrator." Dove stepped back. "That's all I have."

"Why is that?" Dixon scanned the faces he had come to know over the last five years. Faces filled with apathy, defiance, resentment. A band of underachievers. His job was to lead these men, not babysit them. "Kids! How long have we been at this? Six, seven months? What the fuck you guys been doin'?" He turned to his men one by one, challenging them to respond. The room went silent.

"Whoever this guy is," Sam said, "I would bet these girls are not his first victims. From the get-go the crime scenes have been spotless, no prints, no DNA, his only signature is orange twine."

"Where are the profiles on these cases?" Dixon asked, eyeing everyone in the room. "See—this is what I'm talking about boys, do your fucking job!

Dove said, "Each scenario is different. Our perp has moved the bodies from the scene of the crime to a new location. Whatever evidence is being left behind remains a mystery. Until we find the location of where the girls are being murdered, we're stumped."

Dixon's eyes grew large, his voice rose a notch, his words mocking Dove's account. "Do we know HOW they are being taken?"

Dove responded, "All of them tested positive for Rohypnol, GHB, and Ketamine."

"You can't just buy that shit without some sort of trail." Dixon clapped his hands loudly, demanding everyone's attention. "Okay, let's get find out who's got the goods and who they're selling to."

"What about Suzanne?" Sam asked. "I'd like to get her on the pay-roll full-time. She's good, and once she gets back from the Durham Psychic Institute, she'll be even better."

"Seriously, Metzger, can't you find a better way to get a woman? Do you have to fuck around at the expense of our taxpayers?"

"We can't all be Casanova."

Dixon cocked his head. "Don't you have work to do?"

"Yes, I have work to do," Sam replied. *And I'm starting with you.*

∾

Suzanne climbed the stairs to the exam rooms, following Olivia, the young docent giving the introductory tour. The first room she entered had black, padded walls. Instruments were set up inside the room and outside. "In here we measure the electromagnetic waves coming from your body. When we are in our psychic mode, we give off more waves. Those in healing mode, register off the charts. We have conducted this experiment all over the world, and the results have been quite remarkable."

The group meandered through the room, checking out the equipment. Suzanne closed her eyes and imagined being alone in the dark. She shuddered when she saw two eyes peering at her, like blurred watercolor paintings, yet the eyes remained, flat, deadly. Suddenly a girl appeared behind Suzanne's lids. Images flashed like lightening. *Cold, afraid, blonde.* The girl's knee bled on a concrete floor. Suzanne gasped. A tiny white object glistened in the palm of her hand.

"Hey!" Bunny stepped up behind Suzanne. "You okay? Looks like you saw a ghost or two, they're not mine, are they?"

Suzanne blinked her way back to the moment. "No

ghosts. Lack of sleep. I could use a gallon of coffee. When do we break?"

"After the tour, we have three more rooms. Seriously, you okay? You're pale."

"Not a morning person, I guess," Suzanne said. "This is so cool. Are you getting anything?"

Bunny shook her head. "But I keep hoping."

"For what?"

"I'd like to tap into the collective energy of the group, wouldn't that be awesome? All thirty of us channeling together. Group consciousness magnified."

Suzanne wondered if everyone concentrated on finding a serial killer...*would they see what I see?* A man who stood nearby made a sour face. "We focus on *positive* energy," he said, his twisted features contradicting his message. Suzanne shot a smile his way and walked into the next room.

"Are you all familiar with the experiments of Dr. Duncan McDougall?" Olivia asked, her Vanna White gesture sweeping towards a low stainless-steel table hooked up to a digital scale. "His work substantiated that the soul leaves the body when we die. A theme that was explored in the movie, "21 Grams." This table was developed by—please, don't touch, sir," she said. Everyone looked around. No one else saw him but Suzanne. *Jack.* Olivia blinked, and he was gone. She chuckled, "Spirits love to touch the equipment."

Suzanne slipped into the hallway. "Jack," she whispered. For the first time in days, he appeared. "I thought you left me, again."

"You must leave here, Suzanne. Go home. She's not doing well."

"Who?"

"The girl. The blonde girl. Hurry." Before Suzanne could ask more, he vanished.

Suzanne raced back to the hotel, packed her things and booked the next flight home.

Christine ached all over. Her kidneys throbbed and burned. Her bladder felt gritty, her mouth, sticky and dry. If she didn't die today, she'd find a way to end her misery. *Bash your head on the concrete*, taunted the voice sizzling in her mushy brain. She had managed to quiet the voice when she lost consciousness some time during the night, but now it was back with a vengeance. Her screams left her hoarse, parched and swollen. She could barely swallow. Her arms were frozen behind her, her hands and feet numb. No more tears. Chills seared her skin and pulsated up and down her spine. Goosebumps gathered, stinging her skin. Bass drums boomed in her head, Bose speakers, best you can buy. Her vision blurred from the pressure behind her eyes. Hallucinations came and went. A man, his uniform tattered, bloody, his face kind, said, "Hang in there, kid." And she did.

D ixon didn't care about his victims. Once he got what he wanted, he became bored, ending the game. His position as Sheriff gave him certain privileges. How else could he maintain his appetite for killing? He thought about Patti. *Patti, Patti, Patti.* Something lyrical about that name. He smiled to himself. The wheels were turning. And then fate intervened.

"Call on line three, Sheriff. Deputy Chief Ipswich from Fresno says a girl called about her missing friend. Thought you'd like to take this one."

He took the call.

"Hey, Blake Ipswich here, got a call from a young lady, a Patricia Watson. Her friend has been missing a few days. Heard you guys were working on a serial murder case. Thought you'd like to question this girl she may be able to give you something you can use regarding your case up there."

"Thanks, Blake. Can't hurt." Dixon jotted down the information, ended the call and placed another.

"Hello, this is the Sheriff of Goldorado County, Jim Dixon, is this Patricia Watson?"

"Yes. My friend is missing. I haven't seen her for days. Her car is in the lot, she's not answering her door."

"What is your friend's name."

"Christine Bonnevier."

"Tell me about your friend. Is she single? Could she be with a boyfriend?"

"No. Chrissy doesn't have a boyfriend—that's why I can't imagine where she'd be."

"Can I get your information Miss—it is *Miss* Watson?"

"Yes—it's Miss. I'm really worried."

Dixon pictured Patti twirling her hair, a nervous habit she admitted to while chatting with him online. "Does this young woman have family?"

"Yes, but they're in Canada. Chrissy stayed behind when they moved back there."

"Have you contacted them?"

"No. I really don't know much about them. They're not close, I mean Chrissy rarely even talks about them. She's very independent."

"Independent?"

"She does what she wants, but she doesn't disappear or anything like that. We talk every day." Patti paused. Dixon sensed discomfort.

"What is it?"

"Well, we sorta had a fight. Nothing major. I had a meltdown, she left my house. I went to apologize—her car was there. She didn't answer the door. I've gone over to her place several times since then. She doesn't answer her phone *or* texts."

If you only knew. "Let's start with her address, I'll see that a patrolman is dispatched there. What's her apartment number?"

"How did you know she lived in an apartment?"

"You mentioned—"

"Did I?"

"Miss, I don't have time for games."

"I apologize. I'm being paranoid."

"If you can't trust the police, who can you trust?"

"I'm sorry. She lives at 321 Crest Drive, Fresno."

"Can I get your information as well?"

"It's 733 Brisbayne Road, Fresno. My cell number is 209-555-0809.

Dixon delighted in her naivety, *Patti, Patti, Patti.*

Patti hung up the phone feeling uneasy about Chrissy's disappearance. Speaking with the Sheriff made it worse. She expected him to say something comforting like "don't worry, or "I'm sure your friend is fine. Instead his words lacked empathy. Maybe he felt put upon because Christine's case was out of his jurisdiction. Whatever the reason, Patti felt low, and poured herself a glass of wine. *Settle my nerves*, she convinced herself. She mentally replayed her conversation with Dixon. She couldn't recall mentioning that Christine lived in an apartment, and it disturbed her. Something else niggled at the back of her mind. He asked if she were single. Why did that bother her? Perhaps her feelings were still raw from being kicked to the curb. Who does that? Who invites a lady on a date and disappears while she's in the john?

At least he paid the check. Big deal. She deserved better than that, right?

Chrissy always knew what kind of guy she was dealing with before she accepted a date. Of course, she didn't cruise singles sites. Guys gravitated towards her like bugs to a lightbulb. Patti was careful. She selected Jerod from hundreds of single prospects, read his profile, read between the lines. She had a pretty good sense of what was bullshit, what was truth. Being single was the pits. *Single.* Why did Sheriff Dixon want to know if she was single? "It is Miss, isn't it?" It wasn't the question…it was the way he asked it.

Dixon whistled along with Merle Haggard, "That's the Way Love Goes." In two hours and twenty minutes he would face his next victim, Patti. He had two hours and twenty minutes to come up with a story to convince her he was a nice guy, and how difficult it was for cops to date, and how he wanted nothing more than to help her find her friend.

About the conversation he had had with Patti earlier… she had questioned him about the apartment thing. He could've sworn she had mentioned Christine's apartment. What did it matter? Once he had her, his only concern would be how to punish her.

Sometimes he copied the work of the masters. The internet was a treasure trove of documented cases waiting to be recreated, like serial killer Alberto DiSalvo. *The broom stick jammed in Amy Fitzpatrick's vagina was a nice touch.* No, Patti deserved better. *Inspiration. That's all I need.*

S am sat behind his desk reviewing the reports he had collected over the months. He paid close attention to time codes; when the bodies were found, when his men were dispatched, when everyone checked in at the scene, when they checked out. Dixon had rarely made an appearance. He had a phenomenal team working for him, and no one complained about his absence. Dixon had a way of getting things done without exerting much effort. Once in a while he reined everyone in for a shit storm, but for the most part, he was easy going—*if you don't cross him.*

Sam ran his finger down the list of possible characteristics of their unsub. Handsome, gregarious, intelligent—Dixon fit the bill. *So do a million other guys.* He tossed his pen on the pile and leaned back in his chair. He wondered if anyone else noticed Dixon's dark side. *Something in his eyes. Something he hides quite well.*

The dispatcher poked her head in. "Seen Dixon?"

"Earlier this morning, why?"

"He left right after that call came in, and I didn't have a chance to ask him about taking next Thursday off. I have a dental appointment. Root canal."

"Who was the call from?"

"Deputy Chief Ipswich from Fresno. He had some info he wanted to share. May be a connection to the murders. Dixon didn't tell you?"

Sam picked up the phone and dialed.

"Dixon."

"Jim, where you at?"

"Who wants to know?"

"Kelly said you got a lead."

"Kelly is talking out of her ass."

"She said the deputy chief called from Fresno, said he had a lead."

"Some girl reported her friend missing, and he thought it was connected to our guy. Turns out the two girls had a fight, nothing more. Anything else?"

"No, I'm good."

"I'm headed to Tahoe to meet a farmer about some land he owns up there," Dixon said, "What do you think about a shooting range? Maybe set up a virtual site?"

"I'm sure the guys would love it."

"Cool. See you when I get back."

Same distain he always felt when he and Dixon got into a confrontation. The man was a pro at putting people in their place. *One more feature of a coldblooded killer?* Sam's thoughts were interrupted by the vibration coming from his shirt pocket.

"Detective Samson Metzger."

"Sam? It's Suzanne. I'm calling from the Raleigh airport. I'm on my way home."

"What happened? Are you okay?"

"Jack is back. He told me another girl is in danger. He said she's not doing well."

"Did he tell you where she is?"

"No. But I keep seeing cows."

"Cows? There are cows from here to—" Sam's words came to a halt. *Dixon.* He said he was on his way to Tahoe to speak with a farmer. "Call me when you land, I've got to tie up a few loose ends."

What were the chances Dixon was their guy? He dialed a person he could count on to help.

"Dove, it's Sam. I need a phone number tracked."

"What's up?"

"Just a hunch I'd like to eliminate."

"It's not my fortè, but I can run the number."

"I'll be right over."

Dixon made a U-turn and headed for Placerville. He had an inkling that Sam wasn't finished digging. He needed an alibi and a place to stash his phone. *Just in case.*

When he pulled up to the Liar's Bench bar, he saw Laura Hughes leaning against the entryway smoking a cigarette. He parked at the curb, dropped his cell phone into the padded envelope he had tucked away in his glove compartment, and rolled down his window. "Hey darlin', don't you know by law you're supposed to be fifteen feet away from the building if you're going to kill yourself with one of those things?"

"Why Jim Dixon, I didn't know you cared." Laura

took a long drag, tossed the butt to the ground, and smashed it with the heel of her boot. She sashayed to the window and bent down, giving Dixon an eyeful of plump flesh. "Where you been, stranger?"

"Around. Miss me?"

"You know it. Got a few minutes for a quick romp?"

"Not today sweetheart, I'm late for a meeting. Thinking about buying some property up here. Just stopped by to say 'hello' and yank your chain a bit."

"You know I like when you're frisky."

"Have you seen Detective Metzger hanging around?"

"Stiff dick?"

"Yeah, that's the one."

"Nope. Should I?"

"He's sniffing out a case. Thought he might start here."

"Any message if he comes by?"

"If he asks, tell him I went to see a man about a horse." Dixon picked up the padded envelope and handed it to Laura. "Will you hang onto this for me?"

"Does it bite?" she asked, pinning his eyes with hers.

"Just a little insurance. Be by later to pick it up. Maybe we can hang out for a while," he said with a wink.

Laura winked back. She reached in her purse, pulled out a cigarette and lit it, blowing smoke toward Dixon's car. He chuckled. *Bad girl.*

Christine mumbled a prayer. "Dear Jesus, I promise if you help me out of here, I'll change my ways. I'll be better. Smarter. Kinder." A pain shot from her abdomen to her back and she whimpered. "Please," she begged. "Either save me or let me die."

By the time the sun poured between the cracks in the blackened windows, she was still there, raging fever and all. She tried to open her clenched fists, but her hands were frozen. The tiny white object mocked her. She wondered who the tooth belonged to.

She gagged. Pain in her torso competed with the fire in her brain. Heat radiating from her face warmed the metal around her neck. When she exhaled, her breath felt hot on her chin. Something skittered across her feet. She was too weak to scream.

Patti peeked through the curtain when she heard her doorbell ring. A tall man stood on her stoop his hands shoved in his pockets. He did a little impatient dance as he waited. She couldn't see his face. Before she unlatched the lock, she called out, "Who is it?"

"It's Sheriff Dixon from the Goldorado County Sheriff's Department. I'm here to speak with Miss Patricia Watson."

When Patti opened the door, her jaw dropped. "Jerod?"

Dixon pushed the door open, stepped inside, and closed the door behind him. "This is awkward, Patti. I had no idea."

"What are you doing here? You're a cop?"

"Sheriff." He lowered his eyes and shuffled his feet. "When we spoke on the phone I had a sneaking suspicion it was you, but I wasn't sure. Have you heard from your friend?"

"No. I haven't." Confusion remained on Patti's face.

"Can we sit? I am here on official business, but first, I think I owe you an explanation."

Dixon placed a hand on Patti's shoulder and steered her into the living room. "Sit," he said softly.

She obliged, but her hands clung to each other between her knees.

"It's good to see you again. I feel like such a schmuck for running out on you like that, but I had to. There was someone across the room, a young lady, I picked up for prostitution a while back, and I didn't want to make a scene. It's not easy dating when you're the Sheriff of a small town. I try to keep my social life as private as possible. Sorry for lying to you. I would've confessed if we had had the chance to get to know each other better." Dixon reached out and touched her hand. "But right now, it's important we find your friend."

Patti relaxed. She leaned back against the couch. "I suppose it was my fault. After you left me, I was feeling sorry for myself. I drank too much. Christine isn't used to weakness, she's tough. She doesn't get hurt when she's rejected, as if that would ever happen. She keeps her head. She—she's not like me."

Dixon leaned closer and smiled. "No one expects you to be anyone other than yourself. What do you say we start over, go get a cup of coffee and figure out where to start looking for Christine?"

"Okay," she said, "Let me get a sweater."

Dixon patted the small packets he had tucked away in his shirt pocket. All he needed was an opportunity to slip one in her coffee. Better here than in public. "Hey Patti?"

"Yes?" She appeared in the hallway.

"Let me go get us some coffee. I can bring it back here. It's quiet. Better to talk."

"I can make coffee if you—"

"I saw a Starbucks down the street. I can be back in a flash. What would you like?"

"I like their Ethiopian blend. Two sugars, extra cream."

"How about a pastry or something to go along with your coffee?"

"No thanks. Don't need the extra calories."

He looked her up and down. "Please don't tell me you worry about weight… You're walking perfection."

Patti blushed. "Thank you."

"I'll be right back," he said. Once outside, he

grinned. He had her right where he wanted her. *Patti, Patti, Patti.*

Suzanne's head ached. She had taken two aspirin, but the pain didn't go away. *I never get headaches.* She had asked the flight attendant to bring her water three times, and still, her thirst continued. Her kidneys felt tender and her bladder uncomfortable. Every time she closed her eyes, Jack appeared, dressed in fatigues, his pants torn, his jacket tattered. His face was smudged with black, his hair disheveled.

"Find her, she doesn't have much time" he said, blood oozing between his teeth.

Oh, Jack. Don't leave me. I can't do this without you.

Sam called out Dixon's phone number as Dove typed. A map popped up on the screen, giving the men a look at the area where the signal had appeared last. Placerville. *He said he was going to Tahoe.*

Dove clicked on the plus sign, enlarging the area. "Why does this number sound familiar?"

"No need to know that. I'd appreciate if you kept this between us."

"You think this may be our guy?"

"The signal is stationary."

Dove nodded. "Yep. This person isn't moving."

"Is that Main Street?"

Dove increased the size of the area. "Yep. Liar's Bench to be exact."

Sam patted Dove on the back and left the room. He had to check out the situation himself. Dixon wasn't one to hang out in bars. He knew better. Then again, maybe he was meeting the farmer there. *I have to be sure.*

Dixon paid for two coffees and took them to the condiment counter where he discreetly pulled a packet from his pocket and placed it between two sugar packets. He ripped open the tops and poured them all into one of the cups. He added cream, stirred and closed the lid. He added a splash of Hazelnut flavoring to his cup and a generous amount of cream. He stuck a stir stick in the slot on the lid to make sure he didn't get the two cups mixed up.

Christine and Patti. *Best buds reunite, drum roll please.* Should he ravish Patti first? Or wait and take her in front of Christine? *Won't she be the jealous one?* Little Chrissy, who'd thought she could steal the hearts of Patti's suitors with her rockin' body and wicked ways. *Let's see who's wicked now?*

Dixon remembered the way his mother had manipulated men with her stunning looks and voluptuous figure. He wondered how many times good ol' grandpa had dipped his wick in her tight little ass. *Like a dog with a bone, always wanting to bury it somewhere.*

When his mother was old enough to find her own bones to bury, good ol' grandpa turned to him. Shit runs downhill folks. The family legacy lives on, with one slight difference…*I like to torture and kill.*

His thirst for blood had come at an early age. Killing rats, mostly. There were plenty in the hovels he grew up in. Occasionally, his mom would pawn him off on someone who actually had a bed for him to sleep in. *G-L-O-R-I-A, Glor-i-a.*

Gloria Sutter owned a three-bedroom ranch, but she insisted he sleep in her bed. At twelve years old he had filled out and was one of the best-looking boys in town. He was mature for his age—*getting fucked in the ass does that to a kid.*

Round and robust, Gloria tantalized her little house guest with glimpses of her fleshy parts as often as possible during the day, at night she wore a flimsy nightie that crawled up over her bare ass. The first time she cuddled close, Dixon wasn't sure which part of her doughy body was what. When he slipped her his bone, she bumped up against him so hard she knocked him off the bed. After that she cut to the chase and rode him like a bucking bronco. He remembered once her breasts covered his face and he couldn't breathe.

Their little ritual went on for months. Not once did his mother stop by to check up on him or call to see how he was doing. When summer ended, Gloria was bored and sent him home.

Dixon demonstrated his newly acquired skills on a sixth grader named Kelly. At thirteen, her breasts resembled two sugar cones. She was very proud of her blossoming buds and hinted that she wanted him to touch them. One day after school she placed his hands on her chest instructing him, "Move your hands in circles, like this." When he squeezed, she cried. Later, she told her mother what he did, claiming it was his idea. The next day shit hit the fan. Grandpa had to come to school and bail him out. He spent the rest of the day between grandpa's knees sucking his way to redemption.

Memories ignited the rage that burned deep inside of Dixon. Patti would pay the price. *Just like the others.*

Sam parked on Main Street and walked toward the Liar's Bench. He poked his head inside. It was empty with the exception of a curvaceous redhead standing by the door, smoking a cigarette. "Excuse me," he said, "I'm supposed to meet someone here, tall good-looking guy, dark hair, early forties, have you seen anyone fitting that description?"

"You're a cop aren't you?"

"The court house is up the street. I could be a lawyer."

"I know who you are. If you're looking for your

Sheriff, he left a while ago, said he was meeting a man about a horse. Or was it horse property?" She dropped the cigarette on the sidewalk and crushed it with her heel. "Any message if he returns?"

"No message, I'll catch up with him later.

Patti sipped her coffee as Dixon asked about Christine. "How long have you and Christine been friends?"

"Twenty-two years. We met at pre-school, Chrissy took me under her wing. I–" Patti set her cup on the table. "I can't imagine her taking off without a word."

Dixon took another drink from his cup. "The property manager said her place was empty. There was no disturbance. Maybe she had an emergency?"

"She would've called. She was mad at me, but I know she would've at least texted me that she was leaving." Patti picked up her cup and took a drink.

She began to relax. Her eyes were glazed, her speech dragged. Dixon moved closer to her on the sofa. He kissed her neck, unbuttoned her shirt. She kept talking about Chrissy in words that no longer made sense. Dixon took her to the bedroom. She didn't resist.

Patti's mind seemed like it was skipping tracks. Her thoughts kept wadding up in sticky clumps, her body felt detached. She could hear a voice cajoling her to do things she wasn't sure she wanted to do. She wasn't sure of anything, like whether her arm was really floating above her head or if her knees were connected to her legs. Were those <u>her</u> legs, or did they belong to the beast stealing her soul? He's a pretty beast. Eyes the color of the sky, burning globes piercing her brain with commands. *Move.* What does that mean? Move? She was cement. A sculpture. A Mermaid with shiny green scales and a giant fin.

"Get up," growled the beast.

I want to, I really do. Can you hear me? Her words were clear, but her mouth was frozen to her face. The floor looked so far away. *Where are my clothes?* Firecrackers exploded behind her eyes. *Where are my feet?*

Sam called the office. He needed to check with Dove regarding Dixon's phone. Suzanne was on her way back home, and he had to finish up a few things before he dealt with her. Why had she come back so soon? He hoped he hadn't made a mistake by sending her to Raleigh.

He dug in his pocket for his phone. "Metzger—"

"It's Suzanne. I just landed. Has anything happened?"

"What do you mean?"

"Has another girl disappeared?"

"Not that I know of. Why? What are you getting?"

"She's blond. Young. She's in pain."

"I'll pick you up in twenty minutes."

"I'll be waiting," she said.

Sam swiped his hand over a day's worth of stubble. He was anxious to see her, but now wasn't the best time. He dialed Dove.

"Would we be able to pick up a phone signal if it was out of cell tower range?"

"Not with the equipment we have. Did you hit a dead end?"

"Yeah. The signal stopped at Liar's Bench. The owner wasn't there, but according to a witness, the owner wasn't far away."

"Placerville is spotty, but the signal we had was strong. What makes you think the owner has the phone with him?"

"Can't be sure. The person I spoke with didn't mention that the phone was left there."

"Let me know if I can help," Dove said, ending the call.

Sam stared out his driver's window. His mind executed a run-down of his morning beginning with the conversation he had had with Dixon. Something wasn't gelling. "I'm watching you," he whispered. He picked up the phone and dialed the dispatcher.

"Kelly, it's Sam. Do you have the message from Ipswich?"

"Sure do," she said. "Want me to text it to you?"

"Yes, please."

"Sending," she said. "Anything else? I was planning on going to lunch."

"A little late for lunch isn't it?"

"I promised HR I'd cover phones for them while they went to lunch. They're short-handed today."

"Have you heard from Dixon?"

"Not a word. Is he missing again?"

"Excuse me?"

"Sheriff Dixon does a great job, he's hard to keep track of sometimes."

"He's not answering his phone."

"Which one? He has a few phones."

"How does he rate a few phones?"

"Uh oh, I let the cat outta the bag, didn't I?"

"No, I'm giving you grief. I'm sure Dixon has good reason for having more than one phone. Do you happen to have the numbers handy? I haven't been able to get a hold of him all day."

"I have to get permission from him before I give those out."

"I understand." Sam started his ignition. "Check me out for the afternoon, I'm meeting with someone about the Fitzpatrick case. If Dixon calls in, have him give me a jingle."

"Sure, Sam."

He rolled down the window. The weather was gorgeous, and he needed a little sunshine in his life. He dialed Chief Ipswich."

"Chief, Sam Metzger from Goldorado County. I understand you received a call from someone claiming her friend was missing."

"Why yes, I spoke with your Sheriff about it this morning. He said he would handle it, is there a problem?"

"No. No problem, I would like to follow up on the call. Do you have a description of the missing girl?"

"I do, hold on."

Sam listened to an instrumental version of "Raindrops Keep Falling on My Head" while on hold.

"Sam? Her name is Christine Bonnevier. She's twenty-seven years old, five foot seven, one hundred twenty pounds, blond hair and blue eyes. She was last seen at Patricia Watson's home in Fresno."

"Patricia Watson is the person who reported her missing?"

"Yes."

"When did she call?"

"Few days ago. She said she thought Christine would show up at home. When she didn't, she got worried."

"Was anyone dispatched to check out Christine's home?"

"I sent an officer there when I got the call. There's no sign of wrongdoing. The lock wasn't busted, her place was immaculate–her car was even covered."

"Her car was in the lot?"

"Yep. A pretty little Mustang. According to my deputy, she takes really good care of it. I spoke with Jim Dixon about this case. He didn't think it was connected to your cases up there. Are you disagreeing with his assessment?"

"No. I wanted to follow up to make sure we didn't miss anything."

"If we find anything, I'll let you know."

"Thanks, I do have one question."

"What's that?"

"Are there many dairy farms close by?"

"Is the Pope Catholic?"

"I kept smelling them, seeing them. Cows everywhere," Suzanne said. "I don't know what it means. And Jack—he wasn't the same as when I first saw him. His uniform, it's tattered, he's hurt." She turned to Sam. "Is this ever going to stop?"

Sam took her bag. "I don't know."

She stared out the window as they drove down the freeway. "Hungry?" Sam asked.

"No. Yes. I don't know."

"Okay, the 'no' gets a burger, the 'yes' gets something

a little more substantial, and the 'I don't know' gets a surprise. Which is it?"

"Surprise me."

Sam pulled off at the next exit and wound his way through Folsom. "I hope you like Mexican." He parked and waited until she unfastened her seatbelt before adding, "I'm glad you're back."

They were seated at a booth by the window. "How was Raleigh?"

"Interesting. I met a few nice people. Can't say I made life-long friends. In fact, some were kinda weird." She chuckled. "I guess I fit right in."

"I would never say such a thing about you." He paused, then said, "I missed you."

Suzanne fiddled with her fork. "When this is over, I hope we can remain friends. I do like you…"

"I hear a 'but' coming—"

"But—after we catch our killer, we can talk about how to continue being human. Emotions and all."

"Deal. What are you going to order?"

"She's starving."

"Did you eat on the plane?"

"No, she's starving. She's dehydrated and starving."

He placed the menu aside. "Who is *she*? Can you get a name?"

"Tooth Fairy. I keep hearing 'Tooth Fairy'." She opened and closed her palm. "It's in her hand." Suzanne's face crumbled. Tears sprung from her eyes.

Sam pinched the bridge of his nose. "Amy Fitz-patrick. Many of her teeth were missing."

Suzanne cupped her hand over her mouth.

"What is it?" Sam moved around to sit next to Suzanne in the booth. He gathered her in his arms. "You're safe." He held her wracking body close to his until she stopped shaking. "Shhhh…you're okay, no one is going to hurt you. We'll find the girl. I promise this horror will end."

CHAPTER 23

Patti's hands were tied behind her back. She felt detached from her body parts, especially the parts between her legs. Images of chickens, beheaded with a dull knife, danced in her head. She hummed a tune. A lifeless drone, driving Dixon to the brink. "Shut up you stupid bitch!" He shouted, but Patti didn't quiet herself. Inside her mind, dragon flies with sharp teeth gathered around the headless chickens. Surely it was their buzzing the beast referred to. She had no power to make them stop. *I always thought dragonflies were vegetarians.* In another part of her brain, tiny feet shuffled through sand on a cement floor. Gritty little slides, moving back and forth, back and forth. *Ch-ch, ch-ch.* Her inner child cried out in pain. Her mother's voice responded. *"You poor thing. You miss the beach don't you? Maybe when your body parts return home, you can visit the beach"*

Patti could feel the hot sun beating on her face.

Where's my bathing suit? Can someone bring me a towel? I'm all wet.

Dixon forged ahead, despite the urge to pull over and beat Patti bloody. The tape covering her mouth didn't prevent her from droning on and on. Her humming reminded him of good ol' grandpa after he tied one on and fell asleep in his Barcalounger. Time was ticking away. He needed to dump Patti at the house and get back to Placerville before five. *Doesn't leave much time for a reunion celebration.* "Too bad," he whispered. "I was really looking forward to that."

When he arrived at the house, he parked close to the door and dragged Patti out of the car by the hair. He sang a little ditty. "Get 'em by the hair, yes, get 'em by the hair, *cuzzzz*…when you get 'em by the hair they follow you any-where."

Chrissy opened one eye when she heard the car door slam. Fear pumped the last of her adrenaline to her heart, and it beat like a trapped animal. She didn't expect to see what Dixon was pulling behind him. *Patti.* She swallowed her scream afraid he would kill her or worse. Instead she closed her eyes and pretended to be unconscious.

She heard Dixon talk to Patti as he chained her to metal hoops, fastened underneath the staircase. "There," Dixon said, dropping something on the floor. "You ladies don't stay up too late, now." His laughter, nails on a chalkboard

Chrissy heard him mount the steps, slam the door, and start the car. When she heard the spray of gravel, and the sound of the engine fade, she opened her eyes.

Patti stared ahead as if she were alone in the room. Tape hung loose from her cheek. Chrissy whimpered. *We're fucked now. Really fucked! Who's going to save us? You were my only hope. Damn you, Patti Watson. Damn you!*

"Patti," she whispered. Patti's breathing seemed shallow, and Chrissy noticed blood caked above her right eyebrow, and below left her earlobe. The sun would be gone in the next half hour. The light seeping through the cracks would be gone, and they would be left alone in the dark.

"Patti, it's me Chrissy. Look at me. You can't give in to the pain. We have to get out of here."

Patti remained silent.

Suzanne fought for composure. One thing she had learned in her lone workshop in Raleigh is that fear breeds fear. Her visions were interpretations her brain had compiled from the bits of information she was picking up on. She was a receptor for energy traveling

through the ether. She was the vessel into which the information flowed. If she could focus on the information and put her feelings aside, she would be able to assimilate the message without experiencing fear. She also knew it took practice to be able to separate the two. Right now, her mind was filled with chatter. And humming. Dappled sunlight. Sand. *Where is Jack?* When she opened her eyes, she realized Sam was staring from across the table.

"I—I am picking up something, but I'm not sure what. It's not the same as–"

Suddenly it all made sense. "Oh, my god. There are *two* girls," she said.

Sam turned to the window.

Suzanne placed her hand on top of his. "You're keeping something from me—"

"We got a call from Fresno this morning. A young woman reported her friend missing. I tried to call her to get more information, but she's not answering her phone. Sheriff Dixon claims he spoke with this young woman, concluded the two girls had had a fight, and there was nothing to be concerned about."

"You're not convinced?"

"I suspect there is more to the story."

"Have you discussed it with the Sheriff?"

Sam faced her. "Dixon's the kind of person you don't contradict unless you have all your facts."

"What do you need?"

"A trip to Fresno. You in?"

"I'm in."

Dixon arrived in Placerville at 5:04 p.m. He entered the Liar's Bench and took a seat at the bar. Within minutes of his arrival, he felt warm hands massage his shoulders.

"Didn't think you were coming back, cowboy." Laura's fingers dug deep into his muscles and he moaned.

"And miss out on the best massage in town?"

"My magic fingers can do wonders for your stress. Lover."

"Who says I'm stressed?"

"Muscles don't lie. Unless you been haulin' sacks of cement all day."

"It's been a long day."

"Then let's get you comfortable and see if we can't loosen you up a bit."

Dixon slid off the stool and followed Laura through the bar to a stairway, left of the kitchen doors. The steep entry smelled musty and old, but he didn't mind. He'd been in worse places, and right now Laura was a welcome reprieve. He knew her mouth was as skilled as her hands, and a blowjob was just what the doctor ordered, but before he took another step he asked, "Where did you put that pouch I gave you?"

"It's upstairs. I kept it safe and sound for you."

When Laura handed Dixon the pouch, he patted her backside and excused himself to the bathroom. He closed the lid to the toilet, sat down, and ripped the envelope open. He poured the phone into his hand and tossed the envelope aside. He pressed the "on" button and waited until his phone came to life. Six voice messages. Two from Sam Metzger. One from dispatch. The other three were from ladies he had met on the internet. He listened to Sam's message first.

"Jim, it's Sam. I'll be picking Suzanne up from the airport today. I would like you to meet her. Can we arrange that soon? Thanks. Bye."

He replayed the message, analyzing Sam's words. The last thing he needed was some stiff-dick monitoring his every move. He pressed the button to return Sam's call.

"Sam—it's Jim. The cell service here sucks. I just got your message, what's up?"

"I wanted to let you know Suzanne is back from Raleigh. You two should meet. I think she's going to be very valuable to our investigation."

"I have this deal I'm working on, and I'm in meetings all week with the Mayor. How about next Thursday?"

"Next Thursday? We're dealing with a serial killer!"

"We haven't got a chance in hell of catching this guy until we get more leads—we've already been on this what—six months? Longer? What the fuck is a week?"

"Do you want an update if we come up with anything sooner?"

"Yes. I expect to be kept in the loop."

"How did the meeting go today? Did the farmer agree to sell his land?"

"After a fifth of whiskey and a million stories about him and Old Blue, he said he'd take my offer into consideration." Dixon paused. "Anything else?"

"No, just curious. The range sounded like a great idea, that's all."

"Good. Go home. I've got a date with a beautiful masseuse."

Dixon checked his teeth in the mirror and stuck out his tongue. *Nope, no lies there.* He pocketed his phone and went to join Laura.

He found her already undressed down to her black lace bra, panties and garter belt. For a woman of fifty plus, she was in fabulous shape. Toned, and large breasted. She arranged her hair at the nape of her neck and patted the bed. "Come here handsome. Let mama take care of you."

Dixon unbuttoned his shirt and dropped his pants. Laura took care of the rest. After bending down to remove his socks, she dipped her hand into his underwear and whispered sweet nothings. By the time he was naked, she had him so aroused, he was ready to explode. He grabbed her hair in his fist and thrust his hips into her face.

"You don't have to play so rough, cowboy," she cried, gagging.

"C'mere," he said, pulling her down on the bed. "Is

this what you want?" He slipped his hand between her thighs.

Dixon rolled on top of her and spread her legs. "I have what you want," he said, burying himself deep inside her.

CHAPTER 24

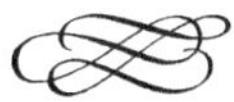

Chrissy stretched her foot toward Patti, but it wouldn't reach. "Patti? Patti, it's Chrissy. Wake up." Patti's limp body didn't move. She looked like a rag doll, chained to a four-by-four post.

Patti stirred. *Or did she?* The room filled with shadows in the evening light. Did Patti's eyes flutter? *Or am I seeing things?* "Patti?" She moaned, "Patti, we're going to die"

She heard metal scrape the floor.

"Patti? It's me Chrissy. I'm here."

"Chrissy?"

"Yes! Oh God, yes!" Chrissy scooted as far as her chains would allow. Her foot stopped inches from Patti's.

"Chrissy?"

"I'm here. Are you hurt?"

"Chrissy?"

"Patti, save your strength. Try and sleep. Tomorrow morning, when it's light, we'll figure something out."

"Have to tell—"

"Shhh, I know, don't talk—"

"The man, he's a cop."

Urine dribbled down Chrissy's leg. This was not good news.

CHAPTER 25

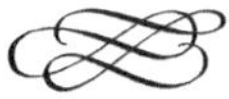

Sam felt good riding next to Suzanne. The sunset cast golden rays across her face giving her an ethereal glow. She smelled sweet, like lemon blossoms and summer rain. He wanted to touch her. Hold her. Kiss her soft lips. Bury his face in her hair. *Never let go.*

As if hearing his thoughts, she turned to him. "How have you been?" Her smile, his kryptonite.

"Busy. Trying to figure out this guy's moves."

"Are you taking care of yourself? Eating, sleeping. Listening to great music and smelling the roses?"

"Now that you're back, I think I can check off most things on that list." He glanced her way.

"I missed you." She blushed. "Even though I shouldn't."

"Any developments with your divorce?"

"Ben is fighting to keep the house. It won't happen.

He can't afford to pay for the upkeep, and I'd hate to let it go."

"Do you plan to stay in the foothills?"

"I don't know. Is there a reason I should?"

"It would be nice to get to know you better. Is that reason enough?"

"I want to stay as far away from Ben as possible. I hope you understand."

"Yes," he said. He turned up the volume on the radio, allowing each of them time to let their feelings percolate.

"My goal is to get a job and to pay my brother back," she said. "He's been more than generous with me. I hope that that this new acquired gift presents me with opportunities to make a living. It doesn't have to make me rich, but I will have to eat, keep the lights on, take in a movie now and then."

"Fair enough. Let's catch our killer and go from there."

"Deal," she said.

When Sam turned into the drive leading to Patricia Watson's apartment, Suzanne groaned.

"What is it?"

"Patti isn't here." She jumped out of the car and ran for the trees

Jack stood between two tall pines, his face filled with worry. He paced back and forth, but he didn't look her way. "You have to stop him, Suzanne." Suddenly the sky went dark. She heard a clinking sound, metal, hitting metal. The stench of cows filled the air.

"Where are they? Help me find them."

She closed her eyes and let the images flow. A stairway, a dank room, cement floor. Chains hung from the rafters. A tooth. She could hear mewling. A car door slammed. Silence. Then screams. Fear, like smoke, flowed through the cracks in the window, rose high in the sky, circled the sun, and exploded into thin air. Darkness fell like a blanket, smothering, suffocating—*I can't move.* Suzanne fought to free herself.

"Suzanne!" She heard a voice. *Far away.* No trees. No birds. Only tall weeds. A rusted tractor stood sentinel in front of a broken-down shack. A tin roof, collapsed on one side, made the place look uninhabitable. Padlocks on the doors said different. Etched patches of black reminded her of kindergarten artwork. *Windows?* The image shimmered, then quickly dissolved. She saw Jack, paler than before. Sadness touched the handsome face she'd once loved. And then he was gone.

She felt a hand on her shoulder. A warm, loving hand. Sam's hand. Somehow that scared her as much as her vision.

"I saw where the girls are being held. It's a run-down shack, in the middle of nowhere." She rubbed her brow. "How are we going to find it?"

"I have an idea," he said, grabbing her hand and helping her into the car. "There's a café nearby. I brought my laptop, we can check Google Earth, see if you recognize the place."

Three miles later, Sam pulled into parking lot of the P-Ville Café.

Once inside, he placed his laptop on the table. Suzanne ordered two coffees from the waitress and got a Wi-Fi password.

"I'm on," he said, typing in their location.

As they sipped coffee and scanned the area, Suzanne's hopefulness began to wane. "I don't see it," she said, her voice dropping low.

Sam keyed in another area. He moved his finger on the mouse, moving the cursor until he found wide open spaces. "Here, take a look." She moved closer. He breathed in the scent of her hair, studied the curve of her jaw, the shape of her ear. Her lashes were long and thick as she blinked. He imagined waking up to her profile every morning and felt more determined than ever to end this nightmare.

"Let's see if we can get a closer look." He moved the cursor to a deserted area and expanded the view. A herd of cows appeared. He zoomed out and moved the cursor.

"Look for a tractor," she said. "There's an old tractor in front of the shack."

"It's getting dark," he said. "If we don't find it soon, we'll have to try again tomorrow."

"She doesn't have much time."

"The blonde?"

"Yes."

He didn't speak. He kept moving the cursor on the screen, zooming in and out each time he saw a structure, or vehicle.

"Stop!" She leaned forward until her nose about touched the screen. "That's it," she said, poking the screen with her finger. "That's the place."

CHAPTER 26

Dixon walked into the night, and gazed at the stars. Exhausted from his romp with Laura, he decided to go home rather than drive back to Fresno. A good night's sleep would recharge his batteries, get him ready for more fun with the girls.

Now that the world was quiet, his thoughts took a left turn and dead-ended with Sam Metzger's voice in his head. Why did Metzger feel compelled to check up on him? And what did that bitch psychic know? He'd worked hard covering his tracks. He had the perfect place to take his victims, he mixed things up so he didn't settle into a pattern. His ego allowed him one signature, orange twine.

No one would ever find the house. Grandpa's house. He had brought his first victim there twenty-two years ago. He was eighteen.

Colleen Crosby was sixteen, a runaway from Des

Moines. Her childhood sounded similar to his. Crack-whore for a mother, deadbeat dad. Uncles who played hide the banana from the time she was seven. He picked her up hitchhiking on highway 99, she was grateful for the ride. She said she appreciated having someone to talk to in her southern drawl, adding, "You're about my age, aren'tcha?"

Her journey west included truckers from all fifty states. She reeked of sex, pot, and beer. Good thing he had a hose to wash her down before he fucked her three ways to Sunday. Unlike the other girls, she knew how to handle her drugs. She enjoyed the sex, went with the flow. No freaking out like the others, in fact, the orange twine was her idea. *Tie me up, baby, do me.* Colleen dug the abuse. So much, she laughed in his face when he slit her throat. He knew then he would kill again, not only for the thrill, but because every bitch he killed lowered the number of women who could reproduce. *Can't stamp out the female population, but heck, I sure enjoy trying.*

CHAPTER 27

Chrissy lost consciousness. How long, she couldn't say. She awoke to her friend's lifeless silhouette dangling in the dark. She shifted her weight to stimulate circulation in her ankles, but as soon as she separated her knees her bladder spasmed, sending a shooting pain from her groin to her back. Urine wicked across her denim shorts. The fabric soaked up the liquid and clung to her skin. A drop in temperature called for another round of spastic chills. Her body shimmied, her skin burned. Her teeth chattered. "Patti. Patti? Patti–p-p-please—*wake up.*"

Sam and Suzanne drove for hours. Miles of open fields, unmarked roads, like searching for a needle in a haystack. Suzanne's head throbbed. She felt as though she were the victim, the prospect, hard to bear. Sam stole glances her way, his expression as weary as hers. She knew he related to her discomfort but felt helpless. Yet, his warmth was genuine, something she could grow accustomed to. Her soon-to-be-ex-husband Ben lacked emotion. She had convinced herself his compassion deficit was due to his illness, a symptom of bi-polar disorder. And so, she dealt with the void. *Even got used to it.* Sam was a breath of fresh air. She wanted to breathe deeply, but fear of another broken heart kept her from letting go. She was drawn to Sam. He excited her. When she wasn't dreaming of Jack, or dead girls, his handsome face filled her dreams and she imagined living her life by his side. Happy. Fulfilled. *Loved.*

Sam interrupted her thoughts. "Over there. Look familiar?"

She recognized star thistle, mare's tail, and fiddleneck. "Can we get closer?"

As Sam steered his Land Rover down a rutted path, a structure appeared in the distance. A high pitch sound rang in Suzanne's ears. There it was, the shack with the collapsed roof. "Yes. This is it."

Sam slowed down. "I don't want to get too close." He shut off the engine. "Listen."

"I don't hear anything."

"That's good. No dogs." Still, the house could be booby-trapped, and he didn't want to take any chances. If Dixon was their killer, they'd need to be cautious. Sam couldn't imagine him being sloppy. "Stay put. I'm going to take a look." Sam switched off the interior lights and opened the door.

"Don't leave me here. I promise to be careful."

"All right, stay close behind me." As they neared the shack, the pain in Suzanne's head increased. Soft cries filled her brain like swarming wasps. She held her head, but the sound didn't stop; the smell of cows so pungent, she wanted to retch. And although the temperature had only dropped to sixty degrees, it may as well have dropped to thirty.

Chrissy shivered. Wet, feverish, and beyond hunger, her sanity hung by a thread. The only thing keeping her from going down the rabbit hole was Patti. As much as she hated Patti for getting her into this mess, she still hoped that once Patti was in her right mind, she would have a solution. Patti was the Girl Scout. Girl Scouts trumped "easy" girls when it came to safety. "Wake up Patti," she whispered. Again. And again.

Patti's lips were glued shut, weren't they? She imagined what would happen if she tried to talk, the flesh on her mouth would tear and bleed. She heard a voice. *Chrissy?* Why would Chrissy be in the classroom with her? She would've stopped the teacher from bashing her head with a two-by-four—wouldn't she? Then again, Chrissy was mad at her. And pigs don't fly, and frogs taste good when served on a bed of spring mix, garnished with goldfish and cheese puffs. She wished she'd never become a ballerina. She wanted her feet to touch the ground, she wanted the horse to quit kicking her in the crotch. She wanted to go home. She wanted to let go of the monkey bars and swim in the deep blue sea.

Sam drew his gun. The world was quiet, with the exception of an occasional screech from an owl, weeds rustling in the wind, and the sound of his beating heart. He nudged the door with his shoulder. It didn't budge. He was feeling along the ledge for a key. He holstered his gun, and retrieved the penlight in his pocket. The light traced the door frame. He noticed the door was nailed shut. He clicked off the light and motioned to Suzanne to follow him to the back of the house. She walked close behind and stopped. Out of the corner of her eye, she spotted the window she had seen in her vision and reached for Sam.

They crouched down and peered through the blackened panes. Sam shined his flashlight in the window. Suzanne stifled a scream.

Chrissy thought she was dreaming. A light beam danced across her foot. "Here. We're down here!" Her prayers had been answered after all. She heard a man's voice, authoritative, yet kind. He broke the window.

"Christine Bonnevier? I'm detective Samson Metzger, Goldorado County PD, can you hear me?"

"Yes," she said. "Get me out of here."

"Is Patricia Watson with you?"

"Yes. She's not moving–*hurry*."

Sam moved quickly. He discovered a cellar door at the back of the shack. A chain and a padlock held the door closed. Sam reached in his pocket for a pouch containing an assortment of tools. He inserted the pick into the chamber and wiggled it until he heard the chamber click. He pulled the lock away from the chain, removed the chain from door and opened it wide. A musty odor assailed his nostrils mixed with the smell of urine and blood. He choked back the acid rising in his throat and shined his light into the opening. A steep staircase led down into a room. The room was empty. He moved cautiously toward another set of stairs. He stepped gingerly, each board creaking beneath his weight. When he reached the top of the stairs, he realized the door leading inside was locked as well.

Sam steadied the penlight between his teeth and went to work. Within seconds, he had jimmied the lock.

Sam found himself in a parlor. An antique dining set, a settee, and a washbowl stand made the room look livable. A large bed with a canopy top loomed in the corner. Next to the bed was a doorway. Before Sam reached the door, he spotted a picture hanging on the wall. A man in overalls, a small, dark-haired boy on his lap. Looking closer, Sam realized the man's features were shredded, unrecognizable—but the boy in the photo, undeniably, Dixon.

Sam followed the beam of light across the room to another door and another narrow stairway. He regretted not being able to call for back-up but knew he couldn't take the chance of Dixon getting wind of his discovery and bolting. He needed absolute proof in order to put the son-of-a-bitch behind bars. A little boy in a photo would never stand up in court as evidence. He needed a positive ID. He needed the girls alive.

"Christine?" He heard a moan coming from the far corner of the cellar. He moved toward the voice. "It's me, Samson Metzger. Don't be afraid. I'm here to help you." He bent down and examined her bindings. The girl smelled like rotted flesh. Her clothes were torn; her hair matted and covered in blood; her eyes swollen; her face flushed; hot from infection. Her limbs were bruised and crusted with blood. One kneecap appeared dislocated, one ankle, twice the size of the other. Her lips were cracked and bloody. He pulled her trembling body close to his. "You're safe, now."

Chrissy found Sam's hand, and pressed something hard against his palm. He recognized the shape. *Amy Fitzpatrick's tooth.*

"Patti said he's a cop," she said.

Once Christine was in Suzanne's care, Sam grabbed a lantern from his trunk and returned for Patti. When he unlocked the chains shackled to the iron ring under the stairway, Patti slumped against him. He eased her to the floor, smoothed her hair away from her face and lifted each eyelid, checking her pupils. Dilated. She was still drugged, suffered a concussion, or both. Moving her could be dangerous, but he had no choice. He had to take the chance and bring her outside while keeping the crime scene as uncompromised as possible.

They would drive to the main highway, dispatch a helicopter to transport the girls to the hospital, and then he'd return to the shack and secure the crime scene. If he was wrong about Dixon, he could kiss his job good-bye. If he was right? The nightmare would end, and that was a risk he was willing to take.

When Sam carried Patti outside, Suzanne felt as though her true purpose had been revealed. Jack had shown her the way. For the first time since the nightmares had begun, she understood her destiny. *Sam, not Jack.* Together, they would save lives.

She bundled the girls in the blankets Sam had stashed in the back of his vehicle. Chrissy cradled Patti in her arms and rocked her like a baby. Neither girl spoke. Suzanne put her arms around them. "It's over. You and Patti are going to be all right."

"I knew he was my angel," Chrissy whispered.

"Who?"

"The guy in the uniform."

"Jack?"

Chrissy's eyes searched Suzanne's. "Do you know him?"

"He's my angel too."

S am glanced at his watch. *9:47 p.m.* He dialed District Attorney George Rader despite the fact he knew the man retired with the sun and woke with the birds. Aside from his job as D.A., George tended forty horses and milked his own cows. Given the man's schedule, Sam anticipated a greeting far from cordial.

"Who the hell is this and what is so important that you felt compelled to interrupt my sleep?"

"George, it's Samson Metzger, sorry to bother you at home, but I need your help."

"You better have a good goddamn reason for calling this late."

Sam explained his dilemma to George Rader, who sounded as if he couldn't get enough air in his lungs to respond. Everyone loved Dixon. He was the town's golden boy. He could do no wrong. "Are you sure?"

"The boy in the photo on the wall—I'm putting my job on the line, sir. It's him."

Once George swallowed the bad news he said, "I'll call the Fresno County Sheriff's Department, you handle things there. We don't want anyone botching our crime scene. This won't go down well in the community. If you can't trust the Sheriff, who can you trust?"

"I understand, sir. Until I can get a statement from the girls, this conversation has to remain airtight. If Dixon finds out we have the girls, he'll disappear. I need to get my forensic team up here first light, and I'll need your help in keeping Fresno's guys out of my hair. I'll need a warrant for Dixon's arrest.

"Let me see what I can do." George paused a moment in silence. "Geez, I still can't wrap my head around this."

Sam hung up the phone and waited for medical help to arrive. When the helicopter landed in a clearing 100 yards from the highway, Sam drove to meet them. Paramedics poured out of the chopper door and rushed toward the Land Rover. Once the girls were strapped onto gurneys, Sam and Suzanne headed for Fresno Surgical Hospital. He hoped to get a statement from the girls before midnight.

CHAPTER 28

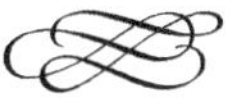

Dixon set a cold beer on the coaster beside his computer, removed his shoes, and unbuttoned his shirt. He sat back in his leather chair and scrolled down his list of dating sites. When he found one of interest, he hit enter and signed in. He perused through "new profile listings" while he sipped his beer. *Too tall, too blonde, too pudgy, too fake, too plain, too short, nope, nope, nope.* He clicked on page two, hoping for better results. When he came up blank, he exited out of that site and explored another. He scrolled through photos until he came upon a woman who fit the bill. *Mia,* 5'5," light brown hair. *No tattoos, loves to cook.* He gave her a "wink", sent his photo and asked for her info. He sat back and waited. By 10:32pm, he had his next victim.

Dear Mia,

It was so refreshing to see someone like you posted

on this site. I can't tell you how disappointed I've been since I joined. In fact, I was about to give up and become a priest. Then I saw *you*. Now I've not only changed my mind about becoming celibate, I now believe in angels!

I too, love to cook. My specialty is Coq au Vin, however, I'm a grilling aficionado, and love to make my own pasta. (My pear and gorgonzola ravioli are truly exquisite) I come from a long line of chefs and foodies, and appreciate a nice meal, paired with a beautiful woman and a bottle of wine. Conversation is a must. I'm a great talker, but an even better listener. I will be in the Portland area this weekend on business. If you would like to meet and share a meal, let me know. My heart is beating out of my chest. Please say yes.

Affectionately,

Christopher

Dixon moseyed into the kitchen, popped open another beer. He tore open a bag of tortilla chip, and searched for a jar of salsa in the back of the fridge. By the time he poured salsa into a bowl, he heard a "ping" coming from the other room. Snacks in hand, he returned to his computer.

Dear Cristopher,

Thank you for your awesome introduction. I would love to meet you this weekend, however, I will be in Seattle until Monday. Perhaps we can meet another time? I love Coq au Vin, but my favorite is Italian. I think we will get along nicely. I'm off to the gym. Lots of energy to work off! Now that I've met *you* wink, wink.

"Wink, wink, your ass." Dixon threw the bag of chips against the wall.

As the Land Rover sped down the highway, Suzanne closed her eyes. Jack waited in her deepest thoughts. She imagined the feel his breath on her cheek as he whispered, "I love you, Suzanne. Always have, always will." He kissed her hair, held her close. *I wonder if he'll find peace now.*

Sam reached for her hand. "You doing okay?"

"I'm tired, but so relieved. How about you?"

"The girls are safe, but Dixon is still out there. It's going to be tricky bringing him in."

"Why's that?"

"Our only hope is getting a positive identification from the girls, and DNA from the shack. I suspect Dixon was careful not to leave fingerprints." Sam squeezed her hand. "We have to be careful not to alert him. Although we have the girls, this nightmare won't end until he's behind bars."

"There *are* others."

"Others?"

"Not all of the bodies have been discovered, and I still feel there's another who has escaped. She's young. Dark hair. She moves like she's hypnotized." Suzanne closed her eyes for a moment. "Jack is showing me a baby."

CHAPTER 29

Sheena Bradford gripped the balcony railing. Wind whipped her long, dark hair around her face. She massaged the bump pushing against the waistband of her yoga pants. *My baby boy*. The city below glittered with lights. Neon signs peppered the streets with artistic flare. She loved living in New York, every day, a new adventure. Soon, she would be exploring the town with her son.

Every night she prayed for her child to be spared the fear she had come to know. She thought moving across the country would make her safe. And, for the most part, she felt protected living with her cousin, Renee. However, there were times when she looked over her shoulder or hid from strangers who resembled Dixon. Soon, she would give birth to his child. Then what? Would her baby grow up feeling deprived of a father? Would he one day search for him? Surely Dixon wouldn't hurt his own flesh and blood. Would he? Sheena wondered. As much as she feared him, she wanted him near. She wanted him to hold her, tell her he loved her, tell her he was wrong about getting rid of the baby, and that he wanted to be a family. Tears filled her eyes. Why couldn't she forget him? Move on? Because— *despite the fact he's toxic, you love him.*

CHAPTER 30

Dixon opened a file he kept for those moments when he needed to fill his head with more than a photo of a pretty girl with a dog or lifting some celebratory drinky-poo. Why did women think guys cared about those things? Show me your tits! Bend over—let me see those firm cheeks.

Dixon collected photos of his escapades. Jennifer—her legs spread wide, her pink bud begging to be kissed. The next photo of Jennifer wasn't as pretty, but it excited him, nonetheless. Her eyes were swollen shut. Blood trickled from the corner of her mouth. He felt himself getting hard. He clicked again. The next photo featured his little coed, Sheena. "Now there's a pair of tits," he mumbled, rubbing his crotch. He scrolled down until he found the photo he was looking for. Sheena, naked in the middle of a field, a flower in her hand. She was stunning. *And stupid.* What had made her think she could trap him into marriage with a baby? He recalled how angry he became when he found her apartment empty. *Bitch.* He imagined her flat tummy big, and round. He suspected she was on the east coast. She didn't have family in California, only her cousin in New York. The reason he didn't pursue her was because she knew nothing about him. *Other than I'm the Sheriff and the best fuck she'll ever have.* His little schoolgirl loved sex. She would do anything to please him, and she was a quick study. Too bad she had to go and get knocked up. He hoped she had enough sense to get rid of 'it.' He hated kids. He'd hated being a kid and had no room in his life for one of his own.

Just like my mama.

CHAPTER 31

Sam and Suzanne waited for the Emergency Room doctor to update them on the girls' condition. Christine and Patti were taken to a private room. A guard was assigned to each girl. No one could enter without an ID.

"Detective Metzger?" A slight Asian man approached.

"Yes." Sam stood and shook the man's hand.

"I'm Doctor Wang. At the moment, both girls are comfortable. We are waiting for MRI results to substantiate the severity of their concussions and CT scans to access their organs. Both girls have suffered fractures to the face, severe contusions and broken bones—Christine Bonnevier is being treated for acute cystitis that has spread from her bladder to her kidneys. Between the drugs, the beatings, repeated rape with unidentified objects, and dehydration, it's a wonder Miss Bonnevier is still alive—I've called in a gynecologist to repair as much of the damage as possible. Miss Watson's trauma is more current. She has five broken ribs and a punctured lung. We've given her antidotal medicine for the drugs in her system. Once she's coherent, we'll go from there." Doctor Wang scratched his brow. "Unfortunately, at this point neither can describe what happened." He shook his head and spoke directly to Sam. "I hope you find the monster who did this, Detective. In my thirty-plus years of practicing medicine, I have never witnessed such brutality. If you had not found them, both girls would have been dead by morning, or soon thereafter."

Sam glanced toward Suzanne. He took the doctor aside. "When will I be able to talk to the girls? Time is critical, Doctor. I can't nail this monster until they identify him."

It was the doctor's turn to show his discomfort. "I can't let you speak with them until we finish our assessment. We are not certain of the magnitude of their injuries. We have barely scratched the surface. Once we get answers pertaining to their medical condition, we will let you get your answers. Until then, let us do our job so you can do yours." The doctor patted Sam's shoulder, turned, and disappeared behind double doors.

CHAPTER 32

After Dixon had relieved his sexual frustration, he showered and climbed into bed. Tomorrow he would drive to Fresno. *Have a little fun.* After all, that's what weekends were for. Maybe he'd look-up Sheena. Say "hello" for old time's sake. He closed his eyes and began drifting off until a memory caused him to stir.

His mother took him by the hand, dragged him across the street to a neighbor's house, where they were greeted by an elderly lady and her Doberman, Brutus. The dog towered over Dixon's head. Paws, the size of cow pies, danced around the woman's legs. The dog's low growl and show of teeth didn't faze him. He knew where the woman kept her toolbox. A hammer to the snout would put Brutus in his place, but who would put his mother in *her* place?

He held her hand tight. "Don't leave me, Mommy."

"Shush now. I'll be back before you know it," she said, pulling a tube of lipstick from her purse. "You behave, or that dog will rip your face off." She smiled and peeled his fingers from her wrist. She pushed him through the door and never looked back.

The old woman slapped a newspaper on the edge of her dining table. "Brutus! You be quiet now. The boy is only here for a visit."

"May I use your bathroom?" Dixon asked.

"Of course. You know the way," she said, wagging her finger. "Wash your hands with soap. I don't want dirt on my clean towels."

"Yes, ma'am," he said, backing his way down the hallway. He slipped into the laundry room, climbed up on the washer, and pulled a wooden box from the cabinet. He held the hammer in his little fist, ready to do battle. As he climbed off the washer, he realized too late the dog was underfoot, and landed on Brutus' paw. Jaws clamped down on his thigh before he had a chance to react. He twisted his body and slammed the hammer into the side of the dog's snout. The dog yelped, freeing Dixon's leg. Dixon slid the hammer under his shirt and tucked the shirt inside his pants.

"What's going on?" asked, the old woman.

"I went into the wrong room," Dixon confessed, "I stepped on Brutus' foot. He hung his head, "I'm sorry."

"Get to the bathroom before you wet yourself," she said, swatting him on the back of the head.

Dixon placed the hammer on the top of the toilet

tank and slid his pants down to inspect his bite. No blood. Just tiny blue-grey dents, but the area around the bite was red and swollen. He pulled up his pants and returned the hammer to his waistband under his shirt. He planned his first kill at four years old.

CHAPTER 33

Suzanne woke with a start. "What time is it?"

Sam smoothed the sleeve where Suzanne had rested her head. "A little after 2 a.m. The doctor should give us an update soon."

"How about some coffee. There's a machine down the hall."

"You stay, I'll get it." Sam rose and stretched.

She noticed Sam's physique. His broad shoulders, trim waist, long legs. Resting against him felt natural. Easy. She didn't want to imagine beyond the here and now, but she had no control of her thoughts. The smell of him lingered. She knew they had far to go before they could get to know each other better, but the prospect warmed her soul.

She closed her eyes and Jack appeared.

"You must stop him, Suzanne. More girls will die."

She ran to the ladies' room, grabbed a paper towel

and turned the faucet to cold. She dabbed the wet toweling across her forehead and pressed it to her eyes.

When Sam returned to an empty waiting room, he saw the contents of Suzanne's purse spilled on the seat. He set the coffee on an end table, gathered her things, and searched the hallway. He knocked on the door to the ladies' room. "Suzanne?" he called softly. She appeared at the door, her face damp, her cheeks pink, her eyes haunted. "What happened?"

"Jack. He says Dixon needs to be stopped before he kills again."

"Tell Jack we got this."

"I don't know Sam, suddenly I'm not so sure."

CHAPTER 34

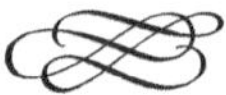

Dixon got out of bed and threw on his clothes. Chrissy and Patti awaited. Two hours before first light. "Can't keep the ladies waiting."

He fixed a cup of coffee, poured it into a travel mug, packed a few protein bars, and bottles of water into a canvas bag while he sang, "On the road again, I've got to get out on the road again…"

Before the creatures of the night retreated and a cool breeze swept stars from the sky, Dixon had jumped into his police cruiser and headed west. As he drove down Highway 50, he keyed the name Sheena Bradford into his dash computer. A series of names scrolled down the screen. He heard a ping. Sheena Bradford had used a credit card in New York. "NYC Memorial Hospital Maternity? What the fuck, Sheena?" Dixon pressed "Save" and increased his speed. "You better not be having that fucking baby." He forgot about Chrissy and Patti and headed for Interstate 80, droning an eerie melody, "Start spreading the news, I'm leaving today, ba-da-da da, da-da-da, New York, New York."

CHAPTER 35

Sheena's sleepy eyes fluttered open with the first light. She never tired of welcoming the rosy bloom in the east. Her bedroom window looked out over the city. The Hudson River, gleaming, and golden, snaked in the distance. She sat up, stretched her arms over her head, and settled her hands on her belly. "Morning little one," she whispered.

She hopped out of bed and went to the window. Filmy curtains billowed around her shoulders. Suddenly, she felt a strong sense of unease. A feeling only one person she knew could provoke. *Dixon.* But how? She'd been careful. Her phone was listed in her cousin's name. The only thing she couldn't use a fictitious name for was her new credit card, but the woman at the bank assured her that her information would not be shared publicly. "We're fine," she promised the bump she fought so hard to protect. "Mama's just being paranoid."

CHAPTER 36

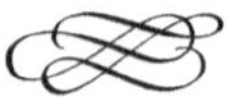

Suzanne sipped coffee, observing Sam in the distance. Light peeking through the blinds of the waiting room's only window highlighted the silver strands running through his dark hair. Daybreak. A fresh new day. How she wished she could spend time strolling through botanical gardens or hiking in the hills. Anything would be better than sitting here *waiting*. Patti and Chrissy were still off limits until later that afternoon. She bristled at the fact that Sam's hands were tied from obtaining a warrant until one of the girls identified Dixon as their captor. At least Jack had given her a break.

She had mixed feelings about Jack. Part of her wanted him to stick around, the other part of her wanted him gone. She had grown weary of the fear, the murders, the helplessness she felt with each clue he dumped in her lap. Training herself as a medium would take time. Interpreting the images would take faith. She wondered if faith was something she still possessed. It seemed her faith had been shattered when Jack died, and Ben did nothing to rebuild it. Then again, she had never given him a chance. She had never stopped loving Jack. She feared she never would. *Until now?*

Suzanne knew once Dixon was behind bars, she would see a different Sam emerge. He could be a positive light in her world. *If you let him.*

The worry on his face dissolved as he drew near. He smiled.

"What's up?" she asked.

"I should get to the station. From there I can at least keep an eye on Dixon."

"It's Saturday."

"I'm going into the office anyway. Maybe it's better if he's not there. I can do a little snooping."

"I have a better idea."

"What's that?"

"Breakfast. My treat."

They arrived at Morning Toast just as the manager unlocked the doors. They sat in a booth next to the window where they could watch an azure blue-sky transition to rose gold. They ordered fresh squeezed orange juice, Mediterranean omelets with sour dough toast and coffee. When their food arrived, Suzanne didn't hasten to slather her toast with whipped butter and homemade Marionberry preserves.

"I can't remember when I've been this famished," she declared.

"It's been quite some time since our last meal." Sam held his fork mid-bite. "Why do I feel so comfortable around you?"

"Please Sam, don't—"

"We're having breakfast. We're talking like we've known each other forever. We're sharing an experience that will haunt us for a lifetime. We're a team. We're on the same page, the same wavelength. We're good together. If you don't want to move to the next step, so be it, but for now, I am going to enjoy every moment I can with you."

Suzanne picked up her juice. "I like you. I like being around you, but for now that has to be enough. I don't know what the future is going to hold. I have two men rocking my boat now, and it's all I can handle."

"Fair enough."

Sam's phone vibrated on the table. "Detective Samson Metzger."

Suzanne could hear the man speaking on the other end of the phone. Doctor Wang. Watching Sam's face process the news, she realized he had found his way into her heart.

"Patti is awake. She's weak, but she's stable. We can see her at noon. The doctor wants to make sure she's strong enough to handle questioning." He grabbed Suzanne's hand and gently squeezed. "I couldn't have cracked this case without you. Thank you."

Patti winced. Her brain fought to process her surroundings. The last thing she remembered was sitting next to Chrissy in a car. Her vision blurred momentarily, adjusting to the figure standing nearby.

"Do you remember me?" Sam pulled a chair close to the bed.

"Not really," she said, struggling to sit up.

"I'm Detective Sam Metzger, this is Suzanne Cash. She's responsible for locating the place you were being held captive."

Suzanne stepped forward. "Hi. I'm happy to see you're awake. How are you feeling?"

Patti turned to Sam. "Where's Chrissy?"

"She's still in critical condition, but the doctor assured me she's going to recover."

"Did you catch the guy yet? He's a cop, you know."

"I need *your* help putting him away. Can you identify him?"

Sam opened his phone, pressed record and opened an app containing photos of six different men. Patti did not hesitate picking Dixon out of the mix.

"That's him. That's the cop." Her finger shook as she pointed at the screen. "*He's* the monster."

Sam had witnessed Dixon's bullying for years, but never imagined he was capable of such evil. He spoke into the recorder. "The witness has identified Sheriff

James Dixon from the Goldorado County Sheriff's Department as her captor and assailant."

Suzanne excused herself from the room as Sam continued his questioning. The judge was on his way with a warrant for Dixon's arrest, but Suzanne's gut told her the chase had just begun. Dixon had no plans to return to Goldorado County. He was on his way to claim his next victim. She knew he was not only after the girl he was after something else. *The baby.*

CHAPTER 37

Dixon detested sloppy. *You left the girls alive, dumb shit, and now you have to flee.* "That's okay, no one will find them. Besides, I've got another mission." Michael Jackson sang in his head. "Gonna make a change, gonna make it ri-i-ight."

He had ditched his police cruiser outside of Salt Lake City. After bundling up the police scanner, his laptop, and radio, he took a chance on hitchhiking. A lonely truck driver took pity on him, drove him into Bountiful and even bought him breakfast.

The Toyota pick-up he purchased from the used car lot ate up a good deal of his travel time, but he was able to close the transaction using fake I.D.s and credit cards he'd been saving for this very occasion. How easy it was to scam people when you knew the ropes. Law enforcement afforded him a valuable education. And with a whore for a mother, and a pedophile for a grandpa, he had all the encouragement he needed to succeed in life.

In a drugstore outside Chicago, he placed a box of platinum hair color, a pair of hair-cutting sheers, a package of eyelash extensions, and self-tanning lotion in his basket. Next, he picked out a Cubs T-shirt, a baseball cap, a pair of shorts, and flip-flops, adding the items to his "new look." At the check-out counter, he placed a pair of sunglasses on the conveyer belt and pulled out his wallet.

The clerk was slow and chatty. "I tried that hair stuff on my daughter Gwen. Prit-near made her bald. Be careful with that stuff. And if it doesn't work for your wife, or your girlfriend, you tell'er to bring back the box, and we'll give her a refund." With that said, she picked up the self-tanner, examined the box and said, "Remember when people went to the beach to get a tan? Geez, what's next?"

"You know women, they'll do anything to make themselves beautiful." He flashed the woman one of his killer smiles.

"That'll be $32.56." She bagged the items with the same slow deliberation she used ringing them up. Dixon placed three tens, and three ones on the counter. He waited for her to count out his forty-four cents. He knew leaving without his change would stick in her pea-sized brain. He had already spent too much time in one place.

He drove to a nearby upscale men's store to purchase a new wardrobe. Two pairs of designer jeans; a pair of white linen Prada slacks with matching sport jacket; one pair of black dress pants; five shirts in assorted styles and colors; one pair of athletic shoes; and one pair of black dress loafers. Altogether, it set him back $6300. The young man at the register wasn't impressed. In fact, he didn't give two shits whether Dixon's driver's license matched his credit card. Did he notice Dixon hadn't removed his sunglasses the whole time he shopped? *No wonder there are so many criminals in the world.*

Saturday morning in Indiana was nuts. It seemed every Hoosier alive was heading somewhere. Cars packed with kids and dogs crawled along Highway 69. He was at ease, having changed his look slightly before he hit the road. He was admiring his haircutting skills in the rearview mirror when a BMW pulled alongside him to the left and stopped, unable to move forward. The pretty girl sitting in the backseat looked his way. Her eyes connected with his. He licked his lips, she licked hers. He wiggled his tongue, she popped her pointer finger in her mouth and pulled it out slowly. She leaned into the window, pressing her breasts against the glass. He slid his hand between his legs and massaged his aching groin. He imagined himself taking her from behind, hearing her beg for mercy as he pounded her flesh and slit her throat. He blinked away the fantasy before he exploded in his only pair of clean jeans. He glanced her way. Her smile, salacious as she winked at him. She tossed her honey colored hair and blew him a kiss. Cars began moving forward, ending their little game.

Dixon pulled off an exit advertising gas, food, and lodging in Canton, Ohio. He checked into a Holiday Express, intending to grab a meal, a shower, and get a couple hours sleep. Not a city he would've chose for a good time, but there she was, the girl in the BMW, lounging by the pool wearing a neon pink swimsuit that left nothing to the imagination. She filled the tiny scraps of material in the most delicious way. Full, perky breasts, a flat stomach, and long, slender legs.

"Well, I'll be damned," she said, bending one leg.

"Must be fate," he said, tilting his sunglasses to get a better look.

"You following me?"

"Should I be?"

"Maybe." She patted the chair next to hers.

He pulled his chair closer to hers. "I thought maybe I was dreaming."

She placed his hand on her knee. "See. I'm real." Her eyes reminded him of the first little bitch he had killed. He liked the feisty ones. They made sex fun, challenging, exciting, which made the kill even better. *It comes as more of a surprise.* His hand inched toward her inner thigh. She slapped his hand.

"What's your name?" she asked, removing his hand from her leg.

"Doug Owens. What's yours?"

"Mikala Morgan. I'm from Peoria. I'm traveling with my brother and his wife to New York. My brother is an author. He has a book signing on Tuesday."

"What genre does he write?"

"Mysteries."

"You like mysteries?"

"I guess they're all right. What about you? Where are you from?"

"Chicago. I'm on my way to Pittsburg. Grandmother's not well."

"I'm so sorry," she said, covering a giggle with her hand.

"That's funny?"

"No. Yes. This whole thing is rather fucked up, wouldn't you say?"

Dixon appreciated her candor. "I like the fuck part."

"You're kinda old for me, aren't you?"

"Am I going to need Viagra?"

She stared at him for a beat. "I suppose my brother won't miss me for an hour or so."

On the way to his room, Dixon counted the security cameras. Two looked active, a third looked iffy. Inside the room, he pulled off his shirt and untied the straps holding her top in place. He bent down to kiss each breast before he found her mouth. She tasted like candy. She smelled like spring. Her honey hair cascaded over tanned shoulders and tumbled to her petite waist. She took the lead, exploring his mouth with her tongue, and slipping her hand into his pants. Soon they were wrestling on the bed, shedding clothes and scraps of neon pink. He flipped her over kneading her buttocks and planting kisses inside her thighs. She bucked like a wild horse wanting to be mounted, but he wasn't ready. He knew once he entered her, he would lose control.

"Hold on," he said, catching his breath. "You want this to be hot?"

"I thought we were getting there." Her face blushed, her brow moist and shiny. She collapsed against the headboard. "What the fuck, city boy?"

"Meet me in the parking lot at 9:00 p.m." Dixon handed her a fistful of neon pink. "Put this on, your brother might think you've been a naughty girl."

"What's at 9:00 p.m.?"

Dixon nuzzled her ear and snuck his hand between her legs. Her wetness confirmed his suspicions.

"You'll just have to trust me now, won't you?" He brushed his thumbs across her nipples.

"Fine." She bounced off the bed and got dressed.

"I'm parked in the back lot near the dumpster. 9:00. Don't be late."

She shimmied into her suit, grabbed her towel and slammed the door.

He counted on her temperament. He also counted on the security cameras catching her departure.

Dixon curled up in bed, a pillow clutched to his chest. He slept for three hours, showered and dressed. He grabbed his duffle bag, the room key, and four miniature bottles of booze from the min-bar.

At 8:00 p.m., he jumped into his car and started the engine. He pulled out of his space and drove to the supermarket a block away. In the parking lot, he switched license plates with a dusty car parked in a far row. Work completed, he munched on a bag of potato chips and a warm cola he had stashed in the trunk. He cracked open one of the miniatures and opened the foil pouch from his pocket. He poured the contents into the dime-size opening and replaced the cap. At 8:55 he drove back to the motel. He saw Mikala waiting by the dumpster, dressed in blue jeans and a crocheted halter top. Her hair, swept to one side, glistened under the sodium lighting. He wondered if she had an inkling that her life was about to end. He pulled into a space obscured from the camera and beeped the horn. She turned and walked towards him. His face was hidden in the shadows, but she didn't hesitate to climb into the car.

"This better be good. I told my brother I left my sunglasses by the pool and would be right back."

Dixon slid his hand from her knee to her thigh. "I assure you, what you're about to experience is going to blow your fucking mind." She moved his hand higher up, anxious to get the party started.

They drove to the back of an abandoned warehouse and parked between the two shipping containers. "We don't have much time," she said removing her halter top and pressing her breasts against his face. "You promised me one helluva fuck."

"Hey, what's the hurry?" He flicked one nipple with his tongue, then the other, his eyes fastened to hers. "Your brother is probably banging his ol' lady and won't miss you for at least an hour." Dixon offered Mikala a swig of the miniature he pulled from his pocket. "Take a sip." While she sipped, he reached beneath the seat with one hand and grabbed a ball of orange twine. His other hand snaked around her waist and drew her near. While he kissed her, and sucked on her tongue, he grabbed her wrists and twisted them behind her back. She couldn't scream with her tongue between his teeth. She bumped his chest with hers, trying to break away as he wrapped the twine around her wrists. He released her tongue and cupped his hand over her mouth. "Shush. I told you—I'm going to blow your mind."

Mikala's eyes filled with fear as Dixon reached for the duct tape he'd stashed earlier, tore off a strip and placed it over her mouth. She kicked him. He slammed her down on the seat and removed her jeans and neon yellow thong. "Cute," he said, pulling the stretchy lace over her head and twisting the fabric around her neck. Mikala's head thrashed as he stretched her panties and wrapped the lace around the door handle. "There," he said. "Now you won't head butt me." With her head immobilized and her body pinned beneath him, he began nibbling her breasts. He moved down her belly and spread her legs. He wasn't at all surprised when he heard her catch her breath as he tasted her. "Isn't that nice?" he asked. Darting his tongue inside her soft flesh, she relaxed, and began to moan. At the moment her breathing slowed, he bit down, drawing blood. Her snorting and gasping behind the tape made him giggle. He slammed her knees together, grabbed a bare breast in each hand and squeezed until he took her breath away. When he released her breasts, she panted and whimpered like a trapped animal. He looked deep into her eyes, relishing her pain and fear. "I know, little darlin', you're not happy," he said, reaching into the glove compartment, removing the remaining glass bottles, "but this will all be over soon."

One by one, he drank the contents, shattered the bottle tops and set them on the dash, admiring their jagged edges in the moonlight. "Oops, I almost forgot." He reached behind the back seat and grabbed a plastic drop cloth. Mikala tried to scream as he slipped the sheeting beneath her. "If there's one thing I don't like, it's a messy car." Her eyes opened wide in terror. He jammed the jagged opening of two bottles into each orb, and cut her throat with the third.

"Goddammit," he groaned, lifting her body from the front seat. He dragged her to the edge of the shipping container and shoved her underneath. He watched as her blood pooled beneath her head and shoulders. He faced the heavens with a sense of relief. Mikala would be dead in minutes. One more whore removed from the face of the earth.

CHAPTER 38

For the next several days, Sam kept Suzanne near him. He was sure Dixon was somewhere in the Midwest, but he took no chances, and brought Suzanne to work with him. As they pulled into the lot of the Sheriff's office, Sam knew from Suzanne's expression that she'd just gotten a psychic hit. He leaned over. "What is it?"

"I'm feeling closed in, like I'm trapped beneath something large. I see graffiti everywhere." She closed her eyes. "Jack is showing me a dark highway."

"Can you see where it leads?"

Suzanne closed her eyes. "Thirteen miles to Paris."

"Paris?"

"Yes. Paris." Suzanne opened her eyes and rubbed her temples.

"You saw the word *miles*?"

"Yes."

"Then it must be a town or city in the United States." He withdrew his phone from his pocket and keyed Paris, U.S.A. into Google. "Great. There's a Paris in just about every state."

"I'm sorry. That's all I'm getting for now."

Sam reached for Suzanne's hand. "You never have to be sorry with me. I don't yell, or punch walls. I feel very fortunate to have you by my side, and I hope this ends soon, because I don't know how long I can refrain from kissing you."

Suzanne leaned forward. Her mouth found his. Their lips fit together like puzzle pieces and moved at a gentle pace. Sam circled his arms around her waist and pulled her close. For a moment, time stood still until Suzanne pulled away.

"I shouldn't have done that," she said. "It complicates things."

Dove Johnson knocked on the driver's window. Sam hit the power button.

"Sorry for the interruption, I've been looking for you everywhere. We got DNA results back on the girls. James Earl Dixon. AKA Earl Ray Freeman, and who knows how many other aliases."

Sam shook his head. "Great. Now all we have to do is find him."

"Follow the trail. A body was found a few miles outside Canton Ohio with the same M.O."

"Orange twine?"

"That, and she was about the same age as the other girls.

Sam pulled out his phone and googled Ohio maps. He slid the map around his screen until he found what he was looking for. "Bingo."

Suzanne peered over his shoulder. "There." She pointed to a marker pinpointing Paris, Pennsylvania.

Sam settled back in his seat. "Why Paris?"

"He's going through Paris, not to Paris." Suzanne turned to Sam and Dove. "He's headed for someplace with a large population. People everywhere. Bright lights." Deep inside the chasms of her mind, Jack hummed a tune. "*New York.*"

Dove shook his head. "I still can't believe it. I know he liked young girls and we all kidded him—but this?"

"Did you know any of the girls he dated? Maybe we can get a hit on who's in New York."

"Let me make a few calls. I'll get back to you." Dove said.

"What about the girl, Suzanne? What can you tell me about her?

"I remember she was young, long dark hair—there was something about," she rubbed her stomach, "a *baby.*"

CHAPTER 39

Dixon drove through the town of Paris before dawn. The streets, empty, just like his life. His biggest thrill to date was killing, and even killing seemed mundane after the fact. He needed more excitement. He knew he couldn't return to California. Time to start anew, be someone else. He had plenty of identities to choose from. He had the means to go anywhere and do anything he pleased. "Good planning," his dear ol' Grandpa use to say, mostly while unzipping his fly. "Gotta have a good plan." Too bad Grandpa didn't plan on his "baby boy" slitting his throat.

After a meagerly attended funeral, Dixon discovered Grandpa was a man of his word. He had somehow stashed away $3.5 million in silver certificates and bearer bonds in his shack. According to the collector Dixon contacted, the silver certificates were worth 50 times their face value, due to their rarity and pristine condition. He had no clue where the money came from, and frankly, he didn't care. Being on the road, at night, all alone, dredged up things he had buried. He deserved that money.

He remembered the day he discovered Grandpa's stash. Dear ol' Gramps had him working in the field, picking green beans and turnips. He hadn't seen his mother in months. She was in Vegas with a high-roller named Frederick Fallahey, who drove a Jaguar, and spoke like he shit money. And as much as Dixon loathed her, he prayed she'd show up and whisk him off to anywhere— other than the hell hole his Grandpa called "the farm".

Eating raw green beans in the hot sun, in addition to the sour milk and bug infested cereal he had choked down that morning, made his stomach churn. Diarrhea hit so fast, he had to squeeze his butt cheeks together to keep from messing his one pair of pants. He scrambled into the cellar entrance just in time to see dear ol' Gramps reposition a rusted refrigerator in front of a hole in the wall. Dixon flew passed him yelling, "Gotta go, gotta go." Out of the corner of his eye he caught a glimpse of what appeared to be bundles of cash piled neatly behind the wall.

Dixon sat on the commode until the wooden seat dug a groove into his backside. He was about to flush when he heard footsteps outside the door.

"Whatcha doin' in there, precious?" the ol' man asked. "Churnin' peanut butter? Or making *cream*?" The man's soft chuckle turned Dixon's bowels to water, and he sat back down on the commode, clenching his teeth. He knew by the sound of the ol' man's voice that he was feeling randy, and Dixon knew what would happen once he opened the door.

"Got the squirts, I'll be awhile," Dixon said, groaning for effect. "Ate too many green beans."

"Stupid ass," the ol' man grumbled.

Dixon listened for his grandpa's footsteps to retreat. When they did, he finished his business, and waited until he heard the screen door slam. While he waited, he hatched a plan. Grab a knife from the kitchen and end the madness, right here, right now.

More than thirty years had passed, but he still enjoyed the memory…the shock on the ol' man's face when his baby boy came barreling out the front door wielding a butcher knife, the realization that he was about to die.

After he had slit his Grandpa's throat, he pulled the body out to the yard, placed it beneath the tractor to make it look like he was repairing the axle. He placed a wrench in his Grandpa's hand, started up the tractor and let the vehicle roll over the ol' man's head. The weight of the back tire crushed his skull like a watermelon.

Dixon hitchhiked into town and reported the accident. Grandpa didn't believe in telephones.

It took two days for the County Sheriff's Office to track down his mother in Vegas. Meanwhile, Dixon stayed with the Sheriff's sister Brenda, and her deputy husband, Andrew. Drew for short.

Once Grandpa was buried, his mother dropped him off at the farm, and took off to Canada with Frank. She swore she'd be back in a week, but Dixon knew better. Frank bought him a bicycle, shelled out ten one hundred-dollar bills, and hit the road.

Dixon didn't mind being left on his own. He survived just fine. He cooked his own meals, washed his own clothes, and taught himself how to make phony IDs. By the end of the summer, he was an expert. He paid visits to Drew, and in time, Drew became his role model. Drew taught him how to shoot, hunt, and fish. Hunting skills certainly came in handy. He learned how to skin a squirrel, decapitate a rattler, gut a pig, and bury a dog so other animals wouldn't find it. Skills he put to good use over the years. Unfortunately, Drew died before Dixon was sworn in as an officer of the law. *He would've been proud.*

Dixon pulled off the highway in Wilkes-Barre and snaked his way through a gas station until he found a vacant pump. He filled up his Toyota pick-up using a bogus credit card and drove a little further down the highway until he came upon the Microtel Inn. *Sleep.* He needed enough to keep him centered between the lines, no more, no less. Mid-afternoon sun made him drowsy, and he had things to do. He explained to the desk clerk he had an early call in the morning and paid for his room in full. He walked half a block to a Burger Chef, grabbed a salad and a burger, and retired for the evening.

Back in his room, he decided to bleach his hair. He read the instructions carefully. He didn't need his scalp burnt, or some gaudy color that would attract attention. He mixed the ingredients in the package, applied the goop on his hair, turned on the TV, and waited.

He flipped through stations, bored with game shows and news reports. His finger was over the button, ready to change the channel when his face loomed on the screen. He leaned closer and pumped up the volume. "Nationwide search for forty-two-year-old Sheriff from Goldorado County, California, James Dixon. If you see this man, call the number on your screen. This man is armed and dangerous."

Dixon checked the progress on his hair. His dark mane had turned copper. *Fifteen minutes to go. The things that can be accomplished in fifteen minutes.* When the color lifted to canary yellow, he was feeling optimistic. The advertisement on the box promised platinum blond. He was counting on the ad being truthful. His fake ID depended on it.

He shampooed the dye out of his hair and examined the results. "Nice." *Now for the lashes.* He opened the package he purchased at the drug store, pinched three fine hairs in the tweezers, dipped the ends into the glue, and applied them to his own lashes. *Man—if you had boobs, you'd be the most popular babe on the block.*

Dixon chose a tight black T-shirt and off-white linen

pants. The combination was striking with his new hairdo and dreamy eyes. All he needed was a little swish, and a little lisp to make his new identity believable.

He had pulled Jeremy Wentworth over for a routine traffic stop six years ago. Jeremy was as queer as the day was long. No judgement, Dixon didn't give a fig which way the guy swung. What interested him was Jeremy's looks. Other than their hair color, he and Jeremy could've passed for twins. Dixon confiscated the guy's license and looked up his social security number. Later, he pulled a few strings to obtain a copy of Jeremy's birth certificate and opened a checking account under Jeremy's name. Once the account was open, Dixon put in a change of address at the bank and kept the account active. He used the account to deposit "tips" he received for being a good guy and letting all those little scoundrels off of their DUIs, and other charges. The majority of his assets were safe in an account in the Canary Islands under another fictitious name. "Life is good," he mumbled, finger picking the platinum waves. By this time tomorrow, he'd be in New York City. "Lookin' for my *ba*-by."

At nine o'clock, there came a knock on the door. Dixon froze. He listened. The knock persisted. *Shit.* He didn't budge. The knock turned into pounding. "Felicia! Goddammit, open the fuckin' door!" Dixon did just that, startling the man on the other side. "Who the—"

"Do I look like Felicia to you, asshole?"

The man stumbled backwards. "Dude—Sorry, I

guess I'm in the wrong wing." He backed away slowly, his hand reaching for whatever he had tucked in his waistband.

Dixon's eyes followed the man's movement. His smirk dared the man to try something stupid. When the man showed both hands, Dixon smiled and said, "No worries. Have a good night." He turned off the TV and went to sleep.

CHAPTER 40

Suzanne returned home late in the afternoon, followed by Sam. A glass of curdled milk sat on the table beside a half-eaten slice of pizza.

Sam slipped into detective mode, gathering information about Suzanne's lifestyle, and Ben's departure. "Did he tell you he was leaving?"

Suzanne dropped her purse on a camel color leather high-back chair. "No. I haven't heard from him. I imagine he wasn't too happy to receive these divorce documents." She gathered the papers scattered on the floor.

"Looks like he isn't about to make life easy for you."

"No–I didn't expect him to cooperate." She viewed the blank signature line. "He's never made things easy for me. Why should he? I never made life easy for him."

"I can't imagine you being difficult to live with."

"Can you imagine being married to someone who is in love with someone else?"

"No. I'd want you all to myself."

"It will never be just 'me,' Sam."

"If you are referring to Jack, I can handle him. He's no threat to me. In fact, I sorta like the guy…in a way. I consider him a silent partner."

Suzanne tilted her head. "A silent partner?" She burst out laughing. "I need a drink." She dumped the glass of milk in the sink, filled the glass with hot soapy water, and tossed the pizza into the trash. She pulled a long stem glass from the cabinet next to the refrigerator and motioned to Sam. "White or red?"

"Nothing for me. I'm driving remember?"

Suzanne's eyes held his for what seemed an eternity.

"If you get bored while I'm packing, help yourself to music or the TV. I'll be as quick as possible."

"Take your time." He checked his watch. "You've got time for a shower if you like. I haven't given you much time to yourself."

"A shower would be nice—"

"You know what? I could use a shower myself, he said." He ran his hand along his scruffy jaw. "How about if I pick you up in an hour? Will you be all right here alone?"

"I have no idea where Ben is, but I don't expect him to show up just because I'm here alone. Besides, it's not like he's physically abusive."

"Keep your phone close by—just in case."

"Okay. See you in an hour."

Suzanne stripped out of her jeans and a yellow blouse that held every wrinkle from the last twenty-four hours. When she passed the mirror, she expected to see an old woman's face. "They're safe," she told the frazzled image. "They're safe because of you. That's all that matters."

She unhooked her bra and stepped out of her panties. Naked felt good. The hot water massaged her knotted muscles. *Better.* She poured a dollop of shampoo into her palm and worked it through her tangled hair. She stood under the shower head, relishing scented bubbles streaming down her skin. Once the water ran clear, she worked on lathering the rest of her body, as if it were possible to scrub away what she had just experienced.

Stepping out of the shower, she wrapped a towel around her petite frame and headed for the sink. Her dripping hair left a trail as she fluffed the heavy mass with her fingers. Suddenly she felt a chill. The door. *I left it open, didn't I?* She listened for movement downstairs. *Ben?* She held her breath. Silence. "Don't start spooking yourself out—no one is here but you."

"Sure about that?" Ben barged into the room.

Suzanne jumped.

"You scared me! Did you forget how to knock?"

"Why should I knock in my own house?"

"How about so you don't scare the crap out of me?"

"Poor baby," he said.

"What do you want? I'm in a hurry."

"Really? Loverboy?"

"Your accusations are not only unfounded, they're annoying."

"Really? Do you think I'm blind?"

"I've been working with the police on a case. I don't expect you to understand, but what happened to me has changed who I am."

"I'll say."

"I see things."

"Cut the bullshit, Suzanne. You've been looking for a way out for years. Do you think I'm so naïve that I don't see what you're doing?"

"The only thing I'm doing is getting dressed. Now if you'll excuse—"

Ben shoved her into the wall.

"Stop! Just go."

"Who's gonna make me?"

"Me."

Ben spun around. Sam had his hand on his holster.

"What are you doing here? Suzanne is *my* wife, and we are in the middle of a discussion, so back off, before I call the Sheriff and tell him you've entered my home without my permission or a warrant."

"Sam has <u>my</u> permission. This is still my home too, and right now, you're the one who needs to leave, not Sam."

Ben leaned toward Suzanne until his face was inches from hers. "This isn't over."

Sam took a step closer. "Sounds like you're making threats."

Ben backed away. "You two think you can ride off into the sunset and live happily ever after? Leave ol' Ben destitute?" He laughed. "Wrong. I'll see you in court, Suzanne. I'm going to take every cent I can from you." He paused. "At least I'll get *something* out of the last fifteen years. God knows you weren't good for anything else." He stormed out of the room.

"How did you know he was here?"

"I saw him walking toward the house as I was leaving."

Suzanne dropped her gaze. Sam pulled her near, but she pushed him away. "Go. Let me get dressed."

Sam didn't speak. He squeezed her hand and left, closing the door behind him.

Suzanne sat on the edge of the tub, holding her head in her hands. Jack appeared behind her closed eyes. He stood on a ledge, the sun set behind him, setting him aglow like an angel in the hand of God. "Oh, Jack. What now?"

Jack's face showed little emotion as he spoke. "A woman under a spell has no moral compass. The child she carries muddles her good senses."

"Great. Just what I needed. Another riddle."

～

CHAPTER 41

Sheena planned to take the subway to Times Square and draw some sketches. The temperature outside was 72 degrees, and the skies were partly cloudy, making for some delicious light. She regretted not finishing her degree in art at Sac State, but never gave up her passion for drawing, painting, and photography.

After breakfast, she made her bed, and dressed for the day. Yoga pants, a loose tank top, and colorful kimono tied under the bust gave her an artistic appearance. She brushed her hair into a ponytail, wound it into a top knot, and thrust a wooden pick through the middle to hold it in place. She hadn't gained much weight in her pregnancy, but the protruding bump was a dead give-away. She turned sideways in the mirror. There was no denying it. *I'm going to be a mom.*

She thought about her own mom, taken too soon

from the world, along with her dad, while traveling in Budapest. The tour bus they were on collided with another bus, exploding into flames, killing them instantly. A tragic memory she chose not to visit too often. Except for times like this, when she yearned to share her predicament, seek advice from one who filled the role she was about to undertake. She could never imagine anyone's mom being a better mom than hers. She swore her mother came to her in her dreams to console her. She'd wake feeling as though they had chatted all night long. But reaching for the phone wasn't an option, and it still made her sad. Her cousin Renée kept her spirits up, tossing around baby names, and checking out the latest nursery décor on Pinterest, but Sheena still missed her mom.

"Stop feeling sorry for yourself." Sheena placed her sketchpad, pencils, and a bottle of water into her Hobo bag, and locked the door behind her.

The elevator delivered her safely to the first floor, where she greeted Simon, the doorman. His ebony skin glistened with perspiration, alerting Sheena to the rise in humidity.

"Morning Simon," she said.

"Morning Miz Bradlee. Where you off to on this glorious day?"

"Thought I'd go sketch in the park."

"You have a good one, now. Stay hydrated. You don't want that baby swimming on dry land." He chuckled. "You got sunscreen with you?"

Sheena dug in her bag to produce a water bottle and a tube of sunscreen. "Thanks for looking out for me"

"Gotta take care of the mothers in the world, they're God's little jewels."

"Thank you, Simon. See you later." To him, she was Bradlee Tipton, a name she pulled from the telephone book.

Dixon glanced at his image in the mirror across the room. He bore no resemblance to Jim Dixon, the wanted criminal from Goldorado County. He turned his head from side-to-side, admiring his profile. "Handsome devil." Platinum hair took ten years off his looks. "See what you've been missing all these years? Time for this blond to have a little *fun*."

He showered, dressed in his new linen suit and pink shirt, packed his belongings, and dropped the key on the nightstand. Before walking out the door, he wiped his fingerprints off the door handles, TV remote, lamp, and light switches. He shook out the bedding, and tossed it on the floor, then took the aftershave from his bag and sprinkled half the bottle over the heap of linens. *House-keeping will have to wash the whole kit and kaboodle.* No one wanted to sleep in another person's scent. He rechecked the bathroom for any evidence that could incriminate him, wiped down the faucets, and decided he was in the clear. No one knew where he had disappeared to, and

with his new look and ID's to match, chances were, he
would never be found.

Suzanne stared out the window on their drive to the Sacramento airport. The plan was to catch a flight to Akron-Canton Ohio, grab a rental car and meet with the crime investigation team working on what could be Dixon's latest victim. Suzanne felt as though she had stuck her finger in a light socket. She feared they were headed toward disaster. Jack persisted, making sure they followed his leads. She closed her eyes. A young, beautiful, dark haired woman, her life filled with expectations, her womb filled with life.

She chewed her thumbnail. A habit she had never acquired. "I never bite my nails," she said, quizzically, turning toward Sam.

"I did when I was in college. Kept me from being a nervous eater. Helped my food budget as well."

"You? Nervous?"

"I'm dyslexic. It was hard for me to get through

school. But I managed. It took several years to break the nail-biting habit. Better than smoking." Sam smiled. "Your turn."

"My turn for what?"

"To share something about yourself."

"I'm allergic to tomatoes."

"I love tomatoes, but I don't like green beans."

"Okay. I had to wear orthopedic shoes until I was four years old."

Sam peeked down at her perfect feet clad in strappy shoes. "Hard to believe."

Suzanne followed his gaze. "I was pigeon toed. At night I wore a brace that kept my feet from turning in. Eventually they straightened out. It would've been horrible to be saddled with orthopedic shoes in grammar school. It was bad enough I had buck teeth." She saw Sam's shocked expression. "Too much information?"

"I can't imagine you with buck teeth. You're so beautiful, I figured you were born perfect."

"You have a lot to learn about me."

"I'm an eager student."

They drove through the airport parking structure in silence until she pointed to an empty space. "Over there—"

Sam pulled in and cut the engine. "Ready?"

She bowed her head and closed her eyes. Jack filled the blackness behind her lids. "Yes," she said, opening her eyes and raising her head, "We're ready."

When they boarded the plane, Suzanne took a

window seat, and Sam sat on the aisle, setting a small bag on the seat between them.

After take-off Suzanne gestured to the empty seat. "Do you get special privileges or something?"

Sam leaned in. "Nope. Just got lucky," he said. "May I?" He lifted the arm rests between them. "I love taking off and landing the best. The rest of the flight I usually spend snoozing. How about you?"

"I haven't flown much. I've always dreamed of traveling. Maybe I'll visit Europe one day." She turned toward the window. "The clouds look even more amazing from up here."

Sam unfastened his seat belt and moved closer. "Yes, they do." His eyes drifted from the window to Suzanne's lips and back to her eyes. Light played on her blue irises, circled in grey and a ring of black. Her eyes reminded him of a stained-glass window at St. Stephens Cathedral in Vienna he had visited as a boy. He had spent the entire service waiting for the morning sun to turn from cobalt to royal blue. He found the same comfort by her side and wanted more.

It had been years since he had thought about love, and now it snuck between rationality and conviction at every turn. He swore off getting serious later in his career, when he became a detective. Fighting crime was an ugly business. It required one to think like a criminal. Although his sobriety made a difference in his attitude, he still found it taxing to vacillate between being tender and being tough. Through the years, he had witnessed failed marriages and relationships among his peers and decided he'd rather be alone.

Then there was Dixon, who made a sport of using women. And killing them. Between Jack, Ben, and Dixon, he doubted Suzanne would be eager to jump into another relationship any time soon. Just then, the flight attendant interrupted his thoughts. "Cocktails?"

"Not for me, Suzanne?"

"No, not if you're not having one."

They opted for coffee instead.

"It's probably too early for a drink, anyway," she said, pulling down her tray table.

Sam reached in his pocket and pulled out his sobriety coin. He placed it on her tray. "Ten years. Thought you should know."

"Oh," she said, examining the coin. Images sped through her mind, including a pretty young woman with short blond hair. Her face had broken heart written all over it. "The important thing is you recognized you had a problem." She handed the coin back to him. "Besides, it wasn't just your drinking that made her leave."

"How?

"I'm psychic, remember?"

"I needed to tell you. I want everything between us to be out in the open. No secrets. We're partners. Partners in crime." He nudged her shoulder, and she smiled.

"In that case, I have to confess—"

The flight attendant arrived with their drinks. Sam

placed Suzanne's coffee on her tray. "You were about to say?" His eyes found hers.

"I forgot what I was about to say."

When their flight landed, they made their way to the rental car counter. Sam filled out forms, retrieved the keys, and they were on their way.

The crime scene was fourteen miles from the airport. Dark clouds loomed overhead. Sam hoped the crime scene was protected, lest they lose evidence. Not that he expected much evidence.

When they arrived, Sam and Suzanne were met by Detective Hal Jorgensen, from the Akron P.D. "Not what we're used to around here," he said. "A drifter, I guess. We get all kinds because of the interstate."

"Has the girl been identified?" Sam plucked a pen and a note pad from his shirt pocket.

"Her brother is at the morgue right now, identifying her body. They were on their way to New York. He's some mucky-muck author. Mystery writer. Go figure."

"Does he have any idea who could have murdered his sister?"

"No. Said the only time she was out of his sight was when she went to the pool in the afternoon. Right before she disappeared, he said she told him she forgot her sunglasses by the pool. He found the sunglasses in the hotel room. He thought she might have been meeting someone, so he went to the pool to look for her. The rest is history. Damn shame, if you ask me." Jorgensen gave Suzanne the once over. "Who's this?"

"My partner, Suzanne Cash. I'd like to speak with the brother. Can you arrange that? We have witnesses who identified a serial killer back in Sacramento. He's on the move, and it would be helpful if we can connect him to this murder. We think he's headed East."

"I'll escort you myself." Jorgensen turned to his men. "Get the tarps over these spatters here. It's gonna rain like a son-of-a-bitch in the next hour!"

Sam and Suzanne followed Jorgensen into town. Meyers Lake consisted of a small grocer, a Country-Western Bar, McDonald's, a post office, and an assortment of antique and gift stores. Outside of the two-block radius stood open fields.

They pulled behind a cinder-block building painted pea-green. The humidity had made Sam's hair curl, and his temper short. "They can keep this weather."

Suzanne's skin glowed, and the hair that had escaped her ponytail fell in wispy tendrils around her face.

"I've never been in a morgue before," she said, hesitating at the door.

"Would you rather wait out here?"

"Maybe it would be best."

Sam handed her the keys to the rental. "Stay cool, I won't be long." He watched her walk back to the car.

After introducing himself to the Coroner, Sam braced himself for what he was about to see. Another dead girl. The Coroner grabbed the handle of the drawer and pulled. A slender figure, covered in white sheeting, slid into view.

"We're not used to this kind of brutality around here," the Coroner said, his bushy brow cinched together. "The bastard not only slit her throat and left her to bleed to death, he blinded her with broken bottles, and mutilated her vagina." The man paused. "Her hands were tied behind her back with a friggin' piece of orange twine."

Sam said, "That's our guy." He bent forward to examine the girl's wrists. *Same as before.*

Suzanne started the engine. She turned the AC to 'cool' and flipped on the radio. She whipped through the stations, wiped a smudge off of the window, and picked lint off of her aqua green top. It began to rain. The first drops hit the window with a splat. As the drops increased, she peered out the windshield, and saw veins of lightning shatter the sky.

Thunder crashed in the distance. She turned off the air conditioner, rolled down her window, and killed the engine. She leaned back, breathing in the scent of sassafras. Dark clouds danced across the sky, dumping a deluge of rain, and filling potholes in the parking lot. She took it all in. This was not a California rain, this was Mother Nature connecting with the lush overgrowth of Queen Anne's Lace, wild asparagus, day lilies, and pennyroyal, wild ginger, and pigweed. Herbs that she had learned to recognize when Jack was alive. She closed her eyes, recalling fragments of their long talks.

"I believe God put a cure for every ailment the human body manifests; it's just a matter of cracking the code. Once you know what each flower or plant is capable of, you have to figure out how much to give and when."

Suzanne listened carefully to Jack, cherishing his knowledge, and moments shared learning new things. When he died, she tucked their dreams away with the hurt, and the disappointment, and the realization that her future was lost. Ben had no goals, he lived vicariously through others. Perhaps that's why she was drawn to him. The less of her soul she invested in the relationship, the better.

She felt Jack touch her cheek, but when she opened her eyes, it was Sam.

"Didn't mean to startle you," he said, climbing in beside her, his hair wet.

"You missed the good parts," she said, handing him the keys. "Thunder, lightning, the whole bit."

"It looks like the storm is headed east, and so are we. Dixon killed the girl, no doubt about it, unless there is another killer using orange twine."

She shivered. "What now?"

"I'm going to let you tell me."

"New York. He's going to search for the dark-haired girl. And the baby."

"Then that's where we'll head next. Back to the airport."

The next flight to JFK departed in forty-six minutes. Sam and Suzanne returned the car and hurried through the terminal.

"Just made it, the plane boards in eight minutes. We got the last two seats."

"No chance of an empty in the middle this time, eh?"

"No, but if Lady Luck is on my side, perhaps I'll get a seat next to you."

They boarded last, hoping to find two seats together. A woman by the window, held her infant in her lap. The baby wailed, kicked and fussed. Next to the ruckus, two empty seats. Suzanne sat next to the mother, immediately bonding with the fussy infant. Her smile made his teary-eyed face break into a grin.

His mother nodded apologetically and wiped away his tears with her thumb.

"This is Blake's first plane ride. I hope he doesn't disturb you too much." She brushed the boy's hair back. "We're on our way to see daddy."

Blake nestled closer to his mom. "Daddy," he said.

"How old is Blake?" Suzanne asked.

"He's eighteen months. We're on our way to meet his father. Gordy's in the military. He's stationed at NSA in Saratoga Springs for one more year. It's super expensive to live there, so we thought we'd save a little money by remaining in Akron with his mom. He tries to come home as much as possible, but it's tough. We figured Blake was old enough for a plane trip."

Suzanne felt a surge of love when the boy touched her arm. His brown eyes held the secrets of the universe. She heard a whisper deep in her soul, *destined for great things*, and she held out her hand. The boy didn't hesitate, he latched onto her hand and placed it on his head.

"He wants you to pet him. We have a dog at home," his mother said.

Suzanne ruffled his hair, and he squealed in delight. His little pink tongue hung from his mouth, and he panted, like a dog. Suzanne had hoped one day to have children of her own. That ship sailed long ago.

An empty womb can be a hard adjustment for some women. Suzanne filled her void with children who needed more love than most. Her children were ill, and she loved them like they were her own. She hugged them, fought for them, and mourned them when they passed. Not being able to return to her job was the biggest loss of all.

Sam watched the interaction between Suzanne and the child. He imagined her with children of her own. He too had wondered whether he wanted a family. As years passed by, the idea became more distant. He wished he had met Suzanne sooner. Perhaps they would've gotten on the same page and worked toward a goal. Family. He thought about his own Mom, Dad, and sister. He suddenly realized how much he missed them. Suzanne affected him that way, she gave him hope, purpose, opened his heart like a spigot.

By the time the plane landed at JFK, a bond had formed between Suzanne and the young mother. "Blake is destined for great things," she said, touching the boy's cheek. "He's very intelligent, and his purpose is to use his knowledge to help mankind. He's not mainstream, he's beyond. You may have a ball of fire on your hands. But if you let him follow his heart, it will lead to an incredible destiny."

The woman looked at Suzanne like she had two heads. "Wow. My horoscope said I'd receive good news today."

They picked up another rental car and headed to the Marriott Courtyard Hotel. After checking into adjoining rooms, they met in the lobby. "Are you getting anything?" Sam asked. "I feel like we're looking for a needle in a haystack."

"The only thing I'm getting is hungry," Suzanne said. "It's after four. The complimentary peanuts from the plane are wearing off. Can we grab an early dinner?"

Sam glanced at his watch. Although they had lost another hour, he hadn't thought about eating. Their last meal was breakfast. "I guess I'm still on California time. And just for the record—you have to tell me when you're hungry. I keep such crazy hours, food is the last thing on my mind."

"I'll make note of that." She wondered if that was why he wasn't in a relationship. Pretty hard to keep up with dating when you worked 24/7.

He ushered her out the main door and turned to the left. A couple of blocks from the hotel, Sam spotted the One-Forty-Four Restaurant and Grill. "What do you think?"

"It's food. I like it."

They were seated at a table near the bar area. Sam ordered coffee, and Suzanne ordered sparkling water with lime. By the time their drinks arrived, she had decided on grilled salmon over quinoa and mixed vegetables, and Sam ordered roasted chicken with truffle mashed potatoes, and asparagus.

"It's easy to see how one could get swallowed up in this city," Suzanne stated, sipping her drink. "I can't wait to get to Central Park. People watching. It's all about people watching."

Sam's face puzzled. "I didn't realize you'd been here before."

"I haven't."

"Then—"

"I don't know. It just came to me."

"We'll go as soon as we finish dinner," he said. "The faster we get a bead on Dixon, the better."

"The girl–she's an artist." Suzanne squeezed more lime into her drink. "She majored in art."

Sam withdrew his phone and punched in a number. It rang twice before Dove answered.

"Been waiting to hear from you—was it him?"

"Yes. Same M.O. as the others."

"What now?"

"We're in New York. I need a favor."

"Anything."

"Check with Sac State's Art Department—see if there were any sudden drop-outs." Sam did the math.

"Three to six months ago. We're looking for a pretty, dark- haired girl, early twenties."

"Got it."

"Our girl is pregnant. How far along, we're not sure."

"Anything else?"

"Yeah. Talk to the teachers. Get names of friends she may have been close to. One way or another, someone must know why she left suddenly."

"I'll get right on it. Keep me posted."

"Thanks." Sam ended the call just in time to be served his meal. He gazed at Suzanne while she ate.

"This is the best salmon I have ever tasted."

"I'm enjoying it vicariously. You look so happy."

"I love food. Mmm. Tomato, basil and cream cheese on an "everything" bagel sounds good right now. Mike's has the best."

Sam stopped mid-bite.

Suzanne put a forkful of quinoa in her mouth and froze. She hadn't noticed that Sam sat still, waiting for her to speak.

"Mike's Bagel's—we have to find Mike's Bagel's."

Sam keyed the name into Google. "We're in luck. There's only one, and it's in Washington Heights. Unfortunately, they close at 5 p.m."

"Let's check out Central Park, see if I can pick up a vibe. We may be able to get her route."

"This is what I love about you. I can starve you, drag

you around the country, and we're still on the same page."

"Don't get used to the starving part. I can get quite testy, you know."

"I'll take your word for it. Now, are you up for dessert? I hear New York is THE place for cheesecake."

"Can we share?"

"Absolutely." Sam placed an order for a slice of cheesecake with fresh strawberries and two forks.

After dinner they hailed a taxi.

While driving along Atlantic Avenue, Suzanne processed the scenery. She sensed the girl would've taken public transportation to the park. *She tries to blend in.* But the bagel shop was close to home, where she could satisfy her craving at a moment's notice.

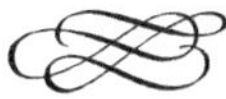

Sheena had enjoyed her day at the park, but was anxious to get back to her part of town before Mike's closed at 5 p.m. When she entered the shop, she was greeted by Marta, employee extraordinaire.

"Hello, Brenda." Sheena had felt bad giving Marta a fictitious name, however, she had rebuilt her life in New York to protect herself and her baby. Lying was a sin, but whatever she needed to do to keep herself safe from Dixon was worth going to hell for.

"Hi Marta, can I have—"

"Tomato, basil, cream cheese, hold the lox, on an 'everything' bagel—right?"

"How do you remember everyone's order like that?"

"I have a photographic memory. My mom said I was foolish for wasting it here, but I love people, and remembering orders is a lot more fun than law codes."

"I wanted to be an artist. Not going to happen now."

"Why?"

"I dropped out of school. I won't be able to afford to go back."

"I can see why you may think you're out of the game," she said, her gaze dropping to Sheena's bump, "But being pregnant may just be the ticket you need to finish school. New York frowns on drop-out mothers-to-be."

"Are you saying I might be able to get a grant?"

"Yep."

"Maybe I'll look into that." Sheena knew it wasn't going to happen. In order to get a grant, she would have to give her social security number to register, and then Dixon would be able to find her. She accepted her bagel, handed Marta a five-dollar bill and said. "Thanks for the tip. Have a good day."

Sheena took her time walking back to the apartment. Renee wouldn't be home for another hour, and she hated being alone at this time of day. The apartment filled with shadows at 4 p.m. and she felt depressed. The lack of light reminded her of afternoons with Dixon. He had demanded the shades be pulled down in her apartment after 3 in the afternoon. Sheena had felt as though she missed half of her day. *He sucked more than light from my life. He stole my soul.*

A block from her apartment, Sheena stopped. She examined her surroundings, but all she saw was an old woman with a shopping cart, and a blond man dressed in a white linen suit, with a pink shirt, talking on a cell phone. He tilted his sunglasses and looked right at her. She pulled her kimono tighter to her breast. She glanced his way. The blond man began shouting obscenities into his phone, his high-pitched whine caused passersby to turn.

"What the fuck y'all looking at! Jesus Norman, people are staring at me. Don't you care?"

Sheena picked up her pace.

Something about the man gave her the willies. When she turned onto her street, she looked back to make sure she wasn't being followed, then ducked into her apartment building. To her relief, Simon was no longer on duty. His shift ended at 5 p.m. He would've picked up on her fear, asked a million questions. The man who relieved him was polite, but not nearly as personable. He tipped his hat, opened the door, and held it until she was inside. "Alonzo, has anyone asked about me?"

"No, Miss Bradlee. Are you expecting a guest?"

"No. Should someone ask for me, or describe me to you, please tell them you have no idea who they are referring to. I encountered a strange man on my walk, he may have followed me home."

"I will be sure to steer him away, Miss Bradlee."

"Thank you." Sheena proceeded to the elevator. When she opened the door to her apartment on the twenty-first floor, she rushed inside and locked the door. "You're panicking over nothing," she assured herself. Yet she went to the window and peeked outside. He was there. Across the street.

Sheena moved away from the window. She had changed her appearance, but was it enough? Her hair was shorter, darker. Her body had filled out. *He's not stupid.* If she could change her image, he could have done the same. Although she couldn't imagine him bleaching his hair or wearing pink, she had to believe he would do anything to find her.

The baby inside her responded to her fear with a tiny kick. She reclined on her bed, willing the fear to go away. She massaged her precious bump. "I promise, he will not hurt you."

Dixon stood outside the high-rise counting the floors. Thirty-nine. Sheena could be in any one of them. Thirty-nine high, eighteen across, times two. Over 1400 residents. Don't forget the doorman. *He probably moonlights as a bouncer in a strip club.* The man was 6'3", and at least 350 pounds. His head was so large, his cap sat on top of his head. His coat fit tight across his chest. *You're a bruiser, all right.* Dixon wasn't worried. *All men bleed the same.* All he needed to do was figure out how to get inside. The rest would fall into place.

CHAPTER 44

S am and Suzanne left the cab a block from the park, and walked to 57th Street. Sam kept an eye on pedestrians, Suzanne kept an eye on subject matter. "I can see why she would love to sketch here."

"Definitely a people-watching wonderland."

"Yes. Bright colors, in all directions. Sad faces. Happy faces. Young and old. Look at the trees, they're lovely."

"Look at the drug deal going down on the corner. *Charming.*" He looped his arm through hers. "The park is going through a shift change. Hold onto me." He glanced her way. "And keep your purse close to your body. This place is a treasure trove for pickpockets and purse snatchers."

Suzanne sighed. "And here I thought we were enjoying the view."

"You enjoy all you want, just hang on to me, and

follow my lead." He nudged her shoulder. "Something you need to know about me—"

"What's that?"

"I'm really a knight in shining armor."

"Does that make me a damsel in distress?"

"I would never call you a damsel."

"What then?"

"Princess."

"Princess?"

Sam stopped. "My queen?"

"Much better," she replied, stepping closer.

As they walked, snippets of people flashed through her mind. She froze, holding her hand in the air. "A woman, waving to a child." She spotted a woman, holding a fist full of balloons in her hand. "She drew a woman and child. The child is holding a balloon, the mother is waving."

"You feel our girl has been here?"

"Yes. She comes here often." Jack showed her more. "I see a man. Fake eyes, and blond hair. He has a knife. Not just any knife. The knife is meant for hunting. For gutting animals." *For getting rid of babies.*

Dixon sat on a bench across the street and waited. He enlarged Sheena's cousin's photo on his phone. He knew all about Renee. She worked as an editor for ABC 7 NY, made a six-figure income, and loved teacup Chihuahuas. When he finally saw Renee walk by, excitement buzzed in his veins. The doorman opened the door to let her in as if expecting her. *He must know everyone.* But how did he get that information? 1400 units—*a lot to keep track of.* Was there a registry with photos and names? Did they all carry some sort of fob that identified them? He wondered. He needed to find out. He waited until Renee was out of sight, then approached the building.

"Excuse me?" Dixon wrapped on the door. The doorman didn't respond. Dixon knocked again this time harder. "I said, excuse me— I have a question." This time the doorman sighed and opened the door.

"I just want to know if they're hiring here. I was a doorman in Portland, and I'm looking for work." Dixon gave the doorman his "poor me" look.

"I don't know if they're hiring, you'd have to check with the office and right now it's closed."

"What time do they open in the morning?" Dixon blinked, portraying an innocent.

"Come back at 9:00, ask for Judy." The doorman handed Dixon a business card.

"Do you have to know everyone here? I mean there's so many people here—"

"We have a monitor. But I've been here thirteen years, so I know just about everyone."

"I think I know someone who lives here. Renee Caperone."

The doorman grinned. He wasn't giving Dixon more than he already had.

"Actually, Renee's cousin and I are friends." Dixon said. "Did she have that baby yet?"

"Not yet. We're all betting on a baby boy. Miss Bradlee is carrying mighty low."

Dixon cringed. Bad enough she's pregnant. A baby boy would be disastrous. He'd grow up without his daddy, then his mama would go whorin' around. History would repeat itself. "Not gonna happen," he hissed.

"Excuse me?"

The doorman's puzzled expression brought Dixon back from his nightmare.

"I'm not so sure." He placed two fingers in the middle of his forehead. "I'm feeling it's a girl."

The doorman shook his head. "We'll see about that."

The sun hid behind the trees, peeking through bushes and casting shadows across the sidewalk. Suzanne let her mind wander. She gravitated toward a bench occupied by an elderly woman clutching two trash bags and mumbling to herself.

"God has forsaken thee!" she seethed through her toothless maw. "Thou shall be sent back to hell to suffer for eternity."

Suzanne was unnerved by the woman's wandering eye. Yet she stepped closer. The old woman cowered and covered her head with her arm. "My spot," she cried. "Here first."

"May I sit down and visit with you for a moment?" Suzanne asked in her softest voice. "I'm not going to hurt you," she said. "My name is Suzanne. I am looking for my friend. She's an artist."

The old woman uncovered her face, sat upright and patted the space beside her. "Do you have any spare change?"

Suzanne dug through her purse, gathering quarters, nickels, dimes, and pennies. "Here." She placed the coins in the woman's outstretched hand. And moved closer. The woman scooted to her right, making room for Suzanne to sit down as she counted the coins one by one.

"Two more dimes and three pennies," the old woman said, putting the coins in her pocket.

"My friend is young, early twenties," she said, reaching in her purse for a dollar bill. "She has long brown hair. She's pregnant. She comes here to sketch. She sits on this bench. Have you seen her?"

The old woman tucked the bill inside the top of her dingy T-shirt. "Miss pretty. She draws Hanna some-times." The old woman began to rock.

"Are you Hanna?"

"I'm Hanna. Hanna Banana."

"My name is Suzanne. My mother called me Suzie Snoozy."

The old woman laughed. "Snoozy, Suzie! That's funny."

"I like Hanna Banana better. Did you see my friend today?"

"She told me a secret. Her name isn't Bradlee, it's Sheena. Sheena Beana!" The woman rocked and cackled, pleased with herself.

Suzanne glanced at Sam. Their eyes connected and held. Then he began texting.

"Do you know Sheena's last name?"

"No. She said no last names, or the devil would kill her baby. Hold him over the fire until he's a tiny crispy critter." The woman opened her bag and pulled out a ragged blanket. "You can't stay here," she said, her eyes narrowing.

"I'll go, but first, does Sheena come here every day?"

"Sometimes."

"Do you know where she lives?"

"On the mountain top. Where God can see her."

Suzanne pulled a twenty-dollar bill from her wallet for Hanna, and then joined Sam. "She was here today. I can feel it. What I'm not getting is where she lives, but I think Hanna said something helpful. She said her name is Sheena, not Bradlee, and she lives on the mountaintop where God can keep an eye on her."

Sam was busy checking the text he received from Dove. A list of students who had dropped out in last six months. Sheena Bradford was on that list. Sam then Googled her name, coming up with a Facebook page that hadn't been updated in weeks. The dark-haired girl was as Suzanne had described her. Young, beautiful. Unhappiness shown in her eyes in the last picture she had posted. Sam clicked on her friends and scrolled through the list. No one with the same last name. He sifted through her posts, looking for something to fill the puzzle pieces they needed. "Bingo," he said, holding up his phone. "She has a connection in New York. Renee Caperone."

He Googled Renee Caperone. A woman matching the photo on Sheena's Facebook page posing with the news team at ABC7NY popped up on the screen. Several photos included Renee, but one grabbed Sam's attention. Renee stood in front of a high-rise building giving a thumbs up. The caption read, "Home Sweet Home."

Suzanne's head began to ache. Jack stomped his feet, his arms flailing like a bird learning to fly. "No, no, no!" he screamed. Suzanne tried to understand the meaning behind his outburst.

"What do you want me to do?" she cried.

Sam grabbed her shoulders. "We got this, Suzanne. We have enough information to find her."

Suzanne shook off the image Jack had planted in her mind. A sharp object, with jagged edges. An object meant for hunting, killing, *gutting*. "We need to find her, NOW."

～

CHAPTER 45

Renee unlocked the door. She had worked overtime on a feature one of the newscasters was doing on runaways. She had the piece ready to go when the man decided he wanted a completely different voice over. Once she disassembled and reassembled the soundtrack, he divulged that he didn't have written permission to use three of the photos he provided. Ugh. Repositioning the only photos they could use threw the story line off completely and the dialog needed be redone. A simple two-hour project turned into a nightmare and a screaming match. She didn't take shit from anybody, let alone some namby-pamby wannabe journalist. She yearned to put her feet up, turn on a mind-numbing chick flick, and drink a glass of Merlot.

Sheena came out of her room, her face practically dragging on the floor.

"Hey Cuz, que pasa?"

"There was this guy—"

"How many times have I told you? You're safe here. No one knows who you are. The staff has been instructed to report any unusual activity to me immediately. I pay top bucks for this kind of security. Now come on, sit. Let's watch girl porn. I haven't seen that new one with Reese Witherspoon."

"Reese Witherspoon is doing porn?"

"Chick flicks. Guys like skin, we get off on cute outfits and happy endings." Renee patted the seat beside her on the couch. "Did you go to the park to draw today?"

"Yes."

"Was that crazy lady there? What's her name?"

"Hanna? She was there. I'm almost finished with the shading on her drawing. Do you want to see it?"

"Absolutely! You know I love your stuff. Let's see!"

Sheena went to her room to get the drawing. When she returned, the house phone rang.

"Are you expecting anyone?" Renee crossed the room to pick up the phone.

"No. Are you?"

"No." Renee picked up the phone. "Yes?"

Alonso said, "There's a man and a woman in the lobby. He says he's a police officer from California and he needs to speak with you."

Renee's brow bunched with worry. "Tell them there must be some mistake. And whatever you do, don't let ANYONE up here."

"Yes Ma'am."

Renee hung up the phone and faced Sheena, who stood in the doorway. "All gone."

"Who was it?"

"Probably someone selling something. Alonso got rid of them."

"I'm scared. I felt someone watching me today."

"You're perfectly safe here. You need to concentrate on being a happy girl. For the baby."

Sheena flopped on the couch. "You're right. What are we watching?"

Renee stroked her arm. "This place is a fortress, no one gets past the guard dogs on duty. Alonso is a trained fighter. He works for us. He won't let anyone in that doesn't belong."

"But who even knew to come here? Doesn't that cause a little concern?"

"I think you're overreacting. But if you want, I can work from home the next few days. I could use a break."

"I don't know what I would do without you. You've been like my mom, dad, and cousin rolled into one."

Renee circled her arm around Sheena and pulled her close. "We're all we got, Cuz, we have to stick together."

Sam left the building feeling defeated. Suzanne took his arm. "It's not a dead end. She's here, I know it. And evidentially they know that someone is looking for them, why else would they lie? You saw how uncomfortable the doorman was when he returned. He knew that we knew he was lying. He had guilt written all over his face."

"You're right. Why did I think this was going to be easy?"

"I say we check out of our hotel and check-in someplace closer so we can keep an eye on the girl."

"And Dixon. He may have tried to contact her already, maybe that's why they're lying."

"The good thing is we found her. The next step is to get to her before Dixon does."

"You think like a cop."

"You must be rubbing off on me."

Dixon hid in the shadows, watching Sam and Suzanne. How did they know about Sheena? Maybe he had underestimated Metzger's little psychic friend. How much did they know? But he was ahead of the game. He had an in with the doorman. And tomorrow he might get the key to the castle.

CHAPTER 46

Sam and Suzanne didn't go back to the hotel immediately. "I'm going to swing by the 34th Precinct, see if I can get more information on Renee Caperone. Her phone number is unlisted, perhaps they can get it for me, or have one of their men call to warn her."

"We don't know that Dixon is here for sure—"

"We don't know that he isn't."

Sam ushered Suzanne into the five-story brick building. They walked past a marble Memorial Wall etched with the names of those who had served the department, dating back to the late 1800's, and towards the desk Sergeant.

"What can I do for you?"

"I'm Detective Sam Metzger from the Goldorado Sheriff's Department in California. We believe a serial killer has traveled to Washington Heights, and that one your residents may be in danger."

The sergeant didn't speak until he had checked Sam's ID and entered his name into his computer. "Do you have the suspect's name?"

"Sheriff James Dixon."

"This some kind of a joke?" The Sergeant looked around, expecting to see a camera. When he realized that Sam was serious, he typed Dixon's name into the computer.

"James Dixon has an APB out on him." The Sergeant turned the screen toward Sam. "This the guy?"

"Yes. However, I doubt he is using that name. We discovered he has several identities."

"Who's the person in danger?"

"We know very little about her. Her name is Sheena Bradford. She was an art student at Sac State. She dropped out six months ago and dropped off the radar. We believe she's hiding out at her cousin's place in Washington Heights. The Belvedere."

"Do you have the cousin's name?"

"Renee Caperone."

"Renee? From ABC7?"

"According to Google—"

"I know Renee. She's friends with my niece. Nice gal."

"We stopped by her apartment to warn her, but—"

"Let me guess," the Sergeant raised his hands to make air quotes, "she wasn't home."

"You guessed it. I wasn't about to argue with the doorman. He looked like he could break my face in a heartbeat."

"Alonso. Yeah, he boxed for quite a few years. He takes his job seriously. We've been called out there a few times. He can be really ugly–but he's there to make sure no one enters the building without permission."

"Well, he's doing a great job. And Ms. Caperone claimed not to be in when we paid her a visit."

Let me text my niece for Renee's number."

Suzanne felt woozy. As if two bodies occupied the same space in her body. She wanted a beer. *I don't drink beer.* She opened her purse and pulled out a compact. She opened it, looked in the mirror, and gasped. Her image was distorted. *Blurry. Blonde.* She blinked her eyes. The image did the same. She felt as though she were morphing into a man's body, yet she felt compelled to do feminine things. *Lipstick.* What is this about? One thing was clear. She did not feel like herself.

"He's disguised himself."

Sam stepped toward her. "This is Suzanne Cash. She's my partner on the case." The reason we've gotten this far is because of this young lady. She's a psychic."

Suzanne expected him to roll his eyes, break out in laughter, but he didn't. Instead he held up his hand and said, "I get it. My Mom believes in all that stuff."

The Sergeant's cell phone beeped. "It's my niece. She gave me Renee's number." He dialed the number and listened. "Renee, this Jerry Veniccio, Lola's uncle calling from the 34th Precinct. I have a Detective Samson Metzger here from California. He says he needs to speak with you right away. Can you call me back please?"

"While we're waiting for a call back, you wanna tell me what this guy is wanted for?"

"He's tortured and killed over a dozen women—that we know of. You have no idea what he's capable of."

"This BOLO doesn't give many details. Let me get this over to my guys."

"Thanks, I appreciate it."

"Grab some coffee, I'll be right back."

Sam poured a cup of coffee in a Styrofoam cup and handed it to Suzanne. "Black, right?"

"Yes, but maybe some cream and sugar this time. You guys like it a little strong."

"It's a wonder I don't bleed caffeine."

"I'm feeling agitated. Jack is racing in my head. Like he has a bus to catch or something." She pressed her palm on her forehead. "I get the feeling that the clock is ticking. That if we don't catch Dixon soon, that baby won't make it to term."

"When we left Sacramento, I thought we were on a wild goose chase. I never dreamed we'd end up this close to the girl. And if we're this close, Dixon can't be far behind."

"Do you have a plan?" Suzanne leaned over to see what Sam was doing on his phone.

"I'm searching for the closest hotel for starters."

CHAPTER 47

Dixon checked into the Hotel Cliff at 7 p.m. He could almost see Sheena's apartment from the window in his room. He wondered what she was doing and realized that he had no idea because he had never taken an interest. He knew she went to Sac State. He knew she had a mole on her left inner thigh. He knew that her mouth was soft, plump, pliable, juicy. He knew he loved her smooth, flawless skin. The way she tossed her hair to the side when she went down on him. Now, those were things to know. But then he remembered she hadn't had her period…they fucked the whole month without interruption. Her breasts had been tender, *fuller*.

His erection strained against his linen pants. He pictured Sheena in her lace bra and panties. She made those Victoria Secret models look like trolls. He imagined her swollen belly, the sound of the knife splitting her taut flesh, *like one of Grandpa's watermelons*. He got off the bed and undressed. He couldn't afford an accident in his one pair of dress trousers. He had a role to play in the morning. Stains were not an option. His plan was to charm the pants off the property manager, get hired as a doorman, and gain access to Sheena.

CHAPTER 48

Renee ignored the call on her cell phone. What she needed most was down time. A rough day at work had her nerves humming, and a headache threatened to develop into a migraine. She was determined to enjoy her glass of wine, a funny movie, and chillax with her favorite person on the planet. She convinced herself that the person who had paid a visit was no danger. *So why is your head throbbing like a MoFo?* Since Sheena had moved in there was always that niggling. What if? What if that asshole decided to track her down? What if he decided he wanted to be the baby's daddy, and haul her cousin back to Sacramento, where she wouldn't be able to watch over her? She cared too much for the girl to let that happen. Soon there would be a little one to dote over, and she didn't want to miss out.

"Let's watch 'Me Before You.' I heard good reviews,

and after the day I had, a good laugh would be welcome."

Sheena clicked on the TV and pressed Netflix. She scrolled through the menu until she found the movie. Before she pressed play, she asked, "Is everything okay? You seemed bothered by something."

"Had a rotten day. But—it's over. We're exactly where we need to be."

"I'm still a little freaked out about that guy."

"What guy?"

"The guy across the street."

"It was probably nothing." She'd lived in Washington Heights Terrace for nine years. Never had she felt more vulnerable. Although the staff looked out for their residents, she knew the doormen made a meager living, and wasn't sure if any of them would accept a bribe. She intended to speak with Judy, the property manager, in the morning to make sure the staff was on full alert.

CHAPTER 49

Sam and Suzanne drove back to the Marriott, checked out and returned to Washington Heights. They found the Hotel Cliff with ease and were checked in within the hour. Sam carried Suzanne's bag to her door.

"I'll be next door if you need anything," he said.

"I'll be fine. Let me know if you get a call."

Sam slid his key card into the slot and turned the handle to enter. Across the hall, an eye peered through the peephole.

"Well I'll be damned," Dixon whispered. "This IS my lucky day."

S uzanne tossed and turned in her bed. Her dreams were laden with snippets from her younger years. *Jack.* They seemed to be in a house of mirrors. Everywhere she looked, he was there. "What do you want from me?" Her voice was hoarse.

"Do you see me," he asked.

"You're scaring me," she cried. But he wouldn't stop.

"Do you see me?", he demanded.

"I see you. Now stop!"

He stood in front of her. The mirror was gone. "Be careful, Suzanne," he said, his voice trailing away.

Suzanne bolted upright. She slowed the stampede in her chest. "It's a warning," she whispered. She felt Dixon's evil intent down deep inside. A dark place. A place where the devil hides in plain sight. She gasped. "He's here."

S am passed his sobriety coin from finger to finger. When his mind was weighed down by stress or worry, he could rely on the trick to reroute his thoughts. It cleared his mind. *Relax.* If he was lucky, sleep would follow.

The red glowing numerals read 2:45. He checked his phone. Renee Caperone hadn't return Sergeant Viniccio's call earlier, so he called her himself and left a message. Was she that scared? Or that naïve? *Why?*

He dozed between 3:09 and 3:30. In his dream, Suzanne lay beside him, her arm, snug around his waist. Her body nestled close to his. Skin to skin. Her heart beating close to his. Her breath whispering across his chest. He wanted to stay in that moment forever. Something jarred him awake.

He heard a muffled noise. He went to the door joining his room to Suzanne's and listened. Nothing. Perhaps she talked in her sleep? He pressed his ear against the door. The wood felt cool against his cheek. When silence prevailed, he got back into bed.

At 5:00 a.m. another sound woke him. His alarm. He showered, dressed, and left his room at 5:30 in search of coffee. At 6:05, he returned with two coffees, and two bagels. He rapped lightly on Suzanne's door. She didn't answer.

Dixon was propped up on one elbow, his face inches from Suzanne's. He moved a lock of hair away from her cheek and studied her ear. He thought about cutting it off and leaving it under Sam's door, but decided he wanted a little fun first.

How easy it had been to break into her room, chloroform her, and steal her into the night. And the cool part was, no one would know. He made sure he avoided the surveillance camera by covering the lens with a piece of gaffer's tape. Once he had Suzanne, he removed the tape, and jiggled the lens with a coat hanger. Next, he went downstairs to the front desk to establish his alibi. The hotel was so ancient, he doubted the cameras worked at all. But he couldn't take a chance. The young man at the desk was very accommodating and fetched an extra blanket. "I'm sorry you couldn't get through.

Our phones are the pits. Is there anything else I can get for you?"

"You been more than helpful," Dixon replied, holding up the blanket. "I almost forgot to ask, is there a flower shop close by? My Grandmother's wake is tomorrow. I want to pick up some flowers. I used to be in the business, and I know what my dear Grandmother would have wanted."

The desk clerk wrote the name of the closest florist.

Dixon smiled. "Thank you, you are too kind."

He left the desk clerk and headed toward the elevator, playing his part all the way up to his room.

He shut the door and sat down on the bed beside Suzanne. "There, my little darling. All done." He snickered. "Won't Sam be surprised to find his personal bloodhound is nowhere to be found?"

He rested his head on Suzanne's breast. He considered fucking the life out of her, but then he'd lose his bartering tool. No, he'd keep her until he had dealt with Sheena. "And then—" he ran his hand along the inside of her thigh, —"then we'll see."

Sam called Suzanne's cell phone. Maybe she was taking a shower. Maybe she was one of those people who could sleep through a mortar attack, an avalanche, or a hurricane. He turned off the ringer on his phone when he needed to sleep. Maybe she did the same. He glanced at the clock. 6:58 a.m. He sipped his coffee. *Give her an hour.* She deserved that much. She'd been up thirty-six hours, maybe more. *She must be exhausted.* His phone rang.

"Detective Metzger, it's Renee Caperone, returning your call. My apologies for calling so early, but I didn't want to talk when my cousin was around. She's still sleeping, I thought now would be a good time. Tell me what this is all about."

"I'm hoping you can fill me in, Ms. Caperone. What we know is that a very dangerous man is on the loose. We think he is in New York, and we think he is after your cousin—and the baby."

"No one knows about the baby."

"Jim Dixon knows."

"How? Sheena didn't tell anyone."

"I don't have that answer. Maybe he figured it out."

"How did *you* find out?"

"I am working with a woman who—" Suddenly everything seemed preposterous. How could he explain Suzanne to this woman? "She's a psychic. She helped us find two girls Dixon had been holding prisoner. Believe me, as farfetched as it may seem, Suzanne has been spot-on with her information." He paused. "She led me to you." Sam heard Renee gasp. "Can we come over and talk?"

"Give us an hour. Sheena is sleeping."

"So is Suzanne. It was a long night for everyone."

"You have the address?"

"Yes. But your doorman is very protective."

"Yes, they all are." Renee said. "We recently lost one of our best. He was sixty-one, ready for retirement. Sudden heart attack. Gone."

"I'm sorry for your loss."

"It means breaking in a new doorman. I'm hoping for someone as dedicated as Clifford was." Renee's voice trailed off. "I'll see you in an hour."

Sam dialed Suzanne's room from the hotel phone twenty minutes later. He could hear the phone ringing in the adjoining room. She didn't answer.

He hung up and knocked on the door connecting the two rooms. "Suzanne," he called, "Are you awake?" No answer. He knocked again this time louder. Still no answer. He called the front desk.

"This is Detective Metzger in room 310. My partner, Suzanne Cash checked into room 312. Have you seen her? Late thirties, five foot-four, petite build, long dark hair. She's not answering her phone.

"I've been at the desk since 5 a.m.. No one has left the building matching that description, but I cannot be certain your partner did not leave before my shift, or during the shift change."

"In that case, please send someone with a house key. I need to be certain she is okay."

"I will send the manager right away."

D ixon opened the bathroom door and grabbed a towel from the rack. "Fuckin' pig," he seethed, mopping up the urine around Suzanne's bottom. He had propped her up against the bathtub, bound her hands and feet with orange twine, and taped her mouth. Once he cleaned up the mess, he removed the tape from her mouth and administered a dose of Ketamine with an eye dropper.

He wasn't expecting her to bite him.

"Goddammit!" He kicked her thigh. "That hurt, bitch!"

She tried to speak, but Dixon tore off a fresh piece of tape and slapped it over her mouth.

"Gotta love the high," he said, checking her bindings. "Now," he said, rising. "I've got a little business to take care of. Do yourself a favor and be a good girl, otherwise I will kill your boyfriend. Understood?"

Suzanne's eyes rolled back. Her head slumped and her body went limp. However, her brain remained active.

She was on a swing. Jack stood behind her pushing, higher, and higher. She touched the sky with her toes.

The sky turned a greenish grey. She let go of the chains. *I'm flying*. Thick, swollen clouds hurried by. Birds flanked her on both sides, their wings flapping hard against their bodies, their beaks chattering in unison. Suzanne could see the down beneath their wings, she sensed the hunger in their eyes. Below, Jack was a tiny speck. She thought she heard him cackling like a crow.

As she soared into the sky, the birds pecked at her body. Drops of blood spattered her arms. She couldn't scream. She had no mouth. *Where did it go?* She touched the place where her lips had been, the surface smooth.

Higher and higher she climbed, until she crashed into something hard. Her head split open like an egg. Her bare legs dangled below her. Blood ran down her face. She reached for her head, but her hands were not her own. *Talons?* If only she could speak. She wanted an aspirin, a band aide to hold her brain in place.

She began to fall.

Dixon dressed in his new white linen slacks, a pale grey shirt, peach color tie, and white jacket. He checked his appearance. *Looking good.* He glanced over his shoulder at the body slumped on the bathroom floor. *She's out.* Good. He had work to do.

At 8:15 a.m., he entered Washington Heights Terrace. The doorman he had spoken with the day before had been replaced by an elderly gentleman, who appeared to have been a Mafia hit man in a previous life.

"I'd like to speak with Judy."

"Do you have an appointment, Mister—"

"Duane. Duane Cooley."

"Mizz Judy doesn't see walk-ins."

"Alonso told me she was looking for a doorman. He said to come back this morning."

The doorman gave Dixon the once over. "Doorman,

eh? I think she was looking for someone with a little more—*muscle*."

Dixon returned the man's smirk. "Should I kick your ass right here?" He swept the room with his hand. "Or are you going to let me see Judy?"

The man studied Dixon's face for a moment. "Absolutely. One moment."

Dixon watched the man's back disappear into the office across from the elevator. As tempted as he was to make a mad dash, he reconsidered. *No, get the job. Get the girl.* He checked his watch. He wondered if Sam had figured out that his sweetie was missing. He wished he could be a fly on the wall for that scene. Maybe I'll let her live. Maybe I won't. Right now, the only thing that mattered was that Sam was detained.

"Mr. Cooley?" A striking woman in her fifties approached Dixon with an outstretched hand. "I'm Judy Wells, can I help you?"

Dixon addressed the woman's shoes. "Jimmy Choo?"

"Why yes, every woman should own at least one pair. What can I do for you Mr. Cooley?"

"I'd like to fill the position you have open for a doorman."

"We haven't advertised, it was only last week that we —how did you hear about the position?"

"Alonso told me. I stopped by yesterday, but you weren't in."

The woman pivoted on her Jimmy Choo's. "Come. We can talk in my office."

Inside Judy's office, Dixon noted the expensive art on the walls. "You have exquisite taste, Ms. Wells."

"Thank you. My husband and I love to travel. I acquire pieces from all over the world. I like the one behind you. Not a collected artist, but I fell in love with his style.

Dixon noticed how she brightened when she said "style." *Probably fucked the guy.* "I can see why. His brush strokes are incredible, and his color choices take your breath away."

"Do you study art, Mr. Cooley?"

"I know what I like," he said.

"Most of our doorman are—how shall I say this without sounding—"

"Ex-thugs?"

"They're trained to be gentlemen, and very good with our residents."

"I agree. Alonso was a prince."

"I have to be honest you don't strike me as the doorman type, Mr. Cooley."

Dixon removed his jacket, rolled up his sleeve, and flexed his muscle. His steely glare trapped her comment in her throat. "Can't always judge a book by its cover."

Judy's expression changed. "You're right. Might be refreshing to have an employee with a little *culture.*" She rose and opened a closet door on the far side of the room. "You look like a 42 long." She produced a red jacket with a Washington Heights Terrace logo stitched across the pocket. "Do you have a white shirt–black pants?"

"Yes."

"Good. Come back at 11:00. If your background checks out, I can get you started then."

CHAPTER 52

Sam stood behind the hotel manager his sobriety coin clenched in his fist. When the man slid his keycard in the slot and opened the door, Sam pushed past him. The room was empty.

"I don't understand," he said. "No one saw her leave?"

"The front desk is always manned, but that's not to say that the employee on duty doesn't step away from time to time. We have security cameras on every floor. No one has reported anything out of the ordinary. Are you sure she didn't just leave?"

"We're working on a case. A very big case. She wouldn't have left without telling me."

"Well, I will have to get in touch with my manager, but I'm sure if she doesn't turn up soon, we can check the security cameras."

Sam glanced at his phone. *Where is she?* "Do what you have to do. I need answers ASAP."

The manager eased his way toward the door. "Probably out for a jog. It's a beautiful day."

Sam looked around the room. He saw the clothes she wore the day before, but not her phone, or her key. *Maybe her phone is on silent?* He checked the closet. Purse. Shoes. "Perhaps you're right. But just to be sure, I'd like to review the tapes."

The manager retreated, closing the door behind him. Sam stood in the middle of the room. What did he really know about Suzanne? What if something had spooked her? What if she had decided this work was too dangerous, not something she wanted to involve herself in, and didn't know how to tell him? What if she had decided to find the girl on her own?

Sam retraced their steps of the previous day. He searched for the homeless woman Suzanne had spoken to and found her collecting cans from the trash one hundred yards from where they spoke.

"Do you remember me from yesterday? I was here with a woman, dark hair, pretty?"

The woman assessed Sam. "Ain't seen nobody this morning." She returned to her can collecting.

"If you see her, please tell her Sam is worried." He dug in his wallet for a twenty-dollar bill. "Please," he said, folding the money into her hand.

When he returned to the hotel, he was met with

concerned faces. The hotel manager stepped from behind the desk. "Anything?"

Sam shook his head. "Let's take a look at that footage."

Dixon slipped past Sam and the manager in the lobby. He entered the elevator and held his breath until the door closed. He avoided looking at the camera in the upper righthand corner. When the elevator stopped, he acted as if he had all the time in the world to exit. Once he was back in his room, he opened the door to the bathroom to find Suzanne still passed out. Her phone vibrated across the floor. He wished he had more time to unclothe her, ravish her body, and kill her properly. But, he had a job, and needed to report to work in an hour.

He filled an eyedropper with Ketamine. "Open up, Bitch." Satisfied that she would be flying high for hours, he quickly changed into his new black pants, a white shirt, and black loafers. He closed the door with such force, he didn't notice the "DO NOT DISTURB" sign fall to the floor.

Sam answered his phone on the first ring, trying not to let his disappointment seep into his tone. "Ms. Caperone."

"I thought you said an hour."

"My apologies. Something has come up." He pinched the bridge of his nose. "Is Sheena awake? I'd like to talk with her."

"My cousin came to me for protection, and to get away from any stress that might impede her pregnancy. You can tell <u>me</u> what's going on. I'll assess whether it's essential she speak with you."

"Do you understand the danger she's in? If we don't find Dixon and put him away, your cousin will be his next victim."

"How can you be sure he knows where she is?"

"I'm working with a reputable psychic."

"Your psychic could be wrong."

"He's here."

"How do you know?" She insisted. "How can you be sure?"

For the first time that morning, he understood. "Because—Suzanne is missing."

CHAPTER 53

Suzanne's world came to a halt. Giant locusts buzzed in her ears. Her blood turned to granite in her veins. Nothing moved. Her eyelashes, heavy ropes that tied her to the floor like *Gulliver's Travels*. How did she end up in Lilliput? It didn't matter. She felt the drops slide down her throat. And before she could say, "None for me, thank you, I've had enough," she spiraled into a dark abyss.

She stood on a rock, fire blazing all around her. She saw Jack on a ledge before her, his outstretched arms seemed suspended in air, his feet crossed in an awkward position. A crown of thorns circled his head. *Jesus.* Blood trickled from one eye.

"I didn't mean to hurt you. It was my duty. My country needed me. It was war."

"I loved you."

"I loved you more."

"You left me behind."

"I'm here now."

"And so am I. Am I dead?"

"No. But if Sam doesn't find you soon—"

"Sam? Where is he?" She ducked, avoiding the beast flying close to her head.

"You have to fight off the demons, Suzanne. There isn't much time."

"Help me, Jack." She ducked again, but this time the beast swallowed her whole.

CHAPTER 54

Dixon entered Washington Square Terrace promptly at 11:00 his red jacket, still in plastic, draped over his arm. Simon greeted him with a broad smile and outstretched hand.

"You must me the new guy–the name's Simon."

"Please to meet you, Simon." Dixon's hand went limp on the handshake. His eyes fluttered. "Miss Judy is expecting me." Dixon cocked his hip and jutted his bottom lip.

Simon chuckled. "She's in her office."

Dixon knocked softly.

Judy appeared at the door a phone cradled at her cheek. "Yes, Renee, I know, I know. No worries, in fact I am training another doorman as we speak." Judy winked at Dixon and motioned for him to enter. "Your cousin is safe, we will make sure of it, and if the police have any questions about the security in our building, they can contact me directly." Judy paused, rolled her eyes, and straightened the pile of papers on her desk. "Yes, absolutely. Bye now." She placed the phone on the receiver and sighed. "Welcome to Washington Heights Terrace."

"Sounds like they keep you on your toes."

"Yes. Your timing couldn't be more perfect. We lost Cliff to cancer. He was with us for twenty-six years, and I have barely had time to send flowers."

"I'm so sorry."

"Thank you. As you may have overheard, the safety of our residents is crucial. When we have a situation, and they don't occur very often, my staff is put on high alert until told otherwise. My apologies for casting you into the mix so soon." She leaned against her desk, her tone matter-of-fact, "I have checked your credentials, and the only flaw you have on record is an unpaid parking ticket from 1983. Is there anything else I should be aware of?"

"I'm gay?"

Judy crinkled her nose, "I hope you're computer savvy. It will expedite your training all the faster."

"I know enough to get by. Where do I start?"

"First, let's get these forms filled out and then," she said, "I will give you a tour of the building."

S am entered the building. Simon tipped his hat. "Morning sir, can I help you?"

"I'm here to see Ms. Caperone. She's expecting me."

Simon picked up the house phone. "Miz Caperone, there is a gentleman here to see you, a Mr.—" Simon paused, his hand covering the receiver. "Who shall I say is calling?"

"Detective Metzger."

"A Detective Metzger is here to see you." Simon glanced at Sam. "Yes, Ma'am, I will send him right up."

Sam saw a man and woman enter the elevator moments before Simon hung up the phone. As the elevator door closed, he glimpsed the man's profile.

"That's Miz Judy. She's the manager here. She must be touring the new hire," Simon said. "He sure gonna make things interesting around here."

Sam cocked his head. "And why is that?"

"Don't get me wrong, Detective, I enjoy every color of the rainbow, but not sure the residents are ready for—"

"For what?"

"My Mama woulda slapped me silly if I sashayed like that in public. Now days, the closet door is off the hinges."

"The new hire is gay?"

"Flame broiled and buttered."

"Interesting." Sam nodded toward the elevator. "Do I need a passkey or something?"

"Oh—almost forgot." Simon walked to the elevator and swiped his badge. "Miz Caperone is in 1308. Thirteenth floor, to your right."

Sam rode to the eleventh floor in a daze. "Where could she be?" he whispered. He caught his image in one of the elevator's four mirrors. He rubbed the stubble on his chin. He hoped Renee Caperone wouldn't judge him by his unkempt look.

He approached 1308 and knocked softly. The door opened to a short woman in her thirties. "Ms. Caperone?"

"Renee," she said extending one hand. "Come in."

Sam eyes soaked in a stunning young lady sitting on a white leather sofa.

"My cousin, Sheena." Renee took the seat beside her.

"I'm Detective Sam Metzger from the Goldorado Sheriff's department in California. I'd like to speak to you about James Dixon."

Sheena's hands went to the bump in her lap. "How did you find me?"

"It really wasn't that hard. Which means Dixon—"

"He can't know where I am. He'll kill me—kill the baby!"

Renee touched Sheena's hand. "Listen–NO one is going to hurt you OR the baby."

Tears gathered in Sheena's eyes. "If this man found me, so can Dixon."

"She's right. Dixon is a pro."

Renee's forehead furrowed. "Pro at what?"

"Dixon is a killer—a cold-blooded killer. He's calculating, maniacal and he'll stop at nothing."

Renee slipped her arm around Sheena and drew her close. "What do we do?"

"Nothing at the moment. Can you stay put for a couple of days?"

"I can work from here, I guess, but how long will we have to be prisoners in our own home?"

"I wish I had the answer to that."

Sheena leaned forward, "Who told you I was here?"

"As I told your cousin earlier, a psychic. Her name is Suzanne."

Sheena turned to her cousin. "Renee, how could you keep this from me? That bastard wanted me to get an abortion."

"I know, but I never thought he was—dangerous."

"He's here because he wants to kill my baby," she cried.

Sam went to window. "The building is secure —right?"

"Yes. Everyone who works here has been checked out thoroughly. Judy is a stickler for background checks. Simon and Alonso are awesome. And Clifford—he was my favorite." Renee paused. "Judy will replace him with someone just as…"

Sheena placed her hand over Renee's. "Judy only hires professionals. Simon and Alonso are both certified to carry weapons and were boxers back in the day. They won't let anyone come near us."

"Nevertheless—keep your doors locked. And if you need anything, call me. I don't care if it's three in the morning."

Both women nodded. Sam stepped toward the door. "Don't get up, I'll find my way out."

As Sam took his leave, he turned to his left. The woman he had seen enter the elevator earlier disappeared into an alcove. Sam heard her say, "This is where our residents can get snacks and sodas. During inclement weather, they change out some of the candy bars for soup. The residents love it."

Dixon saw Sam's back in the hallway. He struggled to focus on Judy's instructions as she led him from the vending area to a lounge with a large flat screen TV and three commercial washers and dryers.

"Each resident has their own unit in their apartment, but the equipment is designed for small loads. We installed commercial grade equipment mainly for comforters, thick blankets, and winter-wear. It does get cold here."

Dixon pictured Judy's pinched features inside the front loader going around and around and around, as the tub filled with her blood. "I'm looking forward to my first snow."

"We pride ourselves on cleanliness, privacy, and protection. New York can be a dangerous city. We get all sorts of riff-raff hanging around our building with the park across the street. Our doormen are the gate keepers."

Dixon nodded. "I totally understand."

"Excellent, Mr. Cooley. I think we are going to hit it off."

"When do I start?"

"Can you be back after lunch?"

"*Perfect,*" he said.

CHAPTER 55

Something fleshy kept getting in the way of Suzanne's teeth. She wanted to yank every tooth out of her mouth, feel the smoothness of her gums rubbing against one another. Enjoy the snakes slithering in and out of her mouth. *I don't like scales stuck between my teeth.* She shivered. Cold air blasted her feet and ankles, and she tucked them beneath her as best she could. She pictured herself as an armadillo. Her eyes lids had stopped working, and her head pounded to the beat of Snoop Dog. Stars shattered all around her as she floated into space. *Good-bye cruel world, I'm off to join the circus.* But the circus wasn't a friendly place. The animals had sharp, gnashing teeth that bit through her armor and nibbled at her intestines.

The pounding continued. A *cannon? Every good circus has a huge cannon.* She imagined herself being blasted from the barrel. The pounding stopped. *Look at me, I'm flying!*

She heard metal scraping metal, a clicking noise she couldn't define. Warm fuzz settled on her shoulders. A voice echoed in her head. You're not in Kansas anymore, Dorothy. *Gimme back those shoes.*

Dixon hurried through the Hotel Cliff lobby and rode an empty elevator to his floor. He slipped his key into the door slot and turned the handle. As he pushed the door open, he noticed the door hanger had been turned. He flipped the sign back to DO NOT DISTURB.

He entered the room with caution. Seeing the unmade bed relieved his angst. He undressed. *First things first.*

"Hello, darlin'."

Suzanne lay in a fetal position on the bathroom floor. Her eyes fluttered.

"Miss me?" he asked, squatting close to her face. He held two fingers against the artery in her neck, checking her pulse. "Let's see what Sam sees in you." He removed the tape from her mouth, and the orange twine from her ankles. His hand reached for her breast and squeezed. "Nice." She squirmed away from his touch.

Suzanne tried to click her heels three times. "There's

no place like home," she heard Jack say. But the face that loomed over her wasn't his. Red glowing eyes, a forked tongue slithered between sharp teeth. The thing touched her, licked her breast. She felt the pressure of its weight settle on top of her. Something hot, molten, seared her cheek. Stars burst in her head and she floated away. When she fell back to earth, she landed on a lamppost. Her body shattered everywhere.

No time to pick up the pieces. The pounding sound returned. Time to get back to the circus—clean up the mess. *Housekeeping*.

Dixon had lifted Suzanne's legs over his shoulders, ready to ram himself inside her again, when the knock on the door came. "What the fuck," he grumbled. He pushed Suzanne aside and went to the door.

"Housekeeping," the woman said, averting her eyes away from his naked chest.

"Can't you read?" he asked, pointing to the sign on the door.

"Sign not there earlier, I come back."

"Well, it's here now, and as you can see," He opened the door wider, making her flinch.

"I come back," she said, motioning to her cart.

Dixon closed the door. "Fuck." He returned to the bathroom to find Suzanne lying in a fetal position. "Great," he snarled. He got in the shower, turned on the water, drowning out the sound of her dry heaves.

Once he finished dressing, he gave Suzanne another

cocktail and packed his bag. She would be dead by morning. *Time to go back to work.*

Dixon followed Judy down the elevator, stopping at each floor so her new employee could acquaint himself with the layout of the building. "My tenants expect their privacy to be maintained at all times. They are to be greeted like they are the most important person on the planet, however, you do not pry. If they offer information about their day, or themselves, you are expected to commit that information to memory. If Mrs. Stein in 1304 rattles on about her six ungrateful children, I expect you to listen, but that doesn't mean you share the fact that two of them are thieves, and the other four are imbeciles. I do not tolerate gossip, tardiness, or insubordination. Are we clear?"

Dixon nodded. "Yes Ma'am."

I like you, Duane. Don't fuck up, okay?"

Sam burst into the building, New York police at his heals. Alonso raised both hands in the air and shouted, "Hey! You just can't just bust in here—this is people's homes!"

Sam flipped open his wallet, displaying his badge. "We have a warrant."

"You let me see that warrant. He paused to study Sam's I.D. "We have rules here."

"Badge, warrant, trumps rules. We're looking for a very dangerous man. 6'2, 185 pounds, wearing a white Prada jacket. Blond hair. May appear gay."

Alonso's eyes lit up. "You mean that Duane Cooley dude? He's with Miz Judy on a tour. She just hired him."

"Where are they now?"

"I dunno."

"One of your residents is in trouble. She's pregnant for Chrissake's."

"You mean Miz Bradlee?"

"The girl's name is Sheena Bradford. Her cousin's name is Renee Caperone. Sheena has long dark hair, early twenties. She's from California."

Alonso squinched his brow. "That's sounds like the girl, but she goes by Bradlee.

Sam turned to address Officer Vespa, the commanding officer in his group. "It's her."

"How do you want proceed?"

"Take your men and block off all the exits. No one is to come or go without my permission. You," he pointed to a muscular young officer.

"Pizzo, sir, Anthony Pizzo."

"Come with me, Pizzo."

Sam headed for the elevator. Alonso swiped his badge, and the door opened. "You gonna need this," he said, handing Sam a temporary keycard.

"Ever shot a man?" Sam turned to Pizzo.

"No, sir," he answered, "I've been on the force six years. Come close a few times. I could shoot someone if I had to."

"Today might be your lucky day."

D ixon stifled a yawn. Judy's droning about this tenant and that tenant bored him to tears. Once he had learned what he had come for, Miss Chatty Kathy had to go. "It's going to be exciting having a little one around."

"How did you—"

"Oh, the mama-to-be came home when I was speaking with Alonso. That's going to be one bea-u-ti-ful child."

"Let's keep focused, shall we?"

"I was just wondering if she requires any special attention. Suppose she goes into labor? Or needs a pickle at two in the morning?"

"Can we keep moving? I have a potential tenant coming in in an hour, I want you acclimated, so you can take your post and shadow Alfonse."

"Where does that door lead to?"

"The janitorial closet. The one next to it is the door to the stairway." Judy gave Dixon a gentle shove. "C'mon, you may as well see the rooftop garden. You'll be locking up at 10 p.m. No exceptions. Tenants tend to whine when it's time to vacate the terrace. They come up with all kinds of excuses." Judy opened the door and climbed the stairs, Dixon followed close behind. The stairwell was well insulated. No noise. He decided it was the perfect moment to pull out the knife he had stashed in waistband.

She didn't expect the knife pressed against her spine. "Is there a problem?"

"What apartment is the pregnant girl in?"

"What are you going to do to her?"

He pressed the knife harder, drawing blood.

"She's in 1308."

Dixon jammed the knife into Judy's spine as hard as he could and pulled it out.

She crawled towards the stairs and collapsed on her face.

Dixon worked fast sorting through her keyring. When he found the key marked Master, he rummaged through the janitor's closet grabbing a drop cloth, and plastic sheeting.

He rolled Judy's body in plastic, then packaged her in canvas. He wiped up blood and dragged her into the closet. He uncovered her face, soaked a rag in turpentine, and stuffed the rag into her mouth. Judy's eyes rolled back in her head. "Thanks for the tour, Judy baby."

Dixon climbed three flights of stairs and turned left. When he heard the elevator he ducked into the alcove of 1308, slipped the master key in the lock, and turned the knob. Renee appeared on the other side of the door.

"What the fu—"

Dixon held his index finger to his lips. "Shhhh. Where's Miss Bradlee?" he whispered.

Renee stepped backwards, pointing toward the bedroom. "What's–"

"Shhh. They're coming." Dixon ushered Renee into the bedroom. Sheena slept soundly.

"Tell me what is going on or I will scream."

"Miss Judy sent me. See? She gave me the key to your place. You are in danger. That detective, the one who claims he's looking out for you and Sheena's baby? He wants to take her back to Sacramento so he can take the baby."

"No—he wouldn't—"

"Miss Judy did a background check on him. He's crooked. He travels with a woman who claims she has psychic powers. Once they isolate the pregnant mother, they brainwash her into giving up the baby. If she doesn't comply—you don't want to hear the rest."

Pounding on the door made Renee jump. "How do I know you're not lying?"

"I just started this gig. If you don't want to believe me, open the door. But—you've been warned."

The pounding increased. Sheena stirred. Renee looked through the peephole. "What do you want me to do?"

"Tell them Bradlee is sleeping, and to be quiet."

Renee went to the door. "Who is it?"

"It's Detective Metzger. We need to talk."

"My cousin is sleeping—I was in the shower. Can this wait?"

"Dixon knows where you live. Do you hear me?" I have an officer outside your door. Don't open the door for anyone."

"Okay. Can I get back to my shower now? I'm dripping water on the carpet. And quit pounding on the door, you'll wake Bradlee."

Dixon whispered. "My names Duane, I'm the new doorman."

"This whole thing is insane, I need a drink," Renee said, walked over to the wet bar.

"I know, crazy isn't it? My first day on the job and all."

"I wonder why Judy didn't call to let me know you were coming."

"She mentioned a potential resident—"

Renee felt Dixon's eyes on her. "Would you like one?" she asked, glancing over her shoulder. Dixon had moved closer. "How silly of me," she said removing the corkscrew from the drawer, "You're on duty." The tiny blade wasn't enough to defend herself. Neither was the metal curlicue at the end. She felt him behind her. She picked up a bottle, swung, and missed.

Dixon slit her throat.

Sam stopped in his tracks. Why would Renee refer to her niece as Bradlee? He had called her Sheena from the beginning. Unless? Sam tiptoed to the door where young officer Pizzo stood and motioned for him to keep silent.

Dixon dragged Renee's body into the bathroom and turned on the shower. Having a cop outside the door up the stakes. If he was lucky, he could lure the cop inside. Kill him and do the ol' switcheroo. He crept into Sheena's bedroom and shut the door. No need for officer do-good to hear Sheena shriek when she realized he had found her. He slipped into her bed.

Sam tapped lightly on the door. He pressed his ear to the door and heard water running. *Perhaps I'm overreacting.* Why had Renee called her Bradlee? He listened for anything out of the ordinary. He didn't hear any variation in the sound of the water. The thrum was consistent. *The water is running, but she's not in the shower.*

D ixon dipped one hand into Sheena's tank top and fondled her breast while he covered her mouth with the other. "Hey baby," he whispered in her ear. "Miss me? Miss your baby daddy?" He squeezed her breast until she gasped. He had never realized how large her eyes were until he saw them filled with terror. He reached into his pocket and withdrew the roll of duct tape he had snagged from the janitor's closet. He heard a light rap on the door.

Sheena squirmed beneath him. She tried to scream, but the tape muffled the sound. "Tsk, tsk, tsk. You don't look happy to see me," he said, his mouth inches from her face. Tears rolled down Sheena's cheeks. "Tears of joy?" Dixon flicked them away. "I think not." His free hand wondered over the mound she had tried so hard to protect as he withdrew a piece of orange twine from his waistband. Her body shook with fear. Her arms flailed and she kicked and punched him with all her might, but she was no match for him. He bound her wrists with the speed of a cowboy roping a calf.

S am stood very still outside the door. He closed his eyes and focused on the sounds coming from the other side of the door. Suzanne's face appeared behind his lids and all at once he knew. He drew his weapon and nodded to the young officer to do the same. "We're going in."

Sam popped a bullet through the deadbolt, grabbed the doorknob and pushed. The door swung easily and both men held their weapons ready for battle. The young officer took off towards the bathroom, while Sam checked the kitchen and one of the bedrooms. The door at the end of the hall was closed.

Dixon jumped to his feet when the door opened, dragging Sheena by the hair. Shielding his body with hers, he withdrew the knife from his waistband and held it near her neck. "You don't want to hurt our little mama now, do you?" His evil grin challenged both men. "Are you ready to risk the life of this girl and her unborn child?"

Sam lowered his weapon. "You disgust me, Dixon."

Dixon drew the knife closer to Sheena's throat. "Maybe I'll just slit her throat and kill them both myself —although I'd prefer to gut her like the pig she is—"

"Put the knife down. Let her go. It's over."

"It's over when I say it is."

"All those women. Why? You had the world by the balls—people admired you, respected you—"

"How did you find me? It was the bitch with the superpowers, right? You certainly couldn't have done it on your own."

"Suzanne led me here. She led me to Chrissy, and Patti, too. They're alive." Sam paused. He softened his tone. "I saw the photo on the wall. You were a boy."

Dixon's eye twitched. "My Grandpa built that place. Little piece of heaven, don't you think?"

"Whatever happened there doesn't justify this—let her go."

"Can't." He ran the blade across Sheena's stomach, "The baby has to go."

"Whatever twisted notion you have about this baby, it deserves a chance."

"C'mon Sam. A chance for what? You think she'll be a devoted mother? You know better. Half the whores we've busted over the years have kids in foster homes. How many find some schmuck to put a roof over their heads only to have him kick the crap out of them when he's had a bad day. Or play hide the banana with the little darlings when the ol' lady is sleeping in the next room?"

Sobs wracked Sheena's body.

"Whatever you endured as a child must've been horrendous Jim, but the killing has to stop."

"Did your psychic bitch tell you how this is gonna end?"

"No."

"Didn't think so. She's a little tied up at the moment."

"What do you know about Suzanne?"

"She's got great tits. Not a bad fuck either, but you must know that."

"Where is she?"

"What do you say we cancel this little soirée. I walk

out of here. And if all goes well, I give you that information."

"Not a chance."

"Gee, that's too bad. I thought you had a thing for her."

"Release Sheena and we can talk."

"Fuck you, Sam." Dixon sliced through Sheena's neck, drawing blood.

Pizzo aimed at Dixon's head and squeezed the trigger, dropping Dixon to his knees.

"Tic-tock," he whispered, crumbling to the floor.

"No," Sam shouted, "No, no no!"

The young officer stood frozen, his gun held high. "He was gonna kill her—kill the baby, I—"

Sam refrained from blowing his top. How could he fault the kid for doing his job? They were there to save the girl, not Suzanne. "Put that thing away and Call 911,"

Sam examined Sheena's wound. "It's not deep, thank God. You're going to be just fine," he said, pulling her close. He peered over her shoulder at the body lying on the floor. Dixon's eyes were fixed on the ceiling, blood pooled beneath his head. "You're safe now, Sheena. You and your baby are safe."

"Paramedics are on their way, sir."

Sam rose, facing the young officer. "First time, officer—"

"Pizzo. Tony Pizzo, sir. Yes, I—"

"What is it?" Sam recognized the angst. It wasn't easy shooting a man."

"We saved lives today, sir, didn't we?"

"Yes, yes we did." Sam patted Pizzo's on the shoulder. "Helluva shot, officer"

Relief washed over the young officer's face.

Dixon was dead, but it wasn't over. Sam plucked a business card from his wallet. "I have another situation to attend to…If you ever need anything—"

Pizzo accepted the card. His hand trembled.

CHAPTER 56

S am returned to the hotel. He knew now Suzanne
hadn't left him in a lurch. *Where are you?*

He raced through the lobby into the elevator, his
shirt, covered in blood. His stomach clenched. He
needed a clear head to see things through. *Where could he
have taken her?* There had to be something on those tapes.
Tic-tock.

He threw on a clean shirt, splashed water on his face,
and grabbed his keys. On the way down to the lobby, he
knocked on Suzanne's door. He didn't expect her to
answer, but he stood there for a moment, hoping. When
he turned to leave, he noticed the DO NOT DISTURB
sign hanging on the door across the hall.

"Detective Metzger," the desk clerk stepped forward. "Can I help you?"

"I need to take a look at those tapes again."

"Come this way." The desk clerk escorted Sam into the back office. "Which day do you want to look at?"

"Show me the tape with the man who asked about the flowers."

The desk clerk typed in his password and scrolled through footage with the time codes Sam was inquiring about.

"There. Stop. Enlarge the frame. What room was this man registered in?"

"Let me look." The clerk disappeared for a moment, when he came back, he said, "1442. His name is Duane Johnson. He's still checked in."

"That's the room across from Suzanne's. Call 911 and give me a key to that room."

"Sir, I can't do that, I—"

"Duane Johnson is James Dixon, and he's dead. Now give me the key. If my partner is in there, she may already be de—we're wasting time!"

Suzanne tried to track the combat boots walking back and forth, but her vision wouldn't cooperate.

"You can't die, we're so close," he said.

Jack?

He lay down on the floor, his face inches from hers. "Breathe."

I can't Jack. I'm too tired.

"I won't let you go."

Suzanne felt her body rise. Jack, carrying her down the hill like he did when they were kids. Bumping along, laughing, so in love. She turned to tell him how happy she was, to taste his lips, but it wasn't Jack. *Sam.*

Sam found her lying on the floor, convulsing.

"Suzanne?" he checked her pupils. "Can you hear me?" She fell limp in his arms.

Sirens blared in the distance. He prayed they weren't too late.

Sam followed the ambulance to Washington Heights General Hospital, on the east side of town.

When he entered the bay where Suzanne was being examined by doctors her petite frame looked small beneath the white sheet. Her face was paler than the first time he had seen her, the night she had been shot, left for dead.

Sam introduced himself to doctors, displayed his badge, and asked for an update.

"Your friend is flying high. We're running toxicology tests as we speak." The doctor examined his watch. "I expect them back within the hour." He met Sam's eyes. "Your friend has been beaten and doesn't appear to be an addict. Can you tell me what's going on?"

"She went missing this morning. I suspect she was

kidnapped between midnight and 5:00 this morning. We're here on a case."

"So, she's a policewoman?"

"No. She's a psychic."

The doctor's reaction took several moments and a series of eye-blinks. "A *psychic*?"

"Suzanne's gift has helped the department immensely. If it weren't for her, we'd still be trying to figure things out."

"Well, you can count your lucky stars you found her. She's in serious condition."

Sam choked back the lump in his throat. "Was she raped?"

"We're getting to that."

"What's your prognosis on her overall condition?"

"Can't say until we get the tox results. We've given her antidotal meds, but my biggest concern is brain damage. She has a serious concussion. Once we get her stabilized, we can get a CT scan." The doctor gently turned Suzanne's head to the left. "Her jaw doesn't appear to be broken, but I'm concerned her temporo-mandibular joint may be damaged, and judging from the bruising and swelling around her orbital bone, I expect fractures."

"Can she hear me?"

"She's someplace in her mind that we may not be able to reach until she comes down."

Sam took Suzanne's hand. "Hey partner. Don't stay

away too long. We have work to do." Sam lifted her hand to his lips.

The doctor patted Sam on the back. "Go get some rest, let me take care of your partner."

Sam squeezed Suzanne's hand. In his mind he whispered three words he vowed never to use again.

As Sam turned to leave, the doctor said. "Before you go, I wanted to ask—who's Jack?"

CHAPTER 57

Suzanne tumbled through space and time. Voices echoed in the caverns of her mind. Bright light blinded her. The sun? No sun in this place, only slithery things and death. She struggled to reach whatever it was that would save her from the darkness. Jack had appeared many times only to be dragged away by a fire-breathing monster. She wanted to help him, fight the demons devouring his face, but she couldn't move. *A pillar of salt. Don't look back.* Now what? She dangled over a pit of fire, her hands cramping, spasming, her grip weakening. A rose petal landed on one hand. The petal lingered there, warm, comforting. And then it was gone.

"Where am I?" Suzanne frantically scanned the room.

A red-headed nurse in eggplant colored scrubs stepped forward. "Washington Heights General. How're you feeling?"

"Where's Sam? Have you seen Sam?"

"There was a man here earlier. I didn't get his name. Handsome, salt 'n pepper hair?"

"Did he bring me here?"

"No, ma'am. You came in by ambulance." She pressed two fingers on Suzanne's wrist and glanced at her watch. "You don't remember, do you? Of course not."

Suzanne contemplated the tubes connected to the crook of her arm. "What's all this?"

"A Flumazenil cocktail. Your tox-screen came back with Rohypnol and Ketamine in your system. The Flumazenil helps reverse the effects of the Rohypnol. You must have a guardian angel. Ketamine is nasty stuff. You've been hallucinating, but the worst is over."

"I'm so tired."

The nurse patted Suzanne's hand, "You rest. I'll be right outside."

She closed her eyes. Jack stepped into view. And then they were back in the pool.

"Look at you!" he shouted. "You're doing it—you're floating!"

Suzanne felt as though she were floating on a cloud

instead of water. She could feel the vibration of Jack's voice on her cheek. She turned to look at him. "I love you," he whispered. "Always have, always will." In his eyes she could see his love, and something more. *Like the first time we met.* "I have to go now, Suzanne. I'm about to start over. We'll meet again. I promise. Until then, follow your path, open your heart. I'll will be with you always, but now, your happiness is within reach. Take the love that is given, fill your mind with new memories, and never forget where it all began."

She understood. *Sam.*

Sam drove to the hospital, anxious to share the good news. While Sheena was in the hospital getting stitched up, she went into labor. Her baby boy was born two weeks early but was in good health.

When he arrived, Suzanne was sleeping. He pulled up a chair and sat, holding her hand. "I think I've fallen in love with you," he whispered in her ear.

Suzanne stirred. Her eyes fluttered. "Sam."

He brought her fingers to his lips. "I'm here. I'm right here. Always."

She closed her eyes.

She floated on sparkling blue waters. The clouds sped by. A young woman with long dark hair stood in a field of gold, Jack by her side. They faced each other, knowing. The young woman's bump had grown. Jack seemed pleased. As the woman massaged her bump, Jack vanished. Time sped up, the sun rising and setting, only to rise again. The young woman remained, her face to the sun. When she turned to go, she was no longer alone. A small boy reached for her hand. Suzanne recognized the woman from her visions. *She's safe.* Suzanne's heart filled with joy.

CHAPTER 58

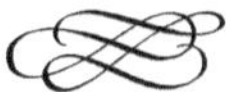

S am knocked on Suzanne's door. Two months had passed since her release from the hospital. The nightmare with Dixon was over. With Ben gone, he felt they were headed for a new beginning. *Partners*. First, and always. *Friends*. He hoped for more, but realized he needed to be patient. Fate had brought them together, his love for her would grow.

"Sam! What a pleasant surprise," she said, stepping into his arms for a hug.

"This came for you," he said, handing her an envelope.

She opened a card addressed to her from New York. The card held a photo of a beautiful baby boy. His smile was infectious. His eyes, unusual, and distinct for his age, one brown, one green. Like *Jack's*. The note read,

Dear Suzanne,

Not a day goes by that I don't think of you, and pray you are doing well. If it hadn't been for you and Sam, my baby boy would not have made it into this world. When I tell him that you were his guardian angel he reacts in a way, well, I don't know how to explain it, he doesn't just smile, he seems to understand. I am eternally grateful to you both, and hope that one day you will meet Emmett, and see for yourself how special he is. Until then, be well, be happy, and God Bless.

Yours,

Sheena Bradford

Suzanne showed the photo to Sam. "It's him, I know it. It's Jack. He said I would see him again. I never imagined it would be like this. She held the photo to her heart. "What do you say we go for ice cream? My treat."

The End

Dänna Wilberg has written, produced, and directed multiple award-winning short films, produced and hosted TV programs in Sacramento for over a decade, and was one of the first writers to be inducted into the "A Place Called Sacramento" Hall of Fame.

Her published romantic-suspense trilogy, "The Red Chair," "The Grey Door," and "The Black Dress," featuring young psychotherapist, Grace Simms, poses the question: What do we *really* know about another person?

Her current work "Borrowed Time," a paranormal-suspense series, features "intuitive" Suzanne Cash, Detective Samson Metzger and villains you will love to hate. Wilberg loves to weave true to life scenarios into her story telling, and gives her muse free rein to steer her in the right direction.

Aside from writing, Ms. Wilberg loves spending time with family, spoiling her grandchildren, traveling the world, volunteering for non-profits, and singing Karaoke. She believes the universe is a mystical, magical realm of which she is blessed to be a part.

Visit the author at her website.

www.dannawilberg.com

ALSO BY DÄNNA WILBERG

NOVELS

Borrowed Time Book 1 - Broken Promises

The Red Chair

The Grey Door

The Black Dress

ANTHOLOGIES

Capitol Crimes 2008

Our Dance With Words

Capitol Crimes 2017

The Second Corona Book of Horror Stories

COMING DECEMBER 2020!

Infinity Books

Borrowed Time - Book 2 - Missing

For psychic Suzanne Cash, life is like having a movie theater in your head. Snippets of coming attractions plague her day and night. She knows she can't solve the problems of the world, yet when a young woman continues to infiltrate her thoughts and dreams, Suzanne is determined to find out more. Even if it means dancing with the devil responsible for a billion dollar human trafficking industry.

From Vienna, Austria, to the Italian countryside, and into the port of Sacramento, California, Detective Sam Metzger joins Suzanne in a search for a missing young woman. *The clock is ticking...and not all is what it seems.*

www.ingramcontent.com/pod-product-compliance
Lightning Source LLC
Chambersburg PA
CBHW070238200726
48293CB00005B/1681